The Social Tutor

A Regency Romance

BRANCHES OF LOVE, BOOK ONE

SALLY BRITTON

Other Titles By Sally Britton

Heart's of Arizona Series:

Book #1, *Silver Dollar Duke*

The Inglewood Series:

Rescuing Lord Inglewood

Discovering Grace

Saving Miss Everly

Engaging Sir Isaac

Reforming Lord Neil

The Branches of Love Series:

Prequel Novella, *Martha's Patience*

The Social Tutor

The Gentleman Physician

His Bluestocking Bride

The Earl and His Lady

Miss Devon's Choice

Courting the Vicar's Daughter

Penny's Yuletide Wish (A Novella)

Stand Alone Romances:

The Captain and Miss Winter

His Unexpected Heiress

A Haunting at Havenwood

Timeless Romance Collection:

An Evening at Almack's, Regency Collection 12

Dedication

To Skye, who believes in me 1000%,
and to Mother, who taught me how to do everything.

Chapter One

NOVEMBER 1ST, 1811

"Waiting on a letter one knows to be full of exciting news is an excruciating experience," Christine Devon said, slumping in her chair in a most unladylike manner.

"Are you waiting for the post again?" Christine's younger sister, Rebecca, glanced away from her book and offered a teasing smile. "Whatever for?"

"I hope the letter will come today and save us all your anxieties on the matter." Julia, the eldest of the three, did not even look up from her stitching as she commented. This meant she didn't see Christine's glare.

"You ought to try reading, Christine," Rebecca said softly. "The news sheets are here on the table. I know you enjoy them."

"I do find them interesting; there is something particularly satisfying about knowing what goes on in the world." Christine glanced at the papers but did not pick them up. "Father says I ought not to read them too much. They are meant for gentlemen."

Julia made a noise which sounded suspiciously like a snort. "He will never know, Christine. If you like them, read them."

Checking out the window once more, Christine darted to the table to snatch the *Times*, a week old now, and went back to her seat.

"There. Now you needn't be so anxious." Rebecca settled more deeply into her chair and lifted her book again. "Reading helps to pass the time, after all."

Despite a valiant effort, Christine could barely read a full sentence without looking out the window in search of the post. Even an opinion piece on the state of the King's sanity couldn't fully capture her attention. The proposal of naming the Crown Prince as Regent did interest her, however, so she vowed to read through the pages again, *after* the post had arrived.

Christine had waited in this manner every day for the last three weeks. Aunt Jacqueline, the widow of an earl, likely did not know how much her niece longed for the missive. The esteemed lady's letter would be positively full of instructions and lists for the coming London Season, because it was, at long last, Christine's turn to make her debut into society. At nineteen, she was on the older side when it came to the hopeful young misses stepping out for the first time, but she felt grateful she was granted a season at all, especially after her sister Julia's spectacular failure four years prior.

Christine did not actually know *what* Julia's spectacular failure consisted of, as no one in the family ever told the whole story outright. All Christine knew of the matter consisted of her father's quiet comments muttered at family dinners, her aunt's vague mention of the "unfortunate affair," and Julia's slow withdrawal from her sisters.

Whatever the past mistake or embarrassment, Christine determined long ago that *her* triumphant season, as one of the most sought after young women in London, would elevate the family to new heights.

"You ought to stop straining your neck like that," Rebecca commented, bringing Christine out of her thoughts abruptly. Her younger sister watched from behind her book, dark eyes twinkling merrily. "You might overstretch it and then where would you be? I doubt goose necks are in fashion in London."

A small chuckle escaped from Julia, and Christine could not help smiling as well. "We cannot have that, I suppose." She pulled her shoulders up and tucked her chin down against her chest. "Do you think a turtle-like posture more the thing?"

Rebecca pretended to consider, and Christine laughed until Rebecca joined in the merriment. It always surprised Christine to see her own features mirrored on her younger sister's face, though they had always looked the most alike of their siblings. They both took after their father with their dark, waving hair and brown eyes. Julia looked more like their mother, her hair a lighter shade of brown and her eyes flecked with copper. Their younger brother, away at school, had light, curly hair and dark brown eyes. Only when they all stood together did they look related.

Christine often wished she looked more like their late mother, if only to feel closer to her.

Their mother passed when Christine was fourteen years old, leaving it to their father's elder sister to turn the sisters out in style for the season. Aunt Jacqueline had immediately taken charge of sponsoring Julia into society, chaperoning her to all the important events, with a promise of doing the same for Christine and Rebecca in their own time. Their father was only needed to pay the bills for the modiste, seamstress, millinery, and whatever else Jacqueline deemed necessary, and he graciously complied. After all, as he said time and again, a woman's first season was an investment poised to benefit the entire family.

At last, Christine saw the footman assigned to retrieve the mail. He fetched it from the inn, where the mail coach stopped twice a day. The poor young man always came the long way around the house to avoid the smells of the stables. Apparently, he had an aversion to horses.

Christine could hardly imagine anything more tragic than to be deprived of horses and daily rides for something as absurd as a damp nose.

Christine hurried from the morning room and across the whole house, choosing to take the servants' stair instead of the main staircase in order to catch the young man more quickly. Today simply *had* to be the day that Aunt Jacqueline's letter arrived. There was much to do to plan for the season ahead, and Christine could not do it without her aunt's instructions.

Mr. Devon planned to remove the family to London immediately following the Earl of Annesbury's annual Christmas ball, and it was already November. That left Christine precious little time to prepare herself for a grand entrance into society.

She flew into the kitchen at the same moment the footman entered and nearly dove at him to retrieve the post.

The startled servant jumped backward as she snatched the letters from his hands. She clutched at the two envelopes and looked at their direction with great anxiety. The first was to their father in a hand she thought to belong to their solicitor; the second was addressed to her.

"Ah, Miss Christine." The butler greeted her dryly from his place at the table. She blushed as she looked at him but made no apologies. She ought to have waited for him to bring the post to Julia.

"I'll take mine now, thank you." Christine tossed the unwanted letter back to the footman without looking and dashed out of the kitchen as fast as she could, going to the garden. She hardly noticed the chill in the air, and thankfully already wore one of Julia's knitted shawls.

She stopped at the first sun-warmed bench she came to, sat, and tore the seal on the letter with abandon, nearly wrinkling the paper in her haste.

My Dearest Niece,

It is with great pleasure that I write to assure you of my determination to sponsor you this season. While it is no secret that I dearly wish to give you this opportunity, your father expressed concern when last we spoke that you might lack another year of experience before entering society. I reminded him that nineteen is more stylish an age and sounds better than twenty to future beaux. If we wait until you are twenty, people will wonder why we have been hiding you. I daresay most have forgotten about Julia's unfortunate season, but there is no reason to dredge up curiosity in any who recall those events...

Her aunt went on to give a detailed list of Christine's needed purchases before her arrival in town, and made a suggestion as to colors and styles that a country seamstress might be able to employ to advantage. The bulk of the shopping would be done upon her arrival in London with her father.

Christine clutched the letter to her chest, her elation filling her with hope until she knew she must glow. At last, her season! Her chance to prove to her father that she was worthy of his affection, worthy of his pride. Her chance to step onto the stage of the world and make a match of such societal importance that other debutantes would positively wilt in comparison.

Her match would be brilliant, no doubt. She hoped for a title, and certainly for wealth, but also to give her father contacts in the upper echelons of society, thus ensuring her family's success in the years and even generations to come.

While her father, and indeed the whole family, benefited from his sister's marriage into the *ton*, he remained on the fringes, an untitled gentleman with business interests shared by several more noble property owners.

Christine sailed back into the morning room to share the wonderful news. Julia sat in her favorite chair still stitching something in a terribly practical shade of gray, likely for one of their tenants. Rebecca was engaged with her novel once more.

Pausing in her step, Christine looked over the scene with a smile. She loved days like this, where they sat together quietly, enjoying each other's company. Horace, the baby of the family and their father's heir, had been away too long. She wondered what he would be doing, were he present. He certainly would not be sitting as quietly as Rebecca, tucked into her chair like a kitten curled in a basket.

Christine finally interrupted the quiet, making her announcement cheerfully. "Aunt Jacqueline has written at last."

Rebecca looked up from her page. "Oh Christine, how wonderful for you."

Julia raised her eyebrows, not even pausing in her work.

Christine stared at her elder sister, perplexed by the complete lack of attention. "I am very excited," she added, still enthusiastic. "She has given me a list of things to purchase before we remove to London."

Julia nodded and this time deigned to speak. "If you will write it out for me, I will make an estimation on the expense for Father to look over."

Rebecca closed her book and stood, coming to peer at the letter over Christine's shoulder.

"What else does Aunt say?" Rebecca asked. "Does she tell you what to expect when you make your curtsy?"

Highly irritated by Julia's lack of enthusiasm, Christine deliberately turned her full attention to her sixteen-year-old sister. "She does. She writes all about it; the dress I will wear and who will make it for me, the ceremony at court. She has included the most wonderful itinerary, though a great deal will depend upon the invitations we receive after we arrive in town."

"I am happy for you." Rebecca looked from Christine to Julia and her smile faltered. "Aren't you happy for her, Julia?"

"Certainly." Julia's fingers nimbly moved the needle up and down, still not looking up. "Christine has been dreaming of this for years."

"Ever since your season," Christine said, lifting her chin. An errant curl fell out of its pin at that moment, spoiling the effect of her now perfect posture. "Four years of dreaming."

Julia paused and glanced up, her staid expression never betraying her thoughts. "A long time indeed. I hope all that dreaming won't spoil the reality for you."

Christine narrowed her eyes at her elder sister, disappointed with Julia's indifference at a time like this. She didn't even feign excitement for Christine's opportunity. "As long as I end the season with a husband of means, I do not think it will be at all spoiled."

Julia shrugged and went back to her sewing, as though completely unconcerned. "If that is your goal, you are likely right. Be careful, Christine."

Christine raised her eyebrows. "Careful of what? Repeating your missteps?"

For a brief moment, Julia's posture stiffened. Christine dared to think she rattled her sister enough, at last, to find out what those missteps had been. Julia, ever the master of her emotions, regained her poise.

"Father is an exacting person. He will expect perfection and, as a mortal being, you will fall short of that. I have no doubt you will do your best, but if you hope to gain his approval by marrying correctly, I am afraid you will be disappointed. His expectations will grow with whatever consequence a good marriage brings you." Julia kept her eyes on the work in her hands, her words falling almost carelessly from her lips.

Hardly believing her sister uttered so many words regarding a topic she normally avoided, it took Christine a short space of time to recover her thoughts. "I do not think it is as impossible as you make it seem. I will succeed in a way that makes Father proud. In fact, I will exceed his expectations." She nodded smartly.

"I suppose nineteen is more mature than seventeen," Julia said lightly. "When I attempted to do the same."

"Precisely why Father made me wait those extra two years,"

Christine said, crossing her arms before her. "Greater maturity of thought. A better understanding of his wishes."

Julia shrugged, her disinterest in the conversation clearly expressed by her lack of attentiveness. "Certainly. I do wish to caution you. Father's ambitions for you may not be entirely what *you* expect. I admonish you again. Be careful."

While Christine loved Julia dearly, there were moments when she wished to throttle her sister for ruining things for the rest of them.

Rebecca interjected with an overly bright tone. "Will you write Aunt back today?" Christine had nearly forgotten her younger sister was present, which happened with greater frequency of late.

Christine ignored her younger sister and took a step toward Julia. "Careful of what, Julia? What sage advice have you to offer, considering your lack of success during your season in London?"

Julia's eyes snapped up and narrowed. "My lack of success, as you call it, happened for a reason. I hope you take care that our father's goals do not overshadow your happiness, Christine."

"Our father's goals are the same as any other father's when a daughter comes of age," Christine argued, clenching the hand not holding the letter. "We should consider and respect his wishes in this matter, as dutiful children."

Rebecca darted forward and stepped between them, clearly sensing Christine's prickly feelings on the subject. "We do respect Father. I think Julia meant that she wants you to be happy with the choice you make this season. That is all. Julia? Isn't that what you meant?"

Julia rose, lifting her sewing basket with her. "Yes. Exactly that. I hope your choice makes *you* happy." As she moved to leave the room she added, in a most unconcerned manner, "If you are given any choices, that is. Receiving an offer is never a certain thing." Without another word, she swept out the door.

"Why does she do that?" Christine asked, glaring at the empty doorway. "Why can she not be happy for me?"

"Her season *was* a failure, Christine," Rebecca said. "I think it hurts her to be reminded of it. Father brings it up so often."

"If she would tell us what happened, we could be more sympathetic to her," Christine huffed, folding her arms across her waist. "Instead, we are left to guess, and she refuses to say a word unless to offer dire warnings."

Rebecca laughed, though it sounded strained. "Come now. You know she loves us. Julia wants us to do well. So we do not end up as she has."

"A spinster."

"That is not kind," Rebecca said, her voice gentle. "She is our sister."

Christine barely refrained from saying more on the subject. Though she may regret her words later, at the moment she wished for someone to be happy for *her*. She thrust the letter out to Rebecca, trying to regain her former excitement. "Here. Read Aunt Jacqueline's letter. I must make a list for Julia."

Christine left the room, determined to do all in her power to avoid Julia's fate of spinsterhood and disappointment.

Chapter Two

T homas Gilbert, lately returned from abroad, walked the grounds of his family's estate. Morning light glowed gold upon the garden walks, the sun doing little to warm the stone, and the shadows in the garden remained a silvery blue. Winter crept nearer every day.

His arrival after dark the night before had left him little time to reacquaint himself with his home. But before his parents woke the next morning, he had already managed a ride down his favorite paths. The exercise had invigorated him and he could not yet bring himself to go inside, despite the chill in the air.

In boyhood he spent hours in his mother's gardens, following behind her to ask dozens of questions, or stealing away to read beneath the trees. He had not realized how much he would miss this small, quiet place until he was abroad, in the rolling hills of the Italian countryside. He'd missed the green grasses and the well-cultivated wildness of an English garden. Coming home this late in the fall, however, meant he must miss them for a while longer. Until spring.

He turned a corner around a wall covered in ivy, where the path led to his mother's hot house filled with more exotic blooms, and stopped when he saw his father. The elder Gilbert was out walking, which struck Thomas as strange. He had never known his father to leave the house before breakfast, as the man spent as many waking hours as he could with Mrs. Gilbert at his side.

Thomas approached him and called out to get his father's attention.

"Good morning, Tom," his father responded, warmly. "I see old habits are still with you. Did the Italians teach you nothing of beginning a day at your leisure?"

Thomas chuckled. "They tried, Father. But there, as here, I find it hard to sleep when there are horses to be exercised." He stopped when he was a pace away from his father. "I have missed our English gardens and lanes. As beautiful as I found the rest of the world, I longed for our quiet country. It is good to be home."

His father made a show of looking him up and down and nodded firmly. "It is good to have you back. We have missed you greatly." He gestured to the path leading to the house. "Are you ready to go in?"

"I think so. I am finally starting to feel the chill." Thomas fell into step with Mr. Gilbert easily.

Since his eighteenth birthday, now ten years past, Thomas had stood at an even height with his father. Looking at the older man now, Thomas had a greater appreciation for their similarities. They were not overly tall men. They would never tower above others at an assembly. But they both bore broad shoulders and they shared the same high cheekbones and angular jaw. Thomas had managed to break his nose by riding into a branch as a teenager, giving him that bit of a difference between them. His father's nose was straight and Roman, while his own was crooked.

"Cook will have meat pies for breakfast," his father said, bringing Thomas out of his thoughts. "And I am likely to suffer many meals of all your favorite foods."

Thomas's smile broadened. "She does tend to spoil me, doesn't she? I wonder if she will make my favorite biscuits."

"She already has a crock filled to the brim with shortbread," his father assured him.

A cloud passed over the sun and both gentlemen looked to the sky. "It looks like we will have a morning storm," Thomas murmured. "I had forgotten how changeable the weather can be."

"It is cold enough now," his father said, "that we should see snow within the month."

"That would be an early winter," Thomas said with a frown. "Are our tenants prepared?"

"Ah. Yes." The elder Gilbert's expression became more somber. "Tom, after breakfast, and after your mother has a chance to bid you good morning, I have need of you in the study. Though I do not wish to burden you, I feel it is important you know the affairs of the estate as soon as possible. Much has happened in your absence."

Thomas raised an eyebrow at his father, taking in the man's expression, noting the tightness in his eyes. He knew his father and he knew if he asked what the man meant now, before they were settled in the study as requested, his father would put off the subject. It would be best to wait and find out what his father wished to discuss after breakfast.

"Yes, Father." He inclined his head respectfully. "I am happy to assist you in any way I can."

"Good man," his father said, reaching out to squeeze his son's shoulder. "Now, to the table with you. Your mother will be distressed we've been out in the cold air."

Thomas laughed and opened the door leading in from the gardens, holding it for his father. He was happy to be home. Whatever troubled the estate, Thomas would do all he could to help.

❦

THOMAS SAT IN HIS FATHER'S STUDY GOING THROUGH THE account books. His father stood by a window, staring out at the gardens Thomas's mother loved. The elder Mr. Gilbert remained silent as his son poured over their records. The way he stared at the gray sky with a heavy countenance, sorrow no longer concealed by his welcoming smile from that morning, put a weight on Thomas's chest.

"I wish you would have told me sooner, Father," the younger man said at last, running a hand through his hair. He wondered when his near-black hair would begin to sprout more silver. He could not remember a time when his father had not been afflicted by the salty strands amid all the pepper, though certainly there was more gray than black upon his head now.

"I wanted you to enjoy your time in Italy," his father answered, glancing over his shoulder. "The money for that was already spent. What good would coming home early have done?"

For two years Thomas had enjoyed himself, not knowing of his family's struggles. He had learned as much as he could from several of the most successful horse breeders in Europe, eager to have first-hand knowledge of what it took to breed champion racers, hunters, and even those docile little ponies that the gentry preferred for pulling ladies' carts. The amount of knowledge he amassed was substantial and well worth the time away from home.

Or so he had thought.

While Thomas pursued his dreams with vigor, his family had fallen on difficult times. They were by no means bankrupt, but their living was far less than it had been.

Thomas's father, a kind and benevolent landlord, had taken it upon himself to assist his tenant farmers the first year that a horrible blight struck their farms. Their income had been inconsequential, nearly nothing, and Mr. Gilbert turned all the funds he could back into the farms. He hired a botanist to look at their fields. He ordered everything plowed under, new seeds brought in and distributed to the tenants.

"Our tenants must be grateful for all your aid," Thomas said as he closed the books before him.

"I could not think another action would be prudent," his father said. "What could I do when they had no funds to pay their rents? It would be folly to cast them out. You know the Jones family has worked the land as long as our family has held it. If the earth itself was blighted, how could I blame them? Or even accept another family in their place to suffer the same fate?"

Thomas agreed that the decision was as logical as it was kind. But the move depleted the family funds a great deal. Then the following year, more disaster struck. A worm of devilish nature invaded and took far longer to eradicate than they had liked. The tenants' crops were nearly destroyed, then finally revived, only to be flooded out with intense spring storms. The already weak vegetation could not handle the excess rains, ending another year without any profit and no income for the tenants to pay the rents. Economies were taken by tenants and landlord alike.

Now, at the end of the second poor growing season, Thomas looked over the many notes of expenditure, the bills, and the farmers' reports of the situation.

"Our funds are low, but we are not in the suds yet," he said as cheerfully as he could, closing another of the books. He rubbed the bump on the bridge of his nose, agitated. "We can still reverse the damages if we have a proper growing season next year. Surely three years of bad luck is unheard of, Father."

"We lack sufficient means to procure enough seed," his father said, not turning from the window. "We have enough to meet the needs of the families. And feed ourselves. That is all."

Thomas froze and stared at his father's back in disbelief. "If we use that, and make no income, there will be almost nothing for next year."

"That is the truth of it, Thomas." He turned slowly and the look in his eyes made Thomas's heart ache. His father's shoulders, once squared, now drooped under the weight of his responsibilities. The lines around his mouth and on his forehead stood pronounced, where no wrinkles had previously been seen. Why hadn't Thomas noticed these things earlier?

His father went on. "We have few options. I do not wish to ask for credit from the banks or from friends. I will not be a debtor."

Thomas knew and respected this. His grandfather nearly ruined the family with debts before his death, and Thomas's father saved them, working hard to right the estate and turn a profit from the land.

Land. They had that in abundance.

"We sell parcels of land," Thomas stated. "Decrease our holdings, sell the house in town."

The senior Gilbert nodded slowly and said with a quiet, defeated tone, "And the horses, Tom. We needn't keep so many."

Thomas drew in a sharp breath and fisted his hands. "The horses? The horses could help our future. I have six strong breeding mares. The three I brought back from Italy are of the finest pedigree. They could save us."

"Tom." His father's voice was kind, understanding even, as he reasoned with his son. "They would fetch a fine price. And how long would it take to breed them? How would you pay for the rights of a suitable stud?"

"I would offer the payment after the foals are born. It would be an investment."

"In the meantime, you would need to pay for all the upkeep that comes with so many animals. We cannot do that, Thomas. Not when our tenants need us to be wiser with our funds. We have made many economies. I would have sold the three you left behind, but I wished you to understand the decision and come to terms with it before doing so. We have carriage horses, you and I may keep our personal mounts, but otherwise we must try for the best price. It will save our family, Tom, and the families over whom we bear responsibility."

Thomas's hopes shattered. He swallowed and stood, the world moving slowly. He came to his father and put a hand on the man's shoulder. "I am sorry, Father. Please give me some time. Let me study the situation out further. There may yet be a way without having to sell our land or the horses. Something we have overlooked."

"We live simply, Thomas. Within our means. Take some time to study the situation if you must. But not too much time. Arrangements must be made soon." He gave his son a pat on the shoulder and shared a rueful smile. "And don't forget, your mother has plans of her own for you. She wants to reintroduce you to the neighborhood. Starting this evening."

Thomas, distracted by the problem at hand, nodded and withdrew into his thoughts, wondering how to achieve his dream with lands that could not even pay for themselves, let alone the beginnings of a horse farm.

Chapter Three

Thomas did not particularly feel like going to a dinner party, even as the guest of honor, but he could hardly refuse. The Littletons lived on the other side of the village and were considered to be socially important in their little hamlet. Sending his regrets would not only greatly disappoint his hostess but would likely be seen as a slight. Having no wish to hurt anyone's feelings, he found himself in a carriage with his father, mother, sister, and brother-in-law, trundling down the gravel drive to Littleton Manor.

"As well intentioned as this party is," he said to the carriage full of his family, "I would like to leave as soon as politely possible."

His sister, Martha Brody by marriage, nudged him with her shoulder. "Tom, as the guest of honor, you are supposed to be the last to leave." Older than him by five years, Martha was as apt to tease him as mother him, and the way her eyes twinkled in the darkness made him smile despite himself. He had missed her greatly during his time away.

"We have the perfect excuse to make a short evening of it," Thomas argued. "Your dear children."

She paused, her hands hovering over a pin she'd been adjusting in her raven-black hair. "Whatever have my children to do with anything?" she asked, obviously perplexed.

"You have five of them. Surely, at least one is ill at the moment and could benefit from maternal care."

George, his good-natured brother-in-law, chuckled. "It *is* the time of year that one or another comes down with a cold or cough." Thomas smiled. At least he had an ally in George.

"Don't hope too much. They are all disgustingly healthy at present." Martha's superior tone made Thomas smile all the more.

Sighing deeply, Thomas crossed his arms and leaned toward the window. "Regretful."

"Dear boy," his mother said, "everyone has missed you. The least you can do is be courteous and even grateful for the special attention being shown to you tonight. Our neighbors wish to hear of your travels."

"And fill you in on all the latest gossip," Martha added helpfully.

"And see if you would make good husband material for any of the local misses," George said, his amusement ill-concealed.

Thomas frowned. Perhaps he couldn't rely on George after all. "You have had a taste of the exotic and come back as a potential prize on the marriage mart, Tom," George continued. "How else is everyone to determine your marriageable worth but through a dinner party?"

Thomas groaned and dropped his head in his hands. "Exactly who else is coming tonight?"

"I already told you," his mother reminded him, sounding as though her patience was being tried by the attitude of her son. "The Littletons invited our family, the Whitsons, the Devons, and the vicar's family."

"In simpler terms, there will be several eligible young ladies present tonight," Martha said.

"If you sounded any more gleeful about this, Martha, I would suspect you had a hand in arranging the guest list." Thomas wouldn't put it past her to meddle in such things.

"She is very good friends with Lady Littleton," George pointed out most unhelpfully, then yelped as his wife likely pinched him for revealing too much to her brother.

Thomas reached up and rubbed both temples to ward off a developing headache. After all his work on the estate books earlier that day, and writing several letters to parties he hoped would have better ideas regarding how to save his family's future, being put up as husband material by the local matchmakers did little to ease the weight he felt upon his shoulders.

If only he'd never left Italy; he much preferred working with horses and staying far out of the way of English society.

THE DINNER PORTION OF THE PARTY LIVED UP TO THOMAS'S LOW expectations. His place at the table wedged him between the vicar's elder daughter, a Miss Ames, and the Littletons' youngest daughter, Miss Hannah. While both young ladies conversed well on topics pertaining to the weather, his health, and his time in Italy, he found himself terribly bored and impatient to get on with the evening. The sooner the meal was over, the sooner they could begin and end the entertainment, and the sooner he would be home where he could pace his father's study in relative peace.

Across from Thomas sat the vicar, one of the two Devon sisters present, and a Whitson lady. Though propriety required he pay more attention to those seated on either side of him, Thomas found himself listening more often to the conversation taking place across the table.

He remembered Miss Christine as a child, though he had not seen her since her mother's death. She had still been in the schoolroom, he thought, when that event occurred. When the tragedy befell the Devons, Thomas mourned Mrs. Devon as though the woman had been family. Hailing from a family of horse-breeders, she had generously made many of his introductions to the Italians possible. Indeed, she herself had been his earliest instructor on the importance of a

SALLY BRITTON

horse's bloodlines. This daughter, he recalled, had often been at her mother's elbow when he was about.

She must miss her mother terribly given how often she had spent time in the woman's company.

Thomas listened with one ear while the vicar, Mr. Ames, attempted to discuss a passage in the Bible with Miss Whitson, and Christine Devon continually interrupted with questions. It brought to mind the numerous times she had interrupted Thomas's conversations with Mrs. Devon, always with an inquiry of some sort. He had never been bothered by her questions, however; Thomas appreciated that she possessed such a curious mind.

"You see, dear ladies," Mr. Ames said with his eyes on Miss Hannah and his shoulders stiff. "King Saul was a complete despot. Though chosen by God, he abused his authority and was therefore removed from power."

"Isn't that what the American colonists claimed about our king?" The Devon girl looked highly interested in the conversation and remained unaware of the frustration her questions caused Mr. Ames, if her wide-eyed stare was any indication. "They said he abused authority and they could not, in clear conscience, follow his governance any more. I believe that many of them justified their actions of rebellion using various religious texts. Kings have long claimed Divine Authority to rule, but it is obvious from Saul's story that such authority can be revoked."

"By God alone," the vicar said with an air of censure, not even turning to look at her. "A group of upstarts can hardly decide for themselves—"

Miss Christine had the audacity to interrupt his explanation. "But a large group of upstarts who are men of faith might perceive things about their rulers that are unjust, might they not?"

The vicar's chest puffed up, reminding Thomas of a rooster attempting to bluster another out of the barnyard. "The King is the Supreme Head of the Church—"

"The Church of England," Miss Christine agreed with a brisk

nod, her brown eyes alight with interest. "There are many churches. I believe that while many profess to be Christian, there are different branches within that belief. It was a king who formed the Church of England, to end Papist rule over the throne, is that not true?"

The vicar turned at last and looked down his nose at the young woman, his hand clutching his napkin. "Of which creed are you, Miss Christine?"

"Church of England." She smiled, her expression without malice or mischief; at least not any that Thomas could detect. Could she be so guileless? "Am I not in your congregation every Sunday, Mr. Ames?"

Thomas tried not to choke on his wine, surprised and amused that she would challenge a man of the cloth. And yet, she sounded so innocent, Thomas still believed her completely unaware of the inappropriate nature of the conversation.

"Indeed. I wonder whether or not you give sufficient heed to the sermons." The vicar's icy tone would have been enough to stop Thomas from saying another word, but Miss Christine seemed undeterred.

"Of course I do." She waved a hand dismissively, either oblivious to, or at least unconcerned about the man's rising ire. The determination on her face reminded Thomas of the late Mrs. Devon. She had often raised her head up in such a manner when making a point to him about her animals.

"That is why I find it so delightful to finally speak to you," Miss Christine went on. "I have many questions about your last discourse. Especially in regard to the rumors about our king's stability and how that might relate to his right to rule both Church and State."

The vicar's other dinner partner alternately blushed and paled as she listened to the discourse and finally broke in with a little giggle. "Oh, Miss Christine, you are quite amusing. Anyone listening would think that you are questioning our vicar's religious teachings. Pray, Mr. Ames, won't you tell me of your recent visits about the parish? I would greatly enjoy hearing of your good works."

Miss Christine, for her part, looked astonished to be cut out of what she clearly considered an interesting debate. She glanced about her, cheeks turning pink. Could she now realize her behavior could be construed as rude or unladylike? Her eyes met his and she raised her eyebrows high.

Thomas had the distinct impression a question was contained in those arched brows. Was she soliciting *his* opinion of the matter? Though he hardly thought their relationship was such that he should acknowledge this silent inquiry, he raised his eyebrows back at her and offered the barest of smiles.

She smiled back, clearly relieved that he would not censure her, and turned her attention to her plate.

The young woman should not have pursued such a topic at dinner and the momentary amusement of her *faux pas* did much to alleviate his headache. The pounding, however, increased with resounding fervor when he realized one of his own dinner companions had repeated the same question a third time.

"I do apologize, Mr. Gilbert," Miss Whitson said. "My mother often tells me my voice is too soft. I shall endeavor to speak up so you may more easily hear me."

Thomas forced a smile, resigning himself to the social niceties that held him bound. "The apology is all mine, Miss Whitson. I was momentarily distracted, but you have my full attention now."

Still, he could not keep himself from sneaking a glance or two across the table, to see if Miss Christine had reengaged the vicar on her topic of choice. Each time, her head stayed bowed over her plate. This afforded him an excellent view of her brown ringlets artfully twisted with pearls, but not another look at her dark eyes or lively expression.

What a shame, he thought, *that we are not dinner partners. Discussing the King's madness or lack thereof would be preferable to describing the color of Italian grapes to Miss Whitson and would be much more diverting.*

After dinner, the ladies excused themselves, and the butler

brought in several bottles of brandy for the gentlemen to choose from for their refreshment. Although not inclined to drink, Thomas thought it best to imbibe a little on this occasion—a necessity if he hoped to make it through the evening in one piece.

The talk immediately turned to the upcoming social season and Parliament's return to the House. None of the men present had any political clout—it was all just talk—but Thomas appreciated the communal desire to be in touch with the current climate.

Thomas noticed that his father, sitting as far away from the bulk of the group as he could get, remained mostly silent. It occurred to Thomas that as badly as he wanted to be gone from this place, his father likely wanted it more. Harold Gilbert knew all the men present quite well, which meant they likely knew of his struggles. It was unlikely anyone in the entire county was ignorant of the difficulties he'd had with the farms. Though they must not know the full extent of the problem, Thomas reasoned, if young misses were still being thrown in his direction.

When the gentlemen finally rose to join the ladies, Thomas made a point to linger back in order to place a bracing hand on his father's shoulder. "Steady, Father. The evening will be over soon."

Harold raised his eyebrows and attempted a smile. "I am getting too old to be away from my own table at night. I look forward to attending fewer social engagements now that you are home. Everyone will wish for the younger Mr. Gilbert. The elder might beg off."

"If you leave me to fend for myself," Thomas said, lowering his voice so that only his father might hear, "I will most certainly exact my revenge. Father or not."

His father chuckled and his expression lightened. "I believe you. Come. Let us see how your mother and sister have fared."

CHRISTINE STOOD BY THE WINDOW, FACING THE ROOM, HER forehead wrinkled in thought. Shifting uncomfortably from foot to foot, she wondered why Miss Hannah kept shooting her disapproving looks. She could hardly guess why or how anyone might find fault in her this evening. She wore one of her newest gowns, her posture remained perfect, her hair done in the latest style, and her opinions given politely and with that air of gentleness her last governess insisted she learn to use.

Yet she obviously fell short of societal expectation.

Julia sat nearby, in deep conversation with Lady Littleton and Mrs. Ames, dressed not nearly so well as Christine and apparently content to sit with the matrons of their country society. Christine did not understand her sister at times, but at that moment, she dearly wished Julia would offer her some hint as to what she had done wrong.

At first, Christine was certain her conversation with the vicar had been appropriate, as religion was generally thought to be an excellent topic for young ladies to consider with some depth. After all, *he* was the one that brought up religion and the rights of kings; she had only done her best to stimulate the conversation. Wasn't that part of a lady's duty at dinner parties? She felt sure it was, though she might obtain one of the guidebooks her aunt mentioned as a directive to a lady's behavior, just to be certain.

But she could *not* have been in the wrong. Hadn't Thomas Gilbert smiled as though nothing untoward occurred? She felt certain his look was one of approval and if a man as well traveled and educated as he could smile at her conversation, she must not have committed too grave an error.

It struck Christine as odd that no one in the company spoke of the King's suspected illness or its ramifications. The topics stayed so trivial, so completely inconsequential.

Why could they never speak of important things in company?

She wondered what foreigners thought of the present troubles in England. Thomas Gilbert would know, having lately come from abroad. And he would not censure her, she felt, for bringing up the subject.

She determined to find an opportunity to ask him. She did not feel at all that this would be ill-advised, as the Gilberts had been their neighbors for several generations and Thomas Gilbert had once been a frequent visitor to the Devon home. He had liked to discuss horses with her mother, when he was still a school lad. Although he must be nearly ten years older than she, Christine remembered he had always had a smile for her and her sisters. Though Christine supposed she saw more of him than any of them, trailing behind him and her mother around the stables.

Julia had once confessed a *tendre* for him, before she was out of the schoolroom, but later admitted she had entertained romantic notions about each of the half dozen bachelors in the area. This confession came before her *Unfortunate Season*, and Julia never said a word about having an interest in any gentleman since.

Christine tried again to catch her sister's attention by moving from the window more into Julia's line of sight. If she could only gain Julia's insight into the situation with the vicar she might be able to relax and enjoy the rest of her evening.

Julia remained completely unaware of Christine's attempts, so engrossed was she in her conversation with the matrons, and the gentlemen entered the room before Christine could go further in her subtle efforts.

The husbands sought out their wives, the younger married men with a lighter step than their elders; and the three single men—one widower, Mr. Gilbert, and the younger Mr. Whitman—joined the circle of young ladies.

Taking advantage of all the shifting of places and changes in conversation, Christine sidled closer to her sister, brushing by the knot of younger people, to stand behind the settee. She bent down to speak in Julia's ear. "Julia."

Her sister ignored her.

"Julia?"

This time she looked up, eyebrows raised.

"Might I have a word with you?" Christine pressed.

Julia blinked and put on her most polite societal smile. "Is something amiss, Christine?"

That gave Christine pause. She could not very well admit to a problem where others might hear and make assumptions. Instead she smiled. "Not at all. I merely have a question."

Julia half-lowered her eyes, her cool demeanor not the least encouraging. "What is it, dearest?"

Dearest. Julia used that particular endearment when irritated by her younger siblings. What had Christine done to irritate her?

"I—" She hesitated, uncertain. "I merely wished to ask if you would be favoring us with a piece tonight?" She winced, knowing full well the question was hardly credible.

Julia's eyes snapped up, the look in them calculating. "Of course not," she answered. "I no longer play in public." Gathering her skirts, Julia rose. "Excuse me." She crossed the room and entered into a conversation with Mr. and Mrs. Brody, a smile already back upon her face.

For a long moment, Christine felt utterly bereft. Here she stood, without a soul to converse with, in the middle of the room, ignored by her own flesh and blood. A lesser woman would have fled the room in tears, or at least blushed, but Christine strengthened her resolve to be the perfect society miss. She lifted her chin, put on her most sparkling smile, and turned to enter the circle of her peers.

Christine took the measure of the others in the group and willed herself to relax. She had known all of these people since childhood. Even Thomas, though newly returned, was familiar to her. A memory flashed into her mind of a late summer afternoon when Mother had sent her out to the garden where Thomas was waiting for a book she'd promised to lend him from her own personal collection. Thomas had taken the book, thanking her and flashing a smile that had made her young heart flutter. Christine wondered if Thomas remembered those years. They felt so long ago.

Joining the circle, Christine feigned interest in Miss Hannah's detailed description of a hat she found at their local milliner's shop. No one could find such inane conversation interesting, could they? One of the things her first governess drilled constantly into her mind was that a lady never spoke unless she had something of great interest to say. A lady should never bore her company.

Christine's patience only lasted a moment. "I hardly think," she said when Miss Hannah paused for breath, "that a hat could really consume so much attention. Surely you saw other things of interest in the village?"

Hannah went pale. The other young ladies in the group blinked and looked from Hannah to Christine, and then back again. Christine looked to the gentlemen to see Mr. Whitman looking away most awkwardly while Thomas Gilbert bit his bottom lip, his eyes lit with obvious amusement.

Oh dear. Had she said something rude or amusing? She had not meant to do either. She only hoped to steer the conversation into more interesting waters.

Christine felt a horrid blush creep up the back of her neck and spread into her cheeks. "Oh, do excuse me," she said. "I think Julia has need of me." She turned abruptly and moved as quickly as she could without running to Julia's side.

Julia gave her a curious glance but said nothing, and then continued to ignore her, while Christine stayed uncertainly in her shadow for the remainder of the evening.

Chapter Four

As the eastern sky changed from deepest blue to gray, Thomas lay wide awake, staring at the ceiling of his bedchamber. Despite the late night of tedium, his sleep was fitful and ended far too soon. He decided he might as well rise and begin the business of the day, but not until after he enjoyed a morning ride. His hunter, a beautiful mare from Italy, would enjoy the exercise and it may very well be one of his last opportunities to ride her. As his father had said, precious few options remained to their family if they wished to avoid debt to institutions or friends.

Thomas marrying for money would be out of the question. His parents would never allow the thought, having formed a love match themselves. After seeing examples of marriage with and without love throughout his life, Thomas would rather decrease his property than attach himself where there could be no true affection.

In less than half an hour, Thomas walked through the stable doors. Six stalls along the back held his most prized possessions. The mares, all beauties with better pedigrees than the nobility of England, were awake and alert as their master greeted each one by name. They were supposed to make his future for him, to raise the status of his family's name and holdings and begin a horse farm he hoped would become well known throughout England. One day, throughout Europe.

Those hopes were crumbling under the realities of his family's financial situation. It was very true that selling even half of his magnificent animals would go a long way to saving their holdings.

Thomas's father thought they all must go, but with the right buyers, Thomas might retain a few of them. His heart ached to even consider losing one, but family duty came before his personal dreams.

After preparing his mount himself, as was his preference, Thomas was soon in the saddle and heading toward the outer fields of his father's estate. His mare was antsy beneath him, so he loosened the reins and urged her into the run she craved. Once the animal had sufficiently winded herself, Thomas led her to the edge of the wood where they took up the familiar paths of his youth. He'd always found the winding forest paths to be peaceful, but that morning, his mind was too occupied to truly enjoy them.

Selling a few of his horses would help their situation, to be sure. But it was only a temporary solution. He had to think more long term. Try as he might, he could formulate no real plan to save his horses unless he found someone willing to allow him use of their stud horses on the promise of a share in the foals. Should there be any. But would even that be enough?

Quite without realizing it, Thomas had arrived at one of his favorite places on the property. He dismounted, allowing his horse to drink from the cool brook.

He had favored the small clearing since childhood, mostly because of how secluded it felt. He rarely saw signs of others passing this way, though the groundskeeper surely passed through on occasion. The trees on either side of the brook opened up, and large rocks poked bald heads up from the ground; the brook tumbled down a short incline at a steady pace, creating a pool that was perfect for watering a horse after a good ride along the boundaries of his father's land. The trees protected the area from strong breezes, and in the summer, the canopy of leaves kept the area cool. It was a perfect retreat from the heat of the day.

With winter approaching, the bare branches reached up to a cold, blue sky, providing no shade, but the familiarity of the location still comforted him. He felt the tension from the last twenty-four hours easing from his shoulders.

Thomas sat on a large, smooth stone beside the water, his eyes watching as it tripped and spilled over stones. He attempted to think on more pleasant things, but found that everything led him back to his family's current predicament.

The one thing that even came close to distracting him was the knowledge that several local mothers were setting their caps at him on behalf of their daughters. He held very little interest in their matchmaking. While he accepted the fact that he would one day marry—he did admire the relationship his parents' shared—he did not feel that now was the correct time to indulge in romance. After all, what could he offer a young lady at present except financial uncertainty?

He sighed and scooped up a small stone to toss into the water. Then he picked up a twig and broke it into smaller pieces, bit by bit tossing each one into the current.

The previous evening's entertainment at least proved to be somewhat diverting. In the end, he had enjoyed seeing the people of the neighborhood more than he had originally anticipated. These were the men and women he had grown up knowing; seeing them had reminded him of their friendships and renewed his interest in their well-being.

The truly amusing moments were all provided by Miss Christine Devon. The young lady, apparently about to make her grand entrance into London society, seemed terribly ill-prepared for the venture. She interrupted conversations, contradicted gentlemen, unwittingly insulted other guests, and then slunk away to hide behind her elder sister like a puppy uncertain of what it had done to

earn censure. While he could detect no malice in the girl, her education might have been lacking in certain respects.

"Oh, hello, Thomas," a merry voice called to him, bringing him
out of his thoughts abruptly. He came to his feet and looked behind
him, then across the brook, to see none other than Christine Devon,
sitting upon a fine chestnut gelding, emerging from the tree-lined
path on her family's side of the divide. "I had no idea you liked this
spot, too."

He was not sure what was more unsettling, that she appeared as
he thought of her or that she was calling him by his Christian name
and acting as though they were well acquainted.

He cleared his throat, squaring his shoulders, and made a brief
bow. "Miss Christine. Good morning."

"I thought I was alone in my terribly unfashionable habits,
waking with the birds for a ride. My sisters, when they go, wait until
midmorning." She brought her horse very near the edge of the brook
before dismounting, quite easily, considering she had no assistance.
The young woman, though dressed in a smart riding habit, looked as
though the wind had played havoc with her hair. Her horse, he noted,
was a beautiful specimen who appeared well lathered from a good
exercise.

"I find morning rides are best for clearing my head," he found
himself saying, still examining the animal more than the rider. "It
prepares me for the day ahead."

"Nearly precisely my view," she said nimbly, and he turned once
more to offer her a polite smile. "It does wonders for easing tensions. I
think if more ladies rode, instead of parading around parks, they
might find themselves with fewer headaches." She said it so matter-
of-factly that he could not help smiling. Once again, he detected
nothing in her tone but an honest opinion, untainted by malice or
criticism. Yet, he could think of several women who would immediately feel offended by her remarks.

"Miss Christine," he said lightly, "I believe many ladies find such exercise unseemly. And many more would prefer to have the excuse of a headache to avoid situations or people they find unpleasant."

She blinked at him, her expression turning thoughtful. "Would they? How strange." Suddenly her eyebrows shot up and she took a quick step toward the bank. "Thomas, I wonder if I might ask you something."

He tried to ignore the discomfort of being addressed with such familiarity. "Please do, Miss Christine. I am at your service."

"Wonderful." She glanced up and down the bank as if to ascertain that they were, most inappropriately, he reminded himself, alone. "I wonder if you could tell me what you made of my actions last evening? I am afraid I am under the impression I did something quite wrong."

He blinked at her, startled by this direct approach, and found himself nearly stuttering out his reply. "Wr-wrong? Last evening? I am afraid I cannot know what you mean."

"Oh, but you must. I know you were listening to my conversation with Mr. Ames. And you were certainly present in the drawing room when I spoke to Hannah. I think I must have committed some gross societal error, but I cannot think what."

Thomas stared at her for several long seconds, trying to gather his wits and figure out what to say. Nothing about such a question was normal or correct in their world. "I believe this is something better discussed with your sister. Or perhaps, your ... governess?"

She shook her head, dropping her eyes at the same moment. "We have no governess any longer, and my sister laughed when I tried to speak to her. That was last night, and she was quite tired by the time we were alone. I did intend to try with her again. But then I ran into to you, and well, perhaps an outside opinion will more beneficial."

"This is an incredibly awkward conversation, Miss Christine," he hazarded to say, reaching up to pinch the bridge of his nose. "I hardly think we should even be standing here, conversing, unchaperoned."

She shrugged her shoulders and paced on her side of the brook. "Thomas, I have known you since childhood. You could hardly have any designs on me. Besides, my mother adored you. I do not think she would mind that I sought your opinion on an important matter."

"Your mother?" He slowly sat back down on the rock. "But it's been years since I have been to your home."

"Five. Since she died." A flash of grief passed along Christine's face but then she smiled, somewhat brittlely. "She liked you a great deal. She thought you had the makings of a fine horseman. I remember your visits. Don't you remember me coming along when you would visit the stables? Mother even required me to fetch and carry books to your home."

Though he would not admit it, he could recall the young girl she was, hair in braids, following him around in her mother's stables.

"I liked her, too. She is the one who gained me an introduction to several breeders," he said. "She was quite the horsewoman. A good judge of animals and an excellent rider."

The young woman before him nodded once, succinctly. "Yes. I miss her greatly, especially now. I'm supposed to be preparing to enter society and I have precious few people willing to offer me direction. I have an etiquette book, but it is frightfully dull reading and contradicts itself. I have asked Julia for assistance, yet I find she doesn't wish to speak to me about anything having to do with the season."

Although he felt some sympathy for her plight, he did not feel it his place to assist her. "I am afraid there is precious little to qualify me as an advisor in such things."

Her smile returned, her eyes dancing as she regarded him with obvious amusement. "You are a well-traveled gentleman who has spent time in London society and abroad. I am certain you have met many well-bred young ladies."

"That is true," he admitted slowly, uncertain as to where this line of thought was leading. "But—"

"And your mother and sisters are very well received in society," she pointed out.

"Yes," he agreed. "They are."

"You likely have some idea of how a young woman ought to behave, and as a gentleman, shouldn't you seek to assist a lady if she expresses a need for help?" Miss Christine spoke that last sentence with narrowed eyes and a sly grin. "So I repeat my entreaty," she continued. As a *gentleman*, could you obligingly assist me by offering your opinion of where I went wrong at the dinner party last evening?"

Thomas stared at her for the space of several seconds before he realized his jaw hung open. He snapped it closed and swallowed his surprise.

He cleared his throat. "Very well. As you are appealing to my honor now, I will tell you that while I believe you made an excellent point when conversing with Mr. Ames, it was neither the right time nor place for you to offer your opposing views on the topic of Divine Right. Further, you tended to interrupt him as he spoke, which he did not appreciate." There was more he could say, but she stood, unblinking, with a surprised look on her face. Whether his words left her confused or hurt, he felt no need to continue. "I believe that is all I am willing to say about it."

Christine's shoulders slumped, but her face regained a look of composure. "I suppose that will do for now," she said. "But I do wish for more assistance. Clearer explanations of things." She sighed. "I need more guidance or I shall be a terrible disappointment to my father when we go to London."

"I am certain you will be a credit to your family, Miss Christine," he said as politely as he could, looking for a way out of the conversation and away from his ruined refuge.

Her gaze was unfocused as she shook her head, not really looking at him. "I worry the opposite is true. After my sister's season did not go as expected, I almost did not get one at all. If I fail to behave properly, I am afraid it will be more than a disappointment for me." Her dark eyes met his again, and the smile she offered was much smaller now, almost sad.

Thomas could not imagine why one difficult evening would have such a disheartening effect on a young lady of her obvious good breeding and cheery personality. But if he saw one of his sisters this discouraged, he would not allow them to remain so.

"You only lack a little guidance, Miss Christine. Surely there are people in our little corner of England who might help you prepare for London. In my time spent there, during the season, every young woman held herself with poise and purpose. Certainly, it cannot be too difficult to acquire that sort of polish." Her frown faded away and her expression changed to one of interest or, he realized in surprise, one of calculation. Her lips then curved upward and her eyes widened.

"*You* could help me obtain the necessary polish, as you say. *You* are a gentleman who is familiar with the ways of society."

Thomas tried to understand her words, not certain what she asked of him. "I don't quite catch your meaning. You wish me to help you? How?"

"Become my tutor. Tutor me in correct societal behavior." She waved a hand in a dismissive manner.

"Tutor you?" he asked, aghast. "How is that at all appropriate? I am a gentleman."

"My dance instructor and music instructor are men," she stated, head tilted to one side as she looked him up and down the way he might look over a horse. Obviously, she misunderstood the situation.

"They likely meet you at home, where you are appropriately chaperoned; the door open, a servant present," he pointed out. "I am not a professional instructor of any kind."

She brought her eyebrows down and he thought he had well confounded her unorthodox plans. Her next words drove that comfort from him. "We are old acquaintances and if we meet in the open air like this, we are unlikely to upset anyone. It is not as though you have any desire to form a connection with me. Everyone knows your circumstances are not conducive to marrying at present, and I do not mind confiding in you that I'm prepared to pursue the most brilliant match in London. My family expects it."

She did not seem to notice or care how affronted he was with her statement of his family's circumstances or how it affected his matrimonial opportunities.

"Miss Christine—"

"Christine, if you please."

Her refusal to even adhere to that simple rule of society gave him alarm. "There is nothing you could do or say that would at all entice me to take up such a position. It is incredibly inappropriate, Miss Christine. I am certain, if you apply to the ladies of your acquaintance, they will be of greater use to you." He bowed, a suitably polite gesture given the circumstances. "If you will excuse me."

"What if I give you stud rights to my horses?" she blurted, clenching her hands at her sides and lifting her chin. "I know you desire to begin a horse farm. The whole neighborhood knows. But *you* lack the ability to procure a sire for your first crop of foals."

He froze, staring across the divide at her, his thoughts suddenly scattered to the wind. "Your stallions?"

"Both of them, if you wish. Castel sired my Ovid and Williomson's Ditto sired my Archer. You ought to recognize those names, even if your tastes run more to the Italian breeds." She raised her eyebrows as she dangled the carrot before him. "They were my mother's treasures and now they are *my* property. I have every right to offer them to you."

Suddenly her proposal no longer sounded absurd. Not with lineage like that in her stables. He had not forgotten those horses, even in five years. He spoke slowly. "You would bribe me with the use of your horses?"

"It is a favor for a favor," she said, jutting her chin out. "An agreement between old friends. An arrangement perfectly appropriate for a gentleman."

Thomas fell quiet.

"Perhaps you would take the time to consider it? I can meet you here tomorrow at the same time." She tilted her head to one side, regarding him with half a smile as if she already knew what his answer would be, the little minx.

Before he knew it, he was agreeing. "Very well. I will be in exactly this spot in the morning."

Her smile stretched as her whole expression brightened and her posture relaxed. "Wonderful. I know if you think on it you will see things my way."

He refrained from denying this, as he was already turning over possibilities in his mind. They went their separate ways after the briefest of farewells. As Thomas headed toward home, he wondered what sort of trouble Miss Christine might cause on a regular basis if she created this much confusion and anxiety after one short meeting.

Chapter Five

C hristine finished dressing for the afternoon just as her
maid came to her door. "Miss Christine," the maid said
respectfully when the door opened. "I was told to inform
you that your father has arrived home. He will join the family for
dinner."

"Oh, thank you, Sarah! We had better find a suitable gown for
dinner. Father insists on our best presentment at meals." It would not
do to disappoint him in his own home, not if she wished to assure him
that her season in London would be a success. "We must discuss the
arrangement of my hair as well." Christine sat down at her dressing
table. "Do you think we ought to try one of the new styles from
Paris?" She bit her lip, studying her brown curls in the mirror. "Can
we try that beautiful Grecian knot?"

"As you wish, Miss Christine. I think that style becomes you," the
abigail said. "What would you like to wear?"

"The blue dinner gown, I should think, with the white ribbons."
Christine stood and went to the wardrobe with Sarah. "Or maybe the
pink? We ought to try both before settling the matter." She sighed. "I
wish Father would've sent word a trifle sooner. He is so particular

about appearances, even at home. And I am certain he will want a full accounting of Aunt's letter."

Christine spent the remainder of the afternoon going over her plans for the season and worrying over her dress for dinner, changing her mind twice before settling on her blue gown more firmly.

Her father had been away on business to London for nearly a month. Christine and her sisters rarely saw him even when he was at home, for he stayed submerged in his business and letters no matter the time of year. Still, she did not feel she could complain about his frequent absences, as he did provide well for his three daughters and school-age son, just as a gentleman should. They were certainly doing well financially, from what she could detect, which was surely all to her father's credit.

Unlike the Gilberts, whose unwise investments and penchant for aiding their tenants left them in a most embarrassing position.

Putting all thoughts of finance from her head, for her father did not like to discuss such matters with his daughters, Christine took a bracing breath and finally left her room. Rebecca exited her bedroom moments after Christine, and the sisters walked the rest of the way together. Julia was already present in the parlor when they arrived.

"Have you seen him yet?" Christine asked, her chest constricting. Father's homecomings always left her nervous. Or excited. It was difficult to tell which until she could more accurately determine his set of mind and mood.

Julia shook her head, not meeting Christine's eyes. "I am told he ordered a change in menu, but that is the only news I have had of him."

"I do hope he is in a cheerful mood," Rebecca said, tilting her head to one side. Christine silently hoped the same.

At that moment, the door opened and in strode their tall, trim, and excessively fierce-looking father. He kept in better shape than most men his age, due to a great deal of sport, and he repeatedly told his daughters that appearance was everything in society. If he looked slovenly, people would assume that to be part of his character and no one would do business with a slovenly man. In keeping with his concern for appearance, his hair remained as neatly trimmed as ever, his face clean-shaven, his clothing immaculate, though appropriate for one of his age and station, and his bearing as ramrod straight as any soldier's.

Like a general appraising his troops, Mr. Devon cast an eye over each daughter as they made their curtsies to him. "Very well," he said, by way of greeting and approval of their persons. "I see the house still stands in my absence, though I have had reports from the staff that leave me surprised at your management, Julia."

Julia stiffened and her eyes went to the floor. "I hope you find the household has been run acceptably in your absence, Father."

"Hardly. We will meet with the housekeeper tomorrow to discuss the problems I have discovered in the kitchens. I should not have to be involved in such domestic chores, Julia. I expect for you to heed my words in the proper management of a house even when I am not present. Am I understood?"

"Yes, Father," she answered dutifully, her eyes still low, though Christine thought she saw her sister's jaw clench.

Well. If Julia ever wants Father's respect, she will have to give in and do things his way. It is his house, after all, and his servants.

Christine never understood why her sister insisted on trying things differently after their father clearly expressed his desires for how they ought to be done. It was a daughter's place to be obedient.

Julia maintained that their father did little more than ignore them, whether at home or abroad, and so they ought to do what they could to please themselves.

"Christine," he said, causing her to snap her attention back to him at once. "I have been speaking with your Aunt Jacqueline at great length and she informed me she would write to you. I would like to have her correspondence and your written preparation for the season on my desk by nine o'clock tomorrow morning."

"Yes, Father," she answered dutifully, her posture stiffening. "We have a complete budget ready for your approval, sir."

"Yes." He cast his eyes over her again in an assessing manner. "Where did you find that hairstyle?"

"In one of the fashion plates sent by Aunt Jacqueline, Father. It is supposed to be all the rage this season. I have asked my abigail to practice it." She and turned her head to the side so that he might admire what the style did to her profile. "It is a most becoming look, Father. It draws attention to—"

"I hardly care what it is supposed to achieve, Christine." His interruption immediately froze her smile in place. "So long as it is deemed acceptable. Take heed to note how other young ladies appear and be prepared to cast aside this style if it is at all out of mode. If you must keep it, I would encourage you to embellish what you can with jewels. Show we are not a destitute house by any means."

His eyes left hers and went to Rebecca. The youngest sister kept her gaze lowered and her expression neutral. Rebecca, younger and of milder manners than her sisters, looked like naught but a meek little lamb.

"Rebecca." His tone was no different with her than it had been as he censured the other two. "Still poring over novels?"

She shook her head slightly. "Not as often, Father. I have been improving upon my knowledge of gardening, as you suggested."

"A very ladylike endeavor and one in which a woman may be seen to be clever, by the arrangement of flowers." He nodded, though no real look of pleasure at being obeyed crossed his expression. "If you must read, read things that will actually be of use to you. I recommend no further novels at all. If you are caught at reading such by the wrong sort of person they will assume the worst of you."

"Yes, Father." Her voice dropped in volume with her response, as did her shoulders.

Christine wondered if this was not a touch harsh, but felt fairly certain that Rebecca would still read whatever she wished. Though she was the youngest sister, and quiet at that, Rebecca knew her own mind.

The butler came in to announce dinner, saving them from further inspection, at least for the space of time it would take to cross the hall to the dining room.

Father went ahead first and they followed after, from oldest to youngest.

Christine thought of reaching out to Julia, to reassure her. But Julia went before her with a stiff spine, squared shoulders, and an air that would likely rebuff any who might approach her, in any circumstance.

Christine sighed and did her best to glide in a ladylike manner into the dining room.

The first several minutes of the soup course passed quietly. The only sound was that of their spoons gently descending into the liquid. The sisters took great care to avoid making any noise at all while they sipped from the spoon. Anything related to a slurp would surely bring on a lecture from their father on proper dining etiquette.

None of the sisters ventured any comment, nor would they. Father would speak first if anyone was to speak at all. Women were ornamentation, he believed, to be brought out when a man wished to show them off or admire them himself. Mr. Devon hardly needed the conversation of his daughters to be part of his dinner ritual.

Yet Christine ached to speak to him about her coming season and all the preparations made thus far. She wanted to ask him about his conversation with her aunt. She wished greatly to ask him all manner of questions about what he expected of her; then she could reassure him of her determination to meet all his criteria with grace and aplomb when she selected a husband from the many admirers that would surely fall at her feet.

They were nearly ready for the fruit course, the whole of the meal passing in silence, when he finally spoke.

"I saw on your menu you planned to serve pears in a red wine sauce this evening," her father said, shooting a look through narrowed eyes at Julia. "Very common, Julia. And not a specialty of cook's. I hired a French pastry chef for a reason."

"Yes, Father," Julia said, her shoulders taut though her eyes remained lowered. "I did not know you would be home when I ordered the menu."

"You should always conduct yourself," he said in a deceptively soft tone, "and this household, the same whether I am in residence or not. I detest pears. They are a grainy, poor fruit with little to recommend them. We do not even grow pears here."

"No, Father," she agreed. "Rebecca does enjoy them, though."

Rebecca sunk somewhat in her chair, her eyes darting from Julia to her father before her gaze fell to her lap. From her place across the table, Christine could not see her sister's hands, but she guessed they would be fidgeting with her napkin. Christine swallowed and looked sideways at their father, trying not to show any outward appearance of worry. Julia often wished to defy the man, but Rebecca would have no wish to do so. It wasn't fair for Julia to drag her into the confrontation like that.

"What Rebecca enjoys is of no concern to me." He did not even look at his youngest daughter, but remained staring at the top of Julia's lowered head.

Christine watched, holding still as a statue, though inside she squirmed at the spectacle Julia made of herself. Why could she not learn to do things Father's way? They could avoid so many of these unpleasant scenes if Julia would only listen.

"Of course not, Father," Julia said at last.

"I expect you to adhere to the meal plans I will lay out for you tomorrow."

"Yes, Father."

He nodded once before the doors opened and the fruit pastries were brought in.

At least they tasted delicious. Christine would give him that. Nothing like the overdone and overly-seasoned pies Julia preferred. Though they were different than the baked goods that were Christine's especial favorite as well. But his daughter's likes and dislikes were of no consequence. Father was lord and master of his home.

Whatever he desired would be served, without question or complaint.

Before touching even a crumb of her pastry, Julia rose from her chair. "Pray, excuse me. I am unwell."

Their father did not even glance up from his plate, dismissing Julia with a short flick of his wrist.

Christine attempted to catch Julia's eye to ascertain the reason for her sister's abrupt departure, but Julia did not look in her direction. She simply turned on her heel and left the room, faster than Christine expected for someone feeling poorly enough to flee.

Poor Julia.

If only there could be more harmony between them all; Christine hated to see her sisters retreat within themselves nearly as much as she hated her father's disdain.

Chapter Six

Dinner at the Gilbert home always served to lift Thomas's spirits. His father presided over the meal with a smile, no matter the circumstances, and his mother, sitting opposite, always matched his expression. His parents often exchanged knowing glances across the room, their affection for each other obvious in their silent communications.

Thomas did not realize how much he had missed their intimate family meals while he was away, not until he was home again. Now, at the table where he had grown up, his parents on either side of him, the only thing that would make the evening more comfortable was the presence of his sisters. A pang of longing welled up inside. Both already married, his sisters were likely tucked up at their own tables, surrounded by their growing families. It wasn't so easy to have everyone together for a family meal; but perhaps it was time for Thomas to plan a visit or two.

Thomas turned his attention to his mother, listening as she spoke freely of her day. She had spent the morning visiting with tenant families and mentioned each person with her customary warmth and concern. She told stories of the children as though they were her own grandchildren.

"They are little imps," his father declared after one especially harrowing tale. "And that Jones boy is going to wind up giving his poor father an apoplexy. He is forever doing the worst things in the name of curiosity."

"Ah, he is a dear boy," his mother countered with a wave of her hand. "Very clever. If he grows up to take over his father's lease, the farm will be in good hands. He is full of original ideas."

"There is nothing original," her husband said drolly, "in putting frogs in places they oughtn't to be."

"Aren't we lucky Thomas never played such pranks." Mrs. Gilbert looked at her son, her gaze full of affection. "It was not in his nature."

His father chuckled and slanted Thomas a look. "No. This boy never noticed anything smaller than a colt."

Thomas laughed. "Father, are you saying you wished me to put frogs in—what was it—cream pitchers? Or my sisters' boots?"

"Would have been more natural," his father said with feigned disapproval. "Instead we were forever pulling you out of the stables."

"Oh, leave him alone." Mother reached out to pat Thomas's hand. "He is a good lad, even if he is horse mad." She sighed. "Although I do begin to despair of you ever marrying, Thomas. Not many gentlewomen spend their days in the stables, after all."

Thomas sat up straighter, noting how quickly his earlier contentment had vanished. For all that Christine Devon said disparaging his ability to find a wife in his present circumstances, his mother did not seem to share those views. "What's this? Have you a mind to be rid of me so soon after I am home?"

She shook her head and smiled gently. "No, dear. But I do have a mother's wish to see you properly settled with a handsome young woman. We would hardly be rid of you, anyway. We would be adding to the table, not losing someone this time." Her eyes twinkled merrily at the idea.

Thomas chuckled and shook his head, not entirely surprised by his mother's plans. "I have not even been home above two weeks and you are playing matchmaker?"

"You are not getting any younger, Tom," she said sweetly. "You've given me plenty of time to plan and scheme on your behalf. I am especially grateful you did not return home from Italy with a bride. I'm so invested now; that truly would have ruined my plans."

Thomas's cravat suddenly felt much too tight. He'd recognized his mother's efforts at the dinner party to make sure there were young ladies in attendance, but nothing about her present commentary felt subtle. "Plans?" His voice caught on the word, and he cleared his throat before continuing. "For me? Involving marriage?"

Mr. Gilbert chuckled. "From the moment each of you were born your mother started making such plans, boy. And I warn you, anyone as ambitious as your mother will eventually get her way."

"I do not think now is the time." Thomas shifted in his seat, his eyes darting from his father's amused smile to his mother's now determined look. "I have only just come home; with things as they are, you cannot hope for me to run off to London to make a match."

Although his mother knew full well the state of the family affairs, Thomas did not wish to speak of it in detail when their evening had begun so pleasantly. Still, it struck him as fanciful for him to consider marriage at such a time as this. Why was Miss Christine the only person who recognized that his family's status would be a problem in finding a suitable mate?

Mrs. Gilbert's expression softened, her look less calculating. "Tom darling, if you find the right young lady, your financial difficulties will not be a deterrent. Indeed, a clever young lady may even help you see us out of it. Or bring a dowry that does the trick."

"A mercenary marriage?" Thomas asked, incredulous.

"Not at all. I want for you what your father and I have." She smiled across the table to her husband, who looked, Thomas noted, much more comfortable with the conversation than he might have expected. "You should have a love match. A partnership built on mutual understanding and respect. A woman who would make such a match with you could hardly care about your present struggles so long as you gave her the security of a good home. We are not paupers. We are a good family. We could provide comfort and security to any young miss, even if our fortunes do not turn around as I suspect they soon will."

Thomas shook his head and slumped back in his chair. "Mother, I knew you had a romantic turn of mind, but I did not think to attach the word 'hopeless' to it."

She rose from her chair, signaling the end of the meal. Her husband and son stood, a habit of respect formed long before. "Dear Tom. There is nothing hopeless about love." She leaned forward to give him a kiss on the cheek. "Are you two lingering over brandies or will you join me in the music room? I have learned a new piece!"

They went with her, willingly on Thomas's part, eagerly on his father's. Thomas hung back and took a seat where he could watch them. His father sat next to the piano stool and turned pages for his wife as she played. Observing their union, their thoughtfulness, even the way they anticipated each other's movements, was an inspiration to Thomas. Despite the difficulty the family faced, Thomas's mother had great faith in her husband and supported him with love and respect.

Thomas understood why she would want such a union for him. He appreciated the rarity of a marriage with such mutual admiration and devotion.

But while his parents gave him hope such a love was possible, he would not enter into a marriage with any young lady unless he could guarantee her a secure future. At present, he he could make no such guarantees. It smarted to think of selling their valuable land and horses in order to meet the current demands of their tenants and household. The future should *not* be sacrificed for the present.

His mind turned to Miss Christine's offer of payment for tutoring. Tutoring in the art of acceptable social behavior.

The utterly absurd idea, in light of his personal hopes and

dreams, struck him as less and less absurd with every passing moment.

⚜

THE FOLLOWING MORNING, CHRISTINE ARRIVED AT SEVEN-thirty sharp, looking less disheveled than the morning before. It led Thomas to believe she had come straight to the brook instead of indulging in a morning ride. A chilly breeze swept through the trees, yet the weather was not yet unbearably cold.

"You appear rather serious," she said cheerfully, by way of greeting. "Does that mean you intend to help me, even if it is against your better judgment?" Her eyes glittered down at him and her smile seemed more suited to a wood nymph than a proper English lady.

Thomas, from his side of the natural divide, kept his tone completely businesslike. "Yes, but I have a few conditions." How she took the arrangement he proposed would truly decide it for him.

She dismounted gracefully, giving her horse an affectionate pat before she turned and delivered another bright smile. "Such as?"

"You must refrain from calling me by my Christian name," Thomas said firmly. "We must maintain an appropriate physical distance so if we are discovered it will not be in a compromising manner. These meetings must remain secret." He ticked each condition off on a finger, holding his hand up in the air and affecting his most stern countenance, which he hoped would give her some indication of how serious this matter would be.

She blinked at him across the way, her arm encircling the neck of her horse, and considered him for several moments. "I understand all but the first condition. Does my use of your name offend you so greatly? We have known each other for many years."

"Even still, ours is not a close connection or an overly familiar relationship," he stated firmly. "And should anyone come upon us, it would be best if we maintain an air of formality."

She nodded, albeit slowly, her countenance at last changing to

49

show a more somber turn of mind. "Very well. I understand your conditions and accept them. Now, I shall give you my terms." She spoke clearly, each word resolute. "My lessons with you will occur every three days from now until the Christmas ball. As it is November sixth, that would mean fifteen separate lessons."

"Fifteen?" he interrupted, eyebrows raised. "Do you anticipate needing that much 'tutoring' in the social arts?"

"You are receiving the stud rights of both my prized stallions, Mr. Gilbert. Surely you expected to put in a little effort to earn them, did you not?" So she was as insistent as he that their arrangement be a business transaction and nothing more.

Thomas sighed and pinched the bridge of his nose with gloved fingers. Miss Christine's horses were well worth his time, but how would he manage to excuse himself so frequently, with his family's financial situation as it stood? He ought to be spending every available moment sorting that business out.

"Very well. I accept those terms," he finally said.

"Excellent." Her smile reappeared, nearly as bright as when she first greeted him. "I believe we will work well together, Mr. Gilbert."

He refrained from commenting on that assessment, still wondering how things had come to this, pressing him into such an unorthodox trade to get what he wanted. He reminded himself again that stud rights to Devon stallions would allow him to hold off on selling his mares for a time and procure investors on the potential foals, a step that could quite possibly secure his family's future without parting with lands, horses, or any prized heirlooms.

"What *exactly* do you wish to learn during our meetings?" he asked, trying not to sound too defeated. He would do well to think of her as his benefactress, even if an unusual one. "You seem to have knowledge of social graces, after all. Where do you find yourself lacking?"

From his distance across the brook, no more than three yards, he saw the sudden blush that stained her cheeks.

"At the dinner party the other night, I had the impression that

Mr. Ames thought my conversation lacking and I might have said something to distress Hannah." She twisted her gloved fingers and looked down at the ground. "I think we should begin there."

"With conversations?"

Miss Christine glanced up and offered a shrug of one shoulder. "My governess always taught me that topics of religious matters, the weather, and the occupations of a lady were appropriate for making conversation. She did warn me to curb my opinions in public but encouraged me to speak my mind in the home. I am afraid I am not certain where the boundaries are when it comes to expressing such opinions."

She looked down again, clearly ill at ease. "I am given to understand that gentlemen prefer to speak of topics that interest them but that a lady should not express differing or too firm opinions. If that is how every lady should speak, how does one stand out in such conversations?"

He blinked, surprised at the perception she offered as well as the difficulty in how such a thing could be taught. Perhaps this was not a completely hopeless endeavor since she could explain her difficulties succinctly. He thought back on his own social forays in London and nodded. "I see the complexity of the situation. Is there more you wish to learn?"

"Yes. How does one flirt without being perceived as a *flirt*? How does one encourage a gentleman in his addresses without being too forward? If it is my duty to please potential suitors by appealing to their tastes in dress, deportment, and opinions, how do I discover such things without being obvious?"

His mind whirled with both the quality of her requests and the idea that she knew not how to accomplish any of these things. In his experience, most of the ladies he encountered were already very adept at such social maneuvering. How did they learn it? He assumed it came naturally or else was passed from one woman to another.

He blurted the question, "Why hasn't anyone taken such matters in hand with you before now?"

Her blush returned and she looked away. "My mother passed when I was fourteen, you will remember. She told me the time would come when I would need to prepare for my come-out, but there was no reason to bother my head with such notions until then. Mostly, she taught me about horses. My governess was a lovely woman but ceased lessons with me shortly after my mother's death. I am afraid I was a poor student and spent more time outdoors than in. She focused her efforts on Julia's societal preparations and Rebecca's eager mind."

"Your honesty on the subject is admirable," Thomas stated slowly. "But it also means we likely have a great deal of work. I am astonished your father did not give you over to some female relative for education before now." Indeed, that would seem to be what most men did: farm out their daughters to boarding schools, governesses, or maiden aunts. *His* father might be an exception, given how often he spoke of his daughters with fondness. Strange, but Thomas had never thought much of the differences between his upbringing and others' before this moment.

"Father rarely bothers himself with our education. I doubt my governess ever informed him of my errant behavior." She smiled in a self-deprecating way. Her shoulders lifted and dropped in a shrug. "He has more important things to take up his time."

Thomas considered this statement, carefully taking in her expression. He wondered what his education would have been like if his father did not, in fact, take an interest in what his son learned. He well remembered his father's visits to Eton and Cambridge, the letters written to and from the schools, and even the introduction to Mrs. Devon with the explanation of Thomas's near obsession over horses.

"I must make a brilliant match," Miss Christine stated firmly, interrupting his thoughts. "And so I *must* be a sensation this season. I am already at a disadvantage, being older than many. The other ladies my age are likely on their second or third seasons, for the most part."

She struck him as quite young, possibly due to her naivete. "How old are you, Miss Christine?" he asked, doing a quick mental calculation. "Nineteen? It has been five years since your mother's passing."

"Yes. I will be twenty in the spring. And twenty sounds ever so much older than nineteen." She shuddered as though the idea disgusted her. "I must make my match before then."

He did not see why it was such a desperate thing, as Mr. Devon was well known in London society and they clearly had financial comfort. Even if she received no offer during her first season, or before the dreaded twentieth birthday, she certainly had enough standing and finances to attract someone in good time. Thomas felt suddenly grateful, at least, that the matchmaking part of Miss Christine's predicament was not of his concern.

It would be wrong to advise against someone with a good head on her shoulders to keep it to herself. Yet this is what Miss Christine asked of him.

"Very well. I will do my best. For today, you have given me much to think on. For the next three days, practice reserving your opinion when in conversation. Instead, encourage others to tell you what they think and feel, before giving in to the inclination to share *your* thoughts on the matter. Try to avoid conflict, not spur it on."

She nodded with a slow deliberateness that lent weight to his words. While he had some difficulty taking this exercise seriously, she certainly did not.

Her dark eyes sought his, widening with an obvious eagerness to please. "Might you give me an example? I merely wish to clarify your instructions." Indeed, her attitude now struck him as that of an apt pupil.

"The vicar's conversation the other evening will serve," Thomas said. "I did not catch the whole of it, but I did hear part of his discourse on Divine authority given to kings."

"Yes." Christine nodded, a frown drawing her eyebrows together and her lips downward. The eager pupil vanished before his eyes and a serious young woman appeared instead. "Wasn't that interesting? He agreed that the kingship given to Saul was taken away because he was unfit, but did not think that the colonists had the right to remove themselves from under King George's reign because of divine right. Yet I would not agree that our king is an overly religious man. Saul's kingship was revoked when he failed to obey a commandment, and I must say that I have heard enough gossip to believe our king might have done the same. The former colonists certainly believe so."

Thomas stared at her, eyebrows raised high, his responsibility suddenly taking on a greater weight. "This is going to be a lot of work," he muttered, looking heavenward. Though her argument interested him, it would encourage her errant behavior to engage her in the same debate. He couldn't encourage the behavior of a blue-stocking.

"What was that?" she asked, stepping closer to the brook.

He shook his head. "Miss Christine, contradicting a vicar over a matter of religion is not at all in keeping with polite conversation."

"I thought religion was an acceptable topic of conversation?"

Her confusion nearly made him groan aloud.

"That is not entirely true. I believe the most acceptable form of conversation in terms of religion is more along the lines of discussing good works. Those done by you, as a lady, and the good works of others. You should never engage in a debate on religious topics, which is precisely what you did with the good Mr. Ames. While a gentle-man, or a vicar, might be free to share his religious ideologies, it is left to a lady in your position to either smile politely and agree or smile politely and keep your opinions to yourself."

"Oh." She bit her bottom lip, her eyebrows furrowed more deeply. "What should I have said?"

He thought carefully, remembering the conversation he had over-heard and pitting that against what most young ladies might have remarked. "You likely should have smiled and thanked him for enlightening you. Then followed Miss Hannah's example and asked after his other Christian endeavors. That would have flattered him, to believe you interested in his occupation." Even as he instructed her, he found his mind going back to her opinions. They were clever and well thought out. But, sadly, they had no place in society while husband hunting.

She nodded, still looking thoughtful, and squared her shoulders. "I should solicit the opinions of others, encourage them to share their thoughts on the subject, and agree with whatever a gentleman says?"

"That would be a good start, yes," he agreed slowly, trying to determine if there was anything amiss with that summary. "That would make most gentlemen inclined to favor you, I would think."

"Gentlemen like to be right, even when they are not," she said, her lips twitching slightly. Her deep brown eyes narrowed again, though they sparkled enough that he realized she saw humor in the statement.

He nearly groaned again but decided it was best to nod in his gravest manner. It was not at all a flattering truth, though it was the way of things in society. "Most believe they are always right. Yes."

"Excellent. I understand. That will have to suffice today. I am due to have an audience with my father at nine o'clock, so I must go if I am to be present in time." She tilted her head to one side, regarding him with a narrow look. "Have you been invited to Miss Hannah's home for dessert and games?"

"I do believe my mother received such an invitation, yes. Will I see you there?"

"Yes, and I will practice what you have taught me." Miss Christine nodded firmly before going to her horse. She led the gelding to the same little rock she used as a mounting block the day before. She climbed atop with ease and offered him a smile and wave.

"Good day to you, Thom—Mr. Gilbert."

"And to you, Miss Christine." He nodded deeply, tipping his hat as well. "I will see you again soon." And until then, he would try to work out how to teach her the things inherent to the rest of the females of society. He hoped, very sincerely, that he had not taken on a task too difficult to complete.

Chapter Seven

"Christine." The two syllables of her name, the only greeting her father gave when she entered his study at precisely the appointed time, came out clipped and precise. "Sit."

She obeyed, walking as gracefully as possible to the chair directly across from his desk. Christine always did her best to be a dutiful and obedient daughter and her father detested an unladylike gait.

"Your lists for purchases?"

She held out the two sheets of paper prepared for this very interview. "The shorter list is for purchases to be made here, the longer are things Aunt Jacqueline wishes me to acquire in town. We estimated the costs, which are noted to the side."

He said not a word as he perused the inventory needed. After a few moments, he turned a page in an account book on his desk and made several notations, then held the lists back out to her. "This appears acceptable. Are you certain this will be adequate?"

Christine swallowed and nodded. "Aunt Jacqueline was very specific. It is not too much?"

Her father raised his eyebrows at her. "As I said, it is acceptable, Christine." He sat back in his chair and steepled his fingers together.

His tone remained even and his cadence deliberate and slow. "You are an investment. I expect that the more I invest in your season, the higher quality the return will be. As a daughter, your use to my household's development is in whatever attachment you make in marriage."

Christine tried not to flinch at his words. She knew she ought to be used to them by now.

"Any assets that are yours, such as the horses, your dowry, inherited jewels, will enrich your husband. If you prove to be a stable marriage partner, able to keep your husband's social standing above reproach, you will be of benefit to him. You understand?"

"Yes, Father." She tried not to fidget, but clasped her hands tightly before her.

"I benefit from whatever connections your new family will have. If you marry a lord, we have access to nobility. If you marry a politician, we interact with those who influence policy and procedure. Should you marry a gentleman of means, his connections will become mine. Do you understand?"

Christine nodded again, firmly. "Yes, Father. I know your expectations."

"Do you? Julia claimed to understand what her marriage would mean for us and yet she failed me abysmally, her season nothing more than a mistake. A wasted investment." He sighed and his eyes swept her figure. "Many girls believe a season to be their due. It is not. A season is nothing more than a business exchange dressed in fine clothing. Negotiations set in ballrooms. Your marriage will be a contract, and a well negotiated contract at that. Do not disappoint me." The last he said with an air of warning, his eyes darkening with disapproval.

Christine swallowed and sat straighter. "I will not fail, Father. I will make you proud."

"That remains to be seen." He looked back down at his books. "That will be all." He uttered the dismissal in the same tone reserved for servants, making his point clear. Like those he employed, she must obey him.

"Yes, Father." She rose, dropped a quick curtsy, and left the study. Once the door closed behind her, she drew in a deep breath, marveling at how stuffy the atmosphere felt in that room. She smoothed down the front of her dress before walking back up the steps to find her sisters. Still jittery from the audience with her father, the comfort of their company felt most necessary.

HANNAH LITTLETON CAME BY IN THE EARLY AFTERNOON TO visit with the sisters, all smiles and excitement over the pending visit of her two cousins. They were both young gentlemen from Warwickshire. One, the heir to her father's estate; the other, a dashing young captain in the army. Hannah obviously thought highly of them as she expounded upon their virtues.

"You remember them. They visited five years ago at Christmastime."

"We were in London at the time," Julia said. Christine recognized the false lightness Julia affected when speaking to others of London. But no one else heard it; Julia carried herself gracefully enough no one would think anything amiss.

Christine realized that last visit to London coincided with the beginning of Julia's season. That year and every year before it, the family had always spent Christmas in London to attend all the events society held to mark the holiday. Now they spent the holiday in the country. Would that change, should Christine marry well?

"It is no matter," Hannah said with a wave. "They were a nuisance then. But twenty-five and twenty-two are ever so much more mature ages, I should think. I saw them last spring and they are both positively charming. I desperately want them to enjoy themselves here so they might introduce me to gentlemen of their acquaintance during the season."

"Oh?" Christine said, tilting her head to one side. "Will they both be there? I should think our military is needed elsewhere at present."

"Nicholas, the second son, has responsibilities in London," Hannah answered primly, barely casting a glance at Christine. Perhaps she had not yet forgiven Christine's *faux pas* a few evenings before. "And his family is well enough known to allow him to receive several invitations to social events. I believe many will think it patriotic to invite a young man in uniform to their parties and balls."

"I suppose," Christine reluctantly agreed, though from what she read in the paper she knew men in uniform would be much more useful elsewhere.

Julia changed the subject subtly, as she always did when London became the focal point of conversations. "You must be excited to have them here for the holiday. What will you do to keep these young men entertained?"

"Oh, we have many things planned. Which is really why I came. I wanted to be certain you accepted our invitation and extend it to Rebecca and your father as well. I want to introduce them to positively everyone. We shall play cards and have a lovely time."

Christine's immediate thoughts were on Thomas's suggestions. Since he would be at the Littletons' home, he could see firsthand how well she performed the assignment given her. An evening out, among gentlemen new to the area, suited her purposes perfectly.

Cards, in fact, would be an excellent testing ground. She could hardly speak about inappropriate topics when the order of the evening consisted of playing games.

Julia confirmed their acceptance, spoke with some delight over what should be worn, and then bid their guest a good day. Once Hannah left, Rebecca voiced misgivings about the evening.

"Do you think I ought to have said I will go? I am not out yet."

"It is only Hannah's family," Julia said. "A neighborhood gathering, and I am certain her younger sisters will be present or she would not have extended the invitation to you."

Christine was on the verge of agreeing when she remembered their father in residence. "Should we apply to Father, to be certain?"

Julia sniffed and the smile disappeared. "Father rarely cares where we are after dinner. I doubt he will care at all whether any of us stay or go."

Christine raised her eyebrows and exchanged a look with Rebecca. "We are going to tell him of the invitation, are we not? He may wish to attend."

Julia stood and gathered her skirts. "You tell him, Christine. I am busy." Without another word she disappeared out the door.

Shaking her head, Christine allowed herself to slump back in her seat. "I cannot understand her."

"No. I do not suppose either of us do. She speaks so little." Rebecca sighed, pushing a chestnut curl behind her ear. "I remember when we used to sit for hours and talk of everything. The inconsequential and the important."

"Then she had to go and ruin her season," Christine added caustically, her eyes going to the window where she could see winter clouds moving in. "And ruin everything for us. At home and in London."

"I doubt whatever happened was something Julia meant to do," Rebecca noted softly. "It is unlikely someone would purposely sabotage their first season, after all."

"First and only." Christine sat up straighter. She needed to change the subject. Thinking on Julia's failure only made her feel more anxious about her own season. She couldn't afford to indulge such fears, even for a moment, else they influence her ability to behave properly. "What are you reading?" she asked Rebecca.

Rebecca blushed and shyly took a book out from under the cushion where she sat. "Nothing of importance. A novel."

Christine rolled her eyes and sighed. "You had better not let Father see."

"When is he ever around to see?" Rebecca asked with a huff, opening the cover of her book. "And I am reading that horticulture book from Aunt Jacqueline as well. Only, it is difficult to remember where I have laid it at times." The airy tone and innocent expression did not fool Christine.

Shaking her head, Christine moved slowly to the window. "Careful, Rebecca. Father expects his daughters to be obedient in all things. I also think he has spies amongst the servants," she added in a lighter tone. "For he seems to know everything that goes on without ever speaking to us."

"The servants like us," Rebecca countered. "They do not care for Father, beyond their appreciation that he provides employment. I'm not even sure they respect him."

The observation was astute and likely true, but Christine remained silent. She watched as the clouds crept across the sky, leaving it gray and dreary. Fall would soon give way to winter, which *should* excite her. The approach of her first season finally gave her the opportunity to experience life! She barely remembered her last visit to London. Before her mother had passed away, the whole family looked forward to visiting the city and enjoying all the entertainments it had to offer.

Her father said having children underfoot was too much of a bother when he went alone, after their mother died. But now, she would be in that great city again, enjoying the festivities, the parks, the libraries and salons, the teas and morning calls. She would be admitted into a new level of society, of sophistication. Plays, operas, musicales, balls, and many other delights awaited her.

She thought again of how important it was that she avoid making a complete fool of herself. Thankfully, Thomas Gilbert was willing to help. She trusted Thomas, just as her mother had; surely he would help her avoid any unpleasantness.

A wave of anxiety pinched up Christine's spine.

He must, for her future depended on it.

Chapter Eight

Thomas arrived at the home of Lord and Lady Littleton with his sister and her husband. His father had turned down the invitation for himself, as Mrs. Gilbert was not feeling well. But his mother desired for Thomas to go out, to see and be seen. She also expected a full report of the evening. She'd spoken from beneath a cool compress as she rested on the couch in his father's study, but her tone left no room for argument.

Knowing Christine Devon would be attending the event gave him something to look forward to, beyond the usual entertainments. He needed to study her behavior, to ascertain if she had understood her first lesson. He hoped her father would be in attendance as well. If he interpreted that gentleman's thoughts on his daughter's behavior, he might help Christine better meet her father's expectations.

Thomas barely remembered Mr. Devon, having met only with Mrs. Devon when visiting the stables. Mr. Devon often left for months at a time. Thomas recalled the inclination he'd once felt to stay out of Devon's way, but now, as an adult, he had no concerns on that quarter.

"I do hope tonight is enjoyable," Martha said as she stepped down from their carriage. "It promises to be a late evening."

"Why are we here if you are reticent about it?" George asked, looking at his wife in puzzlement.

She waved toward her brother. "To make sure this one does his duty."

Thomas chuckled, following them up the steps to the second floor. "I assure you, Martha, I intend to enjoy the evening. A night of games is far less daunting than a dinner party."

She shot a glare over her shoulder at him but said nothing further. They were greeted by Lady Littleton as they arrived at the parlor.

"Oh, thank you for coming," the woman said, her hands fluttering to her chest. "It is good to have you especially, Mr. Gilbert. We have so many young ladies and gentlemen here tonight it makes me feel quite young myself."

"Indeed, Lady Littleton," Thomas said, offering up his most charming smile. "You would fit in with my set in a trice. You look absolutely lovely and your vibrancy is above my own tonight."

"Now I remember why I liked it when Samuel brought you around," she said with a wag of her finger. "Go use that charm on the young ladies, Mr. Gilbert. And see if your behavior might entice my son to do the same. Dessert and coffee are available when you wish it. Cards are in the parlor and some of the men are playing at billiards. Go on, enjoy yourselves."

George and Martha went toward the dessert tables while Thomas decided to make his way to the billiard room first. Upon his arrival, Samuel Littleton intercepted him. Though they attended different schools, they had often kept each other company over the holidays. There were not many young men in the neighborhood, after all, and they were only a year apart in age.

Thomas was introduced and reintroduced to the house guests, the evening guests, and the business associates of Lord Littleton. Most of the men had congregated around the billiards table and, unsurprisingly, the brandy. Mr. Devon was among them.

Thomas wondered if Christine's difficulties arose from her father's social behavior, as he rarely mingled in local society.

It only took a few moments in his company for Thomas to feel as though he had a good read on Mr. Devon. Nothing about the man was reticent. He spoke his mind clearly, succinctly, and somewhat condescendingly.

Thomas listened for a time while he discussed the opening of Parliament for the season, taking the first available opportunity to enter the conversation.

"Mr. Devon, I understand your household has good reason to anticipate the coming season. I admit to being relieved I will not remove myself to London this year, but I can imagine how anxious you must be to have a daughter making her debut." Thomas hoped this was not too forward a comment.

Mr. Devon, holding a glass of brandy, raised his eyebrows at the change of topic. "You are still a very young man, Mr. Gilbert. Which explains why *you* would experience anxiety at such an event. I am not at all concerned. My daughter will do her duty by the family, I am certain, and all will be well."

"Do her duty?" Thomas asked, tilting his head to one side. His sister's words in the carriage echoed in his memory. "Ah, by finding her place in society?"

"By marrying her place in society," Mr. Devon corrected. He traded his glass for the billiard stick, his expression cool. "A daughter is only as good as the son-in-law she brings to her father. I have made certain she understands what I expect of her eventual union." He prepared his shot. "She has been raised correctly. I do not think she will disappoint me."

"You are blessed with an obedient child then?" Mr. Whitson, a man with four children of his own, asked with a chortle. "I confess, I try to know as little as possible of my daughters' preparations to enter society. I do not envy you the task without a wife to oversee it."

"My sister will sponsor her," Devon said without a change in expression. "And she certainly knows what I expect, as well as my daughter."

"Have you not an older daughter?" Thomas asked, feigning confusion. "I believe my sister said it is the middle one who is to have her season."

"Indeed." Mr. Devon's eyes regarded Thomas coolly, chin tipped upward in a way which reminded him of Christine. But Devon's eyes, though a similar shade of brown to his daughter's, were cold. Calculating. Thomas had no doubt that such a glare did a great deal to subdue Mr. Devon's subordinates.

Thomas raised his eyebrows and dared to ask the next question. "Did the elder daughter understand what was expected of her?"

Mr. Devon did not blink. "Not well enough. Her sister is an entirely different being. Much more eager to please. More obedient."

Thomas nodded and offered what he hoped passed as an indifferent smile. "That is good for you, Mr. Devon. I wish you both well for the ordeal." He turned to take part in another conversation, dropping the entire matter with Devon as though it held no real interest but that of idle chatter.

In actuality, the conversation had been quite useful. He now understood why Miss Christine was desperate to understand social graces as he doubted many had been used by her father at home. He could also see why she would want to make her match with all speed; to both get out from under her father's influence and to ease whatever weight Mr. Devon's expectations put upon her.

If her father would speak and behave so coldly in public about her future, what must he say to his daughter in private? No one deserved such constant censure from a member of their own family. Christine struck him as intelligent and lovely. Why not sing her praises in public? Thomas rather thought he would like to, if it could be done without casting suspicion on them both, if only to combat the unpleasantness of Mr. Devon's words.

ALTHOUGH THE EVENING STARTED WITH MOST OF THE LADIES and gentlemen divided, the younger gentlemen soon joined the ladies at the card tables. A whole group of them arrived at once, which led Christine to suspect that Lady Littleton had issued a command upon noticing how short on masculine company her daughters were.

Christine did her best to appease the men around her by smiling, complimenting their plays when it was deserved, and asking for their opinions as though she did not fully comprehend the rules of the chosen games. She felt she had behaved well enough, but the conversation stayed entirely upon the cards. It was hardly a challenge, and she found herself feeling anxious to test her social abilities according to Thomas's recent instruction.

After completing a particularly dull game with Hannah and the Whitson sons, she excused herself from the bridge table and went to find refreshment. Her eyes continuously sought out Thomas Gilbert, but he never even looked in her direction. She had hoped he might have some opinion of how she was doing, but he stayed across the room from her, engaged with others and not venturing near the card tables.

Christine lingered by the refreshment table. She had done well so far; paid the appropriate sort of compliments and plied gentlemen into talking of what they wished. But through it all, Christine found herself bored beyond reason. If *she* found the conversation, surely the gentlemen did as well. An important element still remained missing from the exchanges she had made thus far and she could not entirely understand what it was. Ought she to laugh more? Ask additional questions?

Uncertain of where else to go, she drifted toward Julia. Her sister, dressed more like a matron than a young woman on the marriage mart, stood conversing politely with Captain Markham, cousin to Hannah.

"How do you find your time passing with the Littletons, Captain?" Julia asked politely, her face passive.

"I find it most relaxing to be in the country, away from the rigors of office work," the handsome young man in uniform remarked. "I have always enjoyed my time here."

"How fortunate," Julia stated, again without any real inflection. "I have heard some complain that our entertainments are lacking, but I have thought the quiet life suits a certain sort of person very well."

Julia remained entirely polite, very formal, and not at all flirtatious. Nothing could be learned from *her* behavior.

Even Christine, with all her lack of experience, knew that a smile helped keep a man's attention.

"For myself, I see it more as a respite than a way of life," Captain Markham responded with equal civility.

Julia nodded, raising her eyebrows. "A soldier's life must be vastly more interesting than what we experience here. Especially if you work for the Home Office."

Did Christine have to smile and nod at Julia's conversation as well as the gentleman's? She could not be sure. If this was Julia's attempt at flirtation then at least Christine wasn't the only one without an understanding of the art.

How she wished Thomas would join their little circle! He could at least indicate by expression how she ought to proceed.

She broke into the exchange at last, attempting to change the subject, with a smile. "Tell me please, Captain. How do you find seeing your cousins so very grown up? Miss Hannah is one of our dear friends."

The Captain turned his attention to her, a flicker of interest in his eye.

"It is very good to see her again. She is much younger than I, so when we used to come for visits we did not spend much time in my cousin's company. Now that she has left the schoolroom, it is much different."

"How is a young lady different after leaving the schoolroom?" Christine asked, hoping her face conveyed interest, even if her brain had long since given up.

"Oh, well, you know. They become more interesting to talk to when they are not always thinking on their lessons." He shrugged. "They are more confident in adult company as well. Less inclined to be shy, to stutter and blush, now that their lessons are through."

"Yes," Christine said, turning to share a look with her sister, amused despite herself. "You are saying there is more maturity."

"Indeed. Precisely." He looked between the two sisters. "You both must understand, as young ladies so long out of the schoolroom yourselves."

How did one keep communication going after a particular topic reached a dead end? And was that statement some sort of slight on their ages?

Julia continued the conversation in her easy manner. "And what of your own schooling, Captain? Our younger brother is at Eton currently."

It felt the very dullest sort of exchange. Christine knew not another word to say, though the young captain looked not the slightest bit put out as he described his years of study. The evening would be long if all the male guests conversed in this way.

She really must learn how to liven things up. She would be certain to ask Thomas about it as soon as possible, though tonight he clearly remained content to stay on the opposite end of the room.

Resigned to a long evening, Christine excused herself from that conversation and went in search of Rebecca. Perhaps her younger sister's set would have more interesting things to say. They were far less confined by the dictates of society and proper conversation, in comparison to their elders.

Rebecca and her friends, Master Richard and Miss Lily Ames, sat at their own table and played at spillikins, giggling like schoolroom children half their ages. This was a far more interesting game than whist, and the company more cheerful than at other tables.

Christine moved to stand near their chairs and joined them by commenting in a teasing manner as they played. At least the schoolroom set appreciated her contributions.

69

She glanced up after a completed round and caught Thomas watching her from across the room. He regarded her with a look of puzzlement before turning back to his conversation with Lord Littleton.

Christine immediately felt out of place. Thomas likely felt disappointment that she had removed herself from adult company, thus avoiding any opportunity to practice, as he had charged her to do, agreeing with every inane thing a man in her company might say.

Rising from her seat at the spillikins table, Christine withdrew to a cabinet enclosed by glass at the corner of the room. Lord Littleton kept small curiosities, tokens from his travels, on the shelves within. Christine had been a guest often enough to know the story of nearly every item. Her favorite pieces were the most minute, such as a tiny elephant carved from ivory and painted with gold. She also loved the jade tiger, no larger than her thumb, but carved in such detail as to present tiny bared fangs.

She felt the approach of another person and interrupted her study to see Thomas at her side. She offered him a hesitant smile and raised one hand to tuck a curl back in place, uncertain as to whether or not they ought to converse in public. But of course they could. Speaking with a neighbor at a social function was not out of the ordinary.

"Good evening, Miss Christine," Thomas said with a brief bow.

"Mr. Gilbert," she greeted, returning his courtesy. "How lovely to see you. Are you enjoying the games?" At least she could speak to him intelligently.

"Very much. I find the company entertaining. How do you find the evening's recreation?"

"Excessively diverting," she lied. "Though I am not very skilled at whist."

He nodded and took on a serious expression. "I am abysmal at billiards, though I do enjoy a good game of loo." He gestured to the cabinet, switching topics deftly. "I see Lord Littleton has added several pieces since I last visited. Which is your favorite? I am partial to the tiger."

Christine relaxed. "He is my favorite, too. Though I admit a certain fondness toward the elephant."

"Jungle creatures, both of them. Alas, it is likely as close as either of us will ever come to such amazing animals." His words, spoken in a warm voice, had an immediate effect upon her. She felt comfortable for the first time that evening, knowing she could be herself at last.

"Are there not tigers at the Royal Menagerie?" Christine asked.

"The animals there change often," Thomas told her. "They do have lions fairly regularly. And birds, the likes of which will astound you when you see them. I have been once. I did not enjoy it as much as some."

Christine tilted her head to the side, raising her eyebrows in surprise. "How could you not? There are wonders there from all around the world!"

His look grew distant though his dark gray eyes remained trained on the little tiger behind the glass. "The animals are kept in very close confinement. I cannot imagine a tiger, made to roam miles and miles of jungle, could ever be content to live in a space wherein he can barely take a step. To be built with such power and grace by his Maker, only to be caged and fed on scraps and stray dogs, would be the very worst sort of life."

Her heart felt pricked, listening to his solemn words, imagining the life of a powerful beast confined to a box.

"That would not be a fitting home for anyone," she agreed.

He came out of his thoughts with a shake of his head. "Forgive me, I do not mean to dampen your excitement. You should certainly visit the royal animals so you can tell all your friends how bravely you faced the large cats. I understand some young ladies faint, but I cannot imagine you would do so." The last statement nearly sounded a question, yet the slight twist to his lips made it seem more a challenge.

"Of course not," she answered, narrowing her eyes at him. "I have never fainted."

He chuckled. "If all young ladies had your constitution, we gentlemen would lose a wonderful opportunity to put ourselves forward as champions and saviors when you have a case of the vapors." He nodded back to the case. "What make you of the oriental slippers?"

It took her a moment to respond, as the image of Thomas lifting her to a fainting couch assailed her in a most unwelcome manner. "The what? Slippers? Oh. They are far too tiny," she answered with a shake of her head, hoping to clear the strange vision from her mind. "I doubt I could have worn them at the age of seven. Women of the Orient must have very dainty feet."

"I hear they employ various means to accomplish such a size," he answered. "Every culture, it seems, has certain expectations of their ladies."

"In England," she rejoined, unable to resist smiling, "we put them in long dresses and useless slippers, or gowns made of materials so flimsy, we all catch cold every winter. The most sensible thing I own is my riding habit."

Julia appeared at Christine's side. "Fortunately for you, sister, that it is the thing you wear most often." Her words, though said coolly, bore no malice. Indeed, Julia's smile indicated she might approve the truthfulness of the statement. "I see the two most horse-mad people in the room have found each other. What are you discussing, besides clothing?"

Thomas raised his eyebrows at Christine, but returned Julia's smile. "Nothing of consequence. Tigers and London, the Orient and slippers."

"Far more interesting conversation than memories of the school-room." Julia looked at Christine with a peculiar expression, one Christine thought might be amusement. "Though I am surprised you are not comparing your stables and tack."

"That hardly seems appropriate conversation for a social gathering," Christine said, glancing at Thomas from the corner of her eye to see if he agreed.

"Nonsense," Julia said with practicality. "As long as both parties are engaged, lively conversation may take place on a variety of topics." She waved a hand to indicate the rest of the room and the people in it. "It is unlikely anyone else would be interested in hearing about your fine stables. It is equally unlikely that you have much in common with the other gentlemen."

"Many a gentleman owns a good horse," Christine countered, her cheeks warming as Julia dismissed her ability to converse on any other topic.

Julia chuckled. "Not many would wish to engage in a conversation with a lady who knows more about the species than they do. Oh, do not take on so." She reached out and laid her hand briefly on Christine's arm. "I am trying to say that you have found an apt companion in Mr. Gilbert. You could both discuss your herds until the dawn and likely have more to say. Now, please excuse me. I wish to speak to Mrs. Brody." She barely glanced at her sister as she took her leave of them, vanishing as quickly as she appeared.

Christine felt her blush hot upon her cheeks and turned away from the room, not meeting Thomas's eyes. "I can speak with intelligence about more than horses."

"I believe you," he answered, a twinkle in his eyes. "I have heard evidence of it. You ought to show the others here this evening your capabilities in that regard."

She sighed and looked askance at him.

"Go on, Miss Christine," he said, his eyes lightening a touch with his encouragement. "Practice."

Tilting her chin up, Christine nodded once before stepping back into the thick of it, making her way to an empty chair and another game of whist. Thomas was right. She needed all the practice she could get, especially if she must take part in such drawing-room conversations during her season. Though she had little hope of finding much of interest in her companions that evening. She nearly dozed off when Captain Markham discussed how regimentals fit differently from the common clothes of a gentleman.

She longed to be back at the curiosities cabinet with Thomas, talking of Indian tigers or African lions, or of their beautiful horses. Conversing with Thomas came easily; listening to English bores drone on about their vestments did not.

Chapter Nine

"I think I must be doing something wrong." The first words out of Christine's mouth after she dismounted gave Thomas some surprise.

"Why do you say that?"

"At the Littletons' card party, I attempted conversation with all the unattached gentlemen. I did as you advised and I was frightfully bored all evening." She frowned and paced closer to the brook. "I do not think any of them were entertained either. How does one practice one's wit when trapped speaking only politely? And must I be agreeable to everything? Even when I allow the gentleman to guide the conversation to such boring topics as the tailoring of his clothing?"

He considered her questions, trying not to grin. She spoke rapidly, holding her head at a stubborn angle. Christine would not give up, no matter how exasperated she became.

"There should still be room to make the occasional clever comment," he told her. "And perhaps you should not have given up as you did, joining the schoolroom set a second time for their game. Spillikins, wasn't it?"

"They were at least entertaining to speak to." She waved that advice away. "And the only other person I wished to speak to was you. That would hardly suit our purposes."

Thomas could not help but feel satisfaction from her statement. At least she didn't include him with the rest of the "boring" gentlemen.

"What if there is another element missing altogether?" Christine continued. "I have been considering what could have gone wrong. Aside from our conversations, I felt I could not add a single original thought to the evening without giving offense. I must be missing something." She heaved a sigh and looked up at the sky, shaking her head.

"I suppose that is a possibility," Thomas conceded, regarding her carefully. Thinking over the evening, he had ruminated more upon her father's remarks than on her performance, as she had not put herself in an awkward position similar to the dinner party. No one could accuse her of saying anything remotely impolite, from what he had witnessed.

Christine gestured helplessly with both hands. "But what would it be?"

He thought carefully of the times when he had been on the receiving end of a young woman's attention and what it was that charmed him. The most memorable of such moments included particular young ladies who were, in fact, attractive. "Were you attracted to any of the gentlemen you spoke to?"

"Attracted to?" Her eyebrows shot up and her cheeks turned a becoming shade of pink. "Is that not an impertinent question?"

"It would be, were I not your tutor on the subject." He tried to control his mirth, but failed. At least these conversations with her no longer felt strained. Not now that he understood what she needed from him. "How am I supposed to help you without asking impertinent questions about an entire subject that gentlemen and ladies generally do not discuss?"

"I see your point." She smiled benignly and looked down, her gloved hands twisting one another. "I suppose I found Captain

Markham to be handsome, especially in his uniform." She looked at him through her lashes, tilting her head to one side. "If he didn't speak of the uniform's tailoring with such exuberance, he may have appeared more so."

He bit his lip to hold back a laugh and tried to remain on topic. "Handsome." He raised his eyebrows, thinking of the young man's tall and slender build, his light-colored hair and thin mustache. He supposed some young ladies might like that sort of thing. He was of average height himself and sturdily built with all his time spent in the saddle. "Was there anything to draw you to him? Anything about him that made you wish to learn more of his hopes, dreams, family, or past?"

Christine pursed her lips and shook her head. "I must say, I was so busy trying to curb my tongue that I found little time to feel curious over the other guests. But he did not express himself particularly well. No, I do not think I found him engaging, nor do I wish to learn more of him."

Thomas sighed. His work was certainly cut out for him. "Then I do not think you were attracted to him. You merely found him handsome in a general sense. Miss Christine, you need to take a greater interest in the people around you or else they will think you shallow. As much as a man may want an agreeable wife, he does not wish for a shallow companion."

She lifted both hands and made a sound of exasperation. "I must be agreeable, but not shallow. That seems a contradiction. What does any of this have to do with attraction?"

He answered easily, finding this something he could explain. "Attraction is a great deal like a pull, or a tug you feel when you are with someone. Particularly as you come to know them. For no reason you can be certain of, you will find yourself drawn to spending time in that person's company. At times, you may wish to know them better because you are drawn to them; and at others, you will be drawn to them as you come to know them. It is something of a paradox." He shrugged, not sure if he was helping or confusing matters all the more. Thomas should have spent more time with her that evening, helping to engage her in more stimulating conversation.

She rubbed her forehead. "Indeed. So I should be agreeable, but still try to get to know the gentlemen to see if an attraction will grow?" Christine narrowed her eyes at him. "If I can't decipher why I'm attracted to an individual, is there any way to control whether or not someone is attracted to *me*?"

He sighed and sat on his rock, gesturing for her to take a seat on the fallen tree across the way. He hoped this meeting would not end in a headache. "I believe there are numerous ways to appear attractive and to be an attractive individual. Obviously, physical appearance is the first step. But it is only one of many steps and is not the most important." Thomas paused. He'd had a few friends at Cambridge that seemed to care more for physical appearance than anything else. "At least, not for all."

Christine raised a hand to interrupt him. "Wait. Before we go further, I'd like to be clear on one point. Am I an attractive person? Based upon my appearance?" She turned her head, presenting him with her profile. The pink reappeared in her cheeks, he noted with amusement, but she maintained a calm expression.

Thomas hesitated. How did a gentleman critique a lady with complete honesty on her looks? He supposed he better at least try to be objective.

He took in her profile, eyes skimming from the dark curls at her forehead down the bridge of her nose and across her cheekbones. He noted her long lashes, the pink Cupid's bow of her lips, and her stubborn pointed chin. He took in her posture, her carriage, and tried not to linger overly long on her figure. He cleared his throat at last, surprised by the enjoyment he felt in the exercise. "I would say you are, yes. Physically attractive."

"Is there anything which I could improve upon?" she asked, turning to face him fully, eyebrows raised and laughter dancing in her eyes.

"No." Thomas crossed his arms, pleased he could speak in a calm manner. "You are an agreeable looking young woman." Most agreeable. Delightful, handsome, and charming. He thought it best not to rain all those compliments down upon her, lest she get the wrong idea. "But I think you knew that already."

She bestowed a grateful, glowing smile upon him which heightened the beauty of the features he'd noticed previously. "Thank you. It is nice to have an unbiased opinion, whatever my own may be."

Her humble acceptance of his assessment gave Thomas pause. How many young women would hear such things said and do naught but express gratitude? He had surely paid compliments to young ladies before, but they were often deflected with false modesty or met with no more than a flirtatious giggle.

She continued to surprise him with her next remark. "I shall return the favor and tell you that you are most handsome. Especially when you smile. You far too often look serious." She affected her own serious expression, an obvious mockery of his usual frown, drawing her brows down deeply enough to make a line appear between them.

He couldn't help chuckling, though he shook his head. "As a gentleman attempting to save his family's future, I should say I have reason to be serious."

"True, but I would think it becomes tiresome. If you smiled more, you would worry less." Her smile returned, brightening her side of the brook considerably. "Besides, your payment for helping me should go a long way to assisting your family, should it not?"

"Indeed, it will." He doffed his hat to scratch the top of his head. How had they managed to wander from the topic at hand? "Now. Back to our discussion of attraction. To be attracted to a person involves being interested in them. I doubt you would wish to wed a man who you will find tedious?"

"Well, no." She admitted it with a shrug. "But my priorities must be to find a gentleman of means or title. Or both."

"Yes. As you have said." He shook his head and tried not to sigh. Although he understood her motives, assisting a fortune hunter went against quite a few of his principles. "But if you wish to attract such a gentleman, it would help if you were also drawn to some aspect of his person other than his wealth. If you are bored when you are in his company, he will soon guess it and move on."

"I feel we are talking in circles," she said. "Have you an example of this sort of thing?" Christine tapped one riding boot against the dirt, her expression curious.

He realized his best example, truly the one which inspired him above all, was a story with which he had great familiarity.

"My parents." He sat straighter and made no attempt to contain his pride in their story. "They met at a ball in London, toward the end of the season. My mother told us the story many times. She saw him from across the room and thought him handsome. She asked after him and somehow arranged for a friend to make the introductions. My father had seen her many times, but never paid much attention to her. Then, standing face to face, with her smile lighting up the whole room, they spoke to one another. They discovered a mutual fondness of reading."

Her look turned skeptical, her eyebrows shooting up to her hairline. "That hardly seems promising."

Thomas refrained from laughing at her abrupt statement and continued as though uninterrupted. "My father also said he was immediately struck by my mother's kindness. Before long, he sought her at another event and then decided to pay calls to her home. The more they were together, the more things they found they had in common, and the more attractive they found one another. Until one day, he proposed." His father told the story often, always mentioning his wife's beautiful smile.

Christine had a lovely smile.

There will be a man to notice and appreciate the way her good cheer brightens everything around it. He did not doubt that thought.

"It sounds like a love match," she said barely loud enough for him to hear. He brought his attention back to the present moment, catching the misty look in her deep brown eyes.

He nodded. "It was." The preceding generation had precious few of those incredible couplings. "At a time when such was not common. Theirs is still a love match, I would say."

Her posture jolted suddenly, becoming stiff once more. Christine's lips turned downward and she shook her head. "I do not wish for a love match," she stated firmly, breaking the quiet moment between them with more force than necessary.

Thomas pressed on, knowing she did not yet understand. "The principle is the same. Find common concerns. Expand upon them. Be genuinely interested in what the gentleman says regarding how he spends his time."

Christine stood and resumed pacing, eyebrows drawn together and lips pursed. Thomas thought it a charming way for her to order her thoughts. She hardly ever held still, and the more she thought, the more agitated her movements became.

"Very well. Then, building upon our previous conversation, I should listen to what a gentleman says, ask questions, not disagree with their opinions, and do my utmost to actually be engrossed with their activities instead of focusing on my own goals."

"And do not forget," he added to her very business-like list, "that you are a lovely woman. When you smile."

"I believe smiling was my advice to you," she countered saucily, arching one eyebrow at him. It pleased Thomas to see amusement return to her eyes. He found he liked her best when she teased him, though he knew he ought to keep them on task.

He shrugged. "Such sound advice should assist you as well."

She laughed and he could not help grinning back at her.

"Thank you, Mr. Gilbert. You have given me much to think upon. Shall I see you in three days' time?"

"Of course." He stood and bowed. "Until then, practice all we have discussed and you may report back to me your success."

"Or failure," she countered as she mounted her fine horse. "I am not convinced I can do today's lesson justice."

"I think if you are as determined as you say to marry this season you must make every effort. Good day, Miss Christine."

"Good day, Mr. Gilbert." She waved and moved her horse along, leaving him to his thoughts. He understood her desire to make a good match, but why the vehement refusal of falling in love? Why not hope for such good fortune? Nothing would ever entice him to marry unless he felt a true and deep affection for a lady.

Thomas could not imagine Christine would experience difficulty attracting a husband fitting all her requirements. She possessed a quick wit and an ability to converse with intelligence if she would conform to societal expectations. He spoke truthfully on her appearance as well. The young woman had a lovely face, not to mention a pleasing figure. Indeed, he predicted a very successful season for her.

Even if that success was no more than meeting Mr. Devon's business expectations.

Thomas struggled to find pleasure in the thought. For someone so vibrant and lovely as Christine, it felt wrong to imagine her saddled with a marriage lacking true affection.

Still, no matter the match she made, he must be happy for her. His only obligation to wish for her success in finding the marriage partner she sought, no matter if he found the match, or the gentleman, unsuitable.

Shaking himself out of his brown study, he returned to his horse and decided they both needed more exercise.

Chapter Ten

C hristine sat in the morning room—her mother's favorite in all of the house—and poured over the fashion plates sent by their aunt. She even went so far as to use a pencil to make notes on which particular styles she liked and what could be changed to make a gown suit her. While she normally found very little to care about in the way of dress, except when it came to her riding suits, she knew how essential it was that she wear eye-catching styles and the best that a London seamstress could offer.

It was particularly important that she choose the right shades, those that would play up her coloring. Due to her hours in the saddle, her skin was unfashionably dark. But hopefully, if she wore her hair and clothing correctly, she could turn that problem into an asset.

She appeared healthy, if nothing else.

A sigh from across the room, where Rebecca sat reading, stirred her from her thoughts. Christine glanced her way, seeing her younger sister staring into nothing, the book closed in her hands.

"What are you reading, Rebecca?" she asked, curious.

"A novel," the girl said. "The most delicious thing happened. The heroine suddenly realized that the reason the gentleman has been acting with such care for her family is because he is in love with her."

Christine snorted and waived dismissively. "Romance is the stuff of fiction, Rebecca. You should know better by now. Father says those books are written by fools who wish to line their pockets by telling the world fairytales." She sensed, rather than saw, Julia, who was knitting nearby, stiffen in her chair, her needles falling still.

"I rather like a good fairytale," Rebecca said, looking pointedly at her book. "They are a far better, more pleasant thing to think upon than the realities Father wants us to pursue. I would much rather dream of a handsome hero than pretend an interest in horticulture."

Julia chuckled. "Hear, hear, Rebecca." The needles clicked and clacked together again.

Christine turned in her chair to look at her elder sister, raising her eyebrows and affecting an indifferent tone. "As if either of you know a thing about romance. It is a foolish pursuit. Nothing could possibly induce me to pin my hopes on love. Love cannot pay off accounts, put food on the table, or elevate one high enough to enter the upper *ton*. Love is a distraction from the important things in life."

Julia's expression changed and her eyes took on a narrow, knowing look. "Such as what, Christine? What is so important that love cannot have its place in our lives?"

"Position. Wealth. The ability to increase one's holdings or fortune. Comfort." Christine ticked each item off on her fingers, tilting her chin up and trying to sound more certain of herself than she was. "Love alone cannot provide those things."

"But it can provide happiness," Rebecca said, pulling the attention of both her sisters back to her. "Which is in short supply around here."

"Indeed," Julia agreed softly. "Yet falling in love can also be agony, and a love lost gives naught but heartbreak."

Christine sniffed and turned away. "How would you know? You have one season in London, without a single offer, and you come home acting as though you know everything about courtship."

"Christine!" Rebecca gasped, eyes wide as saucers. "That was incredibly unkind. How could you?"

A scraping sound behind her meant Julia had risen from her position. When Julia finally spoke, her words were quiet, but razor sharp. "She knows Father's words too well and is attempting to adopt them as her own."

Christine attempted not to squirm, wishing her sister would argue with her rather than draw that conclusion.

"We shall see, Christine, what you make of the wide world after you have been in it. I do urge you, as your sister, not to jump so hastily to your judgments until you have more experience." Julia's footsteps moved away until Christine heard the door open and then close.

"That was terrible, Christine," Rebecca said with a look of pain on her pale face. "How could you speak to Julia that way? She is never anything but kind to either of us."

Indeed, Julia's response left Christine rattled. Somehow, she expected to feel better after deflating her sisters' opinions of love. Instead, she felt much worse. Her shoulders sunk and she bit her bottom lip. "I-I don't know. I did not think—"

"No," Rebecca interrupted, standing and clenching her book in both hands. "You did not think. Christine, we are sisters. If we do not protect each other from unfeeling remarks, what hope have we of remaining close and being friends? Mother always wished us to be friends. Or have you forgotten?" Rebecca released a deep sigh. "I will be reading in my room."

"I am sorry, Rebecca," Christine blurted as her sister swept by her.

"I am not the one who needs to hear you say that, Christine," Rebecca said, her tone unforgiving. "Do not forget the Markhams are joining us for tea," she added crisply before snapping the door shut behind her.

Christine sat by herself, alone in the quiet room, with only her fashion plates for company.

CHRISTINE RESISTED THE DESIRE TO DUCK INTO THE LINEN closet when she heard the maid coming to announce the arrival of the Littleton misses and their cousins, the Markhams. She knew she ought to be looking forward to the challenge they presented in honing her skills as a debutante. But being in the same room with her sisters did not suit her fragile mood.

She hovered outside the morning room, still undecided, listening to the soft exchange of voices on the other side of the door.

"Will you all go to London, Miss Devon?" The deepness of the voice identified the speaker as the elder of the two brothers, Mr. Archibald Markham. Christine thought his first name most unfortunate, but otherwise he struck her as the more interesting of the two brothers. He did not go on and on about his clothing, at any rate.

"Not this year, I am afraid. I will remain here, with my youngest sister, and our brother will come home for a short holiday." Julia's voice and tone sounded steady and serene, despite their earlier disagreement. Would that Christine could even have an ounce of her sister's composure.

"Such a shame." Hannah Littleton's voice was familiar enough to identify. "We enjoy London a vast deal at this time of year. I sometimes wish we did not linger in the country for Lord Annesbury's Christmas ball. I am certain there are even better parties and events in London."

"That may be true, but Papa would not ever want to slight our neighbor. It is tradition." Amelia Littleton, the elder of the two sisters, had as much sense as Julia and liberally shared it with others.

If the conversation they shared continued on in such an easy vein, Christine felt equal to it. Trying to remember her mother's graceful, confident movements, she opened the door and swept into the room, affixing a pleasant expression on her face.

"Good afternoon, everyone. Please excuse my tardiness. I came as soon as I learned you had arrived." She made her curtsy as the gentlemen stood to bow.

"Ah, Miss Christine, we were speaking of the earl's Christmas ball." The captain eagerly gestured to an empty chair near his and waited to sit until she'd taken it. Julia prepared a teacup for her at once.

"Oh, the ball. I do look forward to attending. This will be my first year." Christine looked around at their guests, all seated comfortably. The Littletons sat on a sofa, Julia in a chair next to the tea things, and the gentlemen in single chairs across the oriental rug from their cousins. "Will you be there, Mr. Markham?"

"Yes, though we will return home for a time before then, to prepare for London." Though shorter than his military brother, Mr. Markham had a more commanding air. He sat as straight as a soldier, wore a dark coat, and maintained an expression devoid of any true emotion. Christine envied him the ease of such a mysterious countenance.

The younger brother chuckled and took a sip of tea. "Unfortunately, I will not be able to attend the ball in its entirety. I have received word that I must be in town immediately following Christmas, to go to some society events as an aid to the colonel. Officers must be present at the best events, to reassure the populace all is well."

Christine very nearly challenged that statement, wishing to know if all was truly well. Only that morning she read of several frightful engagements on the Continent with Bonaparte troops. She bit her tongue in time, nearly causing pain. She quickly recovered and managed to say something appropriate. "How delightful for you."

"It is a great advantage to being stationed at home rather than abroad," the young man answered with a grin. "I hope I will see you about town, Miss Christine."

"If you are at the best events, I imagine you shall," Miss Amelia Littleton answered, smiling benignly. "Miss Christine will certainly travel in the finest circles with her aunt, a countess."

Julia served Christine her tea and retook her seat, presiding over them as hostess with practiced ease.

"It will be a shame if you miss any of the dancing, Captain. I am certain several young ladies hoped to see you in your regimentals," Julia said. The half-smile on her lips nearly caused Christine to choke on her tea. If her sister was attempting to make the young man start conversing on his attire again, she would have to head that off at once.

"Yes, I understand the earl's ball is always lovely, but woefully short on gentleman to partner with during the dancing." Christine put her cup down and turned to Hannah. "Isn't that so, Miss Hannah? Even the most popular young ladies must sit out a time or two."

Hannah took up that thread of conversation easily. "It is positively dreadful; you will have to dance with everyone, Archibald. I have several friends who must not sit out, if it can be helped."

He nodded to his cousin. "I will do my duty."

Christine relaxed, pleased that she'd managed to steer the conversation. A lengthy monologue on tailoring coats might have been harmless in the end, but she'd take points for the well-executed subject change. Thomas would be proud.

"The young ladies of Kettering will be pleased," Miss Littleton stated from behind the rim of her teacup. "The balls held at the earl's home are lovely events—so amusing and the refreshments are divine."

"Tell me, does Lord Annesbury yet remain unmarried?" Captain Markham asked. "I thought I heard a rumor he was to marry this Christmas. I thought it surprising he would still hold the ball, but given he is something of an eccentric, I wasn't certain what to believe."

Christine's eyebrows shot up and she turned to look at Julia, surprised by the news that the most sought-after bachelor in their county could plan a wedding they did not hear of until that moment. Julia looked calm as ever. "No, his younger brother is to wed. One of my friends, actually. I met her in Bath while visiting a cousin. Miss

Ellen Bringhurst. The Bringhurst family lives on the west side of the county."

"Ah. The earl remains safe." Captain Markham chuckled. "That is well for my cousins."

Both young ladies colored and protested at once.

"The very idea," Miss Littleton gasped, looking suitably shocked.

"Really, Nicholas, that you should say such things." Hannah sniffed and looked away.

Christine bit her lip to keep from laughing. Most of the young ladies of their acquaintance went to great pains to look their best for the earl's ball, but he had not paid anyone attention beyond the most basic of courtesies, not since the death of his countess. Besides that, everyone *did* think him a trifle eccentric. Her father often spoke of his unexpected business decisions, which resulted in unlikely success more often than not.

Christine would rather marry a man she understood than one who constantly went about surprising everyone.

"Who will be the hostess, if Lord Annesbury remains single?" Mr. Markham asked, turning a disapproving eye toward his brother.

"His mother, the Dowager Countess. She delights in such things." Julia stood and lifted the refreshment tray. "Might I interest anyone in another biscuit or cake? Cook's lemon biscuits are a marvel."

As the conversation flowed about her, Christine found she did not have a great deal to say, and the Markham brothers were seemed content to speak with Julia and the others. She nearly spoke up, several times, but thought it might be best to wait until someone drew her out. The fine line between speaking in turn and interrupting remained difficult to discern when everyone felt they had something of interest to share.

How much more difficult would it be to gain attention and conversation in a crowded London ballroom? A room full of people to the point of others calling it a crush. How would she stand out enough that a gentleman would even think he might wish to speak to her? Here she sat, within touching distance of the captain and his brother, and they did not direct their attention to her once.

She tried to sit straighter, to lean forward slightly, and when those small shifts failed she opted to stare directly at Captain Markham for several seconds until he caught the look from the corner of his eye. He actually started, as though surprised by her, and turned to give her a smile that looked half-alarmed.

"Did you need something, Miss Christine?" he asked in a near whisper, as his cousins were speaking about how they hoped the weather would hold.

"Oh." She blinked and shook her head. "No. Nothing."

What a spectacular failure I am, she thought miserably, turning her eyes to the floor. *After all of Thomas's time spent tutoring me, I am still a ninny.*

Rather than turn her attention back to the conversation, which obviously did not need her to continue, she mentally composed a list of questions for Thomas. He would help her and then she need not worry about sitting silently at teas or remaining a wallflower at London balls.

Chapter Eleven

The clouds above threatened to break at any moment, but Thomas kept his word and appeared at the brook early. He checked his watch, hoping Christine would arrive with her usual promptness. He had not long to wait. Christine arrived, coming in at a fast pace, both rider and horse panting.

"I did not think I ought to come," she said, not dismounting. "Because of the clouds. However, I feared you would uphold your end of our deal, and I decided I had better at least tell you we can forgo our lesson today. The sky looks ready to burst."

He directed his eyes upward, checking the progress of the clouds. "I thought of that. But it is hard to get away most days and I would not want to miss the opportunity to continue our lessons. I have a plan. Can you come across the brook?"

"Yes." She tilted her head and regarded him curiously. "It is not so deep to deter me." She tapped the gelding gently with the riding crop in her hand and he moved forward into the water without hesitation. Thunder rumbled in the distance, causing both horses to flick their ears back. "Was that the extent of your plan? That we enjoy the rain from this side instead of the other?" she asked, a teasing sparkle in her eyes.

Thomas wondered at the merit of his idea. The barrier of the brook had been important before. He felt the way one might if a wall was abruptly knocked down in a previously comfortable room: overly exposed and disconcerted.

"Not at all. I thought we would go to my mother's greenhouse. Hers is rather large, and is mostly empty at present. It is warm and dry. Our horses will have shelter in a shed nearby. What do you think?"

"I think we had best make haste." She looked pointedly at the sky, frowning now. "This will not hold much longer."

He strode to his waiting mare and swung up into the saddle. "This way."

They rode quickly down the until they came to his mother's gardens. Thomas dismounted and showed Christine the old gardening shed where they could leave their horses together. Thankfully, the beasts did not mind one another.

"The greenhouse is around that wall," Thomas said. Thunder rolled overhead. Wishing to hurry, Thomas took up Christine's hand and briskly walked down the path to the glass house. With her free hand, she reached up to hold her hat, at its usual jaunty angle, upon her head. She smiled broadly as they came to the entrance, breathing deeply from their pace. He opened the door and allowed her to enter first.

Another crack of thunder echoed through the air, louder now, and the raindrops fell, beating a quick tempo on the glass.

The greenhouse was darkened by the cloudy sky, but there remained ample light to see by, and the room felt much warmer than outside. Thomas shut the door firmly behind them and pointed over Christine's shoulder. "There is a bench there, if you would like to sit."

Christine nodded and went slowly, her eyes likely adjusting to the change in light as his did, picking her way down the aisle of wintering plants. She lowered herself to the bench with a little sigh.

"That was good thinking. This is a lovely place and much warmer than meeting by the brook, too. You do not think anyone will find us here and make assumptions?"

"I highly doubt it. This is my mother's refuge. Even the gardener rarely ventures here. Mother prefers to keep it to herself."

"Then she might happen upon us?" Christine asked, a hint of worry in her voice.

"No. She spent the last several days here, preparing plants for the winter. She finished yesterday morning."

Christine looked around, noting plants with and without greenery. "My sister, Rebecca, has been reading about horticulture. Father says it is a very ladylike pursuit."

Thomas found a stool against one glass wall and lifted it, bringing it to where Christine sat. He did not think sitting directly next to her would be beneficial to their tutoring session. The bench was really too small, unless two people wished to be abnormally close.

After he settled on the seat a few feet away, he looked around the greenhouse again. "I have heard of several noblemen who are dabbling in the pursuit. Especially in terms of growing pineapples and bananas. It is more than growing flowers for adorning homes. Horticulture, agriculture, are important facets of keeping a large household operating smoothly."

"Rebecca does not see it that way. Nor does my father. He believes a woman ought to know how to raise and arrange flowers, for ornamentation."

He could not tell by her tone what her thoughts on the matter were, though his were not favorable. Thomas resisted the urge to make an observation about her father's lack of vision.

"To each their own," he said instead, directing his eyes to her again. He affected a more serious tone. "And how are you since our last meeting? Have you had the opportunity to practice what we discussed? Finding things of interest in the gentlemen you converse with?"

She sat straighter in what he recognized as her "pupil" attitude, ready to focus on the subject at hand. "I had opportunity to practice at tea with the Markhams, and I did find my results improved. To an extent. I still felt like I had to put a great deal of effort into being attentive. Perhaps that is because I am aware that the gentlemen I spoke to are completely inappropriate when it comes to choosing a husband."

"Because they have not the money or connections," Thomas said, crossing his arms and leaning away from her. While he well understood the ways of the world in marriage he did not necessarily like society's expectations. A man could be a good, honest, hard-working member of his community, committed to giving his whole life over to the support and care of a wife, and still be overlooked for lack of material possessions.

While his situation was not entirely desperate, it still rankled that the likes of Miss Christine Devon would never give him a second thought. In fact, she was so certain he was an inappropriate choice that here he was, tutoring her. Like a common tradesman.

"Yes." She looked down at her lap, her eyebrows drawing together. "Father has been very specific about the sort of man I should be pursuing."

That irritated him even more. Devon struck him as the worst sort of gentleman, putting pressure on his children to fulfill his expectations. "I suppose fathers have certain hopes for marriageable daughters."

"Indeed. And specific demands." She forced a smile, which really looked more like a grimace, and took a deep, slow breath before meeting his eyes again. "But I do believe that is the reason I find myself struggling. To put so much effort into a gentleman I know cannot ever be a real matrimonial option feels like playing false. Or being dishonest. I would not like to lead either Markham on."

"How kind of you," he said, listening to the rain beat down upon the glass as the storm grew in intensity. If he followed this line of conversation much longer, he knew he would end up being argumentative. The girl followed her father's orders. Debating with her on the priorities of her husband hunt would help no one. "What would you like to center our efforts on today?"

"Gaining attention," she said at once, "from the sort that I wish to attract. Let us say I wish a gentleman to be introduced, or I want him to notice me. How do I get notice without being too forward?"

"That is the easiest thing in the world," he said, half smiling. Thomas did not doubt her abilities to attract anyone she wished. "And your chaperone can easily manage the more difficult points for you. If you tell your aunt who you most wish to be introduced to, it will be her duty to see it done."

"I still think I ought to know how to go about it for myself," she countered, "in the case of my aunt not having the right connections or being unavailable."

He sighed. His mind stretched back to the flirtations of London ballrooms before his trip to the Continent.

"You make eye contact, Miss Christine. Across a room, or during a dance. Make sure the gentleman catches you looking." He closed his eyes and imagined himself at such an event, standing and looking out over a crowded room. What about her, standing opposite, would draw him in? "Offer the tiniest, barest smile. Too large a smile is considered vulgar. Then look away. Give it the space of, oh, a quarter hour, and then allow him to catch you looking again." He opened his eyes to see her staring incredulously at him. "If that does not do it, he is likely uninterested at that point in time."

"That seems very subtle," she said with obvious misgivings. Her lips pursed as she regarded him earnestly. The range of expressions he watched her go through during their time together always amused him. One moment she laughed and the next looked as though she belonged in Parliament, discussing the weighty matters of the world.

Most young ladies were schooled from a young age to always look pleasant and content without drawing attention to their emotions or thoughts. He hoped she would never learn to keep her face a mask as they did. Such a thing would be a shame when the emotions written on her lovely face were as enlightening as they were engaging.

He chuckled and turned his attention back to the present. "That is the goal. You cannot approach a gentleman and introduce yourself. He must seek the introduction. If you give him reason to think you would like to meet him, most unattached gentlemen will make an effort. They will speak to the hostess or the master of ceremonies. They know their part."

She tilted her head to one side, her eyes narrowed. "Would you have made an effort to meet me? Had we not already known each other, I mean."

Thomas hesitated to answer. Would he? The point did not bare commenting upon, he told himself, brushing aside the unsettling thought. He answered briskly, "You hardly need worry about me, Miss Christine, or my tastes in ladies. We decided I would teach you according to society's likes and dislikes. Not mine."

She released an exasperated sigh. "I know. Society. I merely thought that you, as a gentleman of the right age—"

"But not the right means," he reminded her, turning his attention to a leafy vine growing on the lattice above her. The conversation made his shoulders feel tight and his back stiff. He had no desire to discuss his family's shortcomings. Or his. The entire line of conversation nettled him.

"Do men of varying means think so differently?" Christine asked, drawing his attention back to her. He realized her dark brown eyes watched him carefully, though he did what he could to keep from meeting them.

"We are all flesh and blood, Miss Christine," he answered as lightly as he could. "Our account books and titles affect us very little when we see a pretty face."

"And you do think my face is pretty." In anyone else, the statement would have sounded incredibly vain. But the innocent way she spoke, her voice soft and her eyebrows raised, kept him from passing such a judgment upon her. She sought reassurance, not flattery.

Thomas could not help his smile, his feelings put aside. "Yes. I do think your face lovely. As we have established before. Very well. Let us practice the art of smiling across a crowded room. I believe our current crowd of plants will work well. On your feet, Miss." He stood and offered his hand to her, assisting her to stand. He withdrew it quickly, barely giving himself time to enjoy the warmth of her fingers. He strode down the path between greenery. "We will try this first. An unobstructed view of your quarry."

Her eyes brightened and her smile returned, full force, lighting the whole of the darkened building. "Quarry? Am I a huntress now?"

"All women on the marriage mart are either hunted or hunting," he quipped. She covered her mouth and giggled. He waved the merriment away. "Enough of that. Here. I stand facing you. Give me your best 'I would like to meet you' smile." He put his arms behind his back and affected an indifferent expression.

Christine's smile remained wide and bright, despite his irritation.

"That will never do." Thomas sighed deeply and rolled his eyes heavenward. "Far too forward."

She laughed and raised her hands in a helpless manner. "I cannot help it! Practicing my smile is ridiculous."

"I have heard of young ladies sitting in front of mirrors for hours to practice smiling and pouting. This is nothing compared to that level of dedication. We must hope you are a natural, as we do not have that sort of time. Look away if you must, to compose the expression, and then look up."

Taking his advice, she looked down at the floor to school her amusement. He watched her take a breath before lifting her head slowly and offering him a gentle, small smile.

Thomas's heart skipped.

A natural, indeed. Be careful, Tom, he reminded himself.

"Excellent. Now, do not maintain eye contact for too long. Prolonged staring might actually frighten a gentleman. Or give him the wrong idea about your intentions. Glance away, slowly."

Maintaining the facade, she turned her head as though to look at something to her side.

He relaxed and released his breath, wondering at what point he had started holding it. "Good, yes. Now. I shall turn to one side. My view of you is unobstructed but you must still gain my attention. I can see you in my periphery." He took the position and pretended to be looking into the distance, only slightly aware of her deep red riding habit on the other side of the enclosure. After a moment of apparent indecisiveness, he noted a quick movement from the corner of his eye. He turned his head and saw that she had pretended to wave to someone behind him.

Once he was turned, she directed her eyes to him and offered that little smile and lowered lashes, then looked back as though seeking out the person to whom she had waved behind him.

"Not a bad tactic," he said, voice raised to carry. "But it would not truly be effective unless someone you knew *was* on that side of the room. You may be caught in your ruse."

"Ah." She frowned and raised a finger to tap upon her lips, drawing his attention to them in a manner which made him catch his breath again. "I had not thought of that. Very well. One more time?"

What was she asking? After every smile, it took him more than a breath to recover his thoughts.

"If you wish." He turned again and waited, trying to ignore the lip-tapping. Ought he to mention how distracting a habit that was?

"Miss Christine?" he called out, after several beats of silence.

Her voice carried over from her side of the building. "I am thinking. If I had a fan, I could snap it open dramatically. Would that work?"

"Ballrooms are usually very warm. A fan would not be out of place. But suppose you did not bring yours? Think."

Finally, she simply walked across the room, moving with a slow grace he did not think could be taught, as steady in her movements as when she rode her horse into the clearing, until she stood more in his line of sight. She gave him the now perfected expression, and it was potent enough to cause his disobedient heart to flip.

Thomas shoved the sensation away and attempted to focus on Christine, his pupil and nothing more.

"I suggest you employ the same tactic when the view of the gentleman is obstructed. Keep in mind to never stray too far from your chaperone." He offered her a slight bow. "Well done today, Miss Christine."

"Thank you, Mr. Gilbert." She curtsied, her brighter, less socially acceptable grin appearing once more. Though his heart had stuttered at her attempts at allurement, he found he preferred that beaming expression even more.

Christine looked at the glass roof. "The rain is slowing."

Thomas looked up as well, noting the gray skies above. The patter did seem lighter than before. "Indeed. Is there anything more you would like to discuss today?"

"Not in the matters of flirtation," she answered with good humor, obviously as relieved as he was that the lessons were over for the day. He chose not to comment as he neared where she stood. "Though I do wish to know more about your Italian stock horses. My father's head groom has been to your stables and he is most impressed with your ladies."

"They are quite noble; I suppose ladies is an apt enough word for them. They come from famous Italian lines. I have my Lipizzan from the Pluto dynasty. She was difficult to procure. I had to save the life of her master's groom. My Carmen, a Calabrese, is a beautiful girl. Lively, strong, but with a pleasant temperament. What did you think of her?"

"She is the one you rode today? Oh, I think she is positively marvelous! There is a lightness in her step that makes me believe what you say about temperament. She seems a cheerful mare."

Christine's astute observations pleased him. "Very."

"And your third Italian beauty?"

He took a deep breath and let it out slowly. "She is my youngest. My Sarcidano. I have high hopes for her. Very wild. Flighty. With the right breeding, I could get a racer from her."

"They sound magnificent. I shall have to come up with an excuse to be a legitimate visitor in your home, in hopes that I would be allowed to see them." The comment struck him as wistful and he very nearly asked her to come and see them that very moment. But it would not be at all appropriate. For either of them. She would need to enter his home as a guest of his mother.

"Perhaps I can arrange something," he said at last, watching her expression change into one of appreciation.

"Thank you." She tipped her head to one side. "That might create an opportunity for us to 'negotiate' the breeding rights of our stables. Then it will not be such a surprise when my grooms bring the stallions over after Christmas."

"That is a clever notion." He regarded her seriously before speaking. "What becomes of your horses when you marry?"

"I intend to do all in my power to keep my rights to them. They are my property, not my father's," Christine stated firmly. "There are ways to ensure a wife's property remains apart from her husband's, but I have not broached the subject with my father. I know he does not view the idea favorably."

"I could look into that for you," he offered. "It would make me feel as though we are on more even footing in this bargain of ours." It would be a shame for her to lose the rights to the animals her mother left in her care, especially when she bore such apparent love for them.

"If you would, I would be most grateful." She looked again into the rain-splattered glass and he followed her gaze, enjoying the quiet sound of the ending storm.

They said little else, except to bid each other good day. After Thomas saw Christine safely mounted and on her way, he turned toward the stables but came to a stop when movement on one of the paths caught his eye. His mother stood at the corner of the greenhouse, watching him with raised eyebrows.

Thomas's blood froze.

He and Christine had been found out.

Chapter Twelve

After seeing to his horse in great haste, Thomas nearly ran into the house and went straight to his mother's sitting room. He knew she would be waiting for him. He felt like a boy, summoned to her domain for a correction on his behavior. This time, he certainly deserved it.

He found her there, in her favorite chair, looking as though she had barely situated herself before the fire, adjusting her shawl around her shoulders.

"Mother," he greeted as he came closer and bent to kiss her cheek.

She allowed the kiss, then slowly shook her head at him. "Thomas, sit down here this instant and tell me what is going on."

"Going on?" he asked, making a last effort at innocence, hoping she had not truly seen Christine leave their property with him staring after her.

"Yes. In my greenhouse, of all places!" Her eyes narrowed and she gestured impatiently at the chair behind him. "And I warn you, should I not like what you have to say you will find yourself in very dire circumstances." Her shoulders straightened. "I raised you better than this, Thomas. Philandering with an innocent girl!"

"Now, Mother." He sighed deeply and rubbed his forehead, still standing. "It is not at all what you are imagining. I am not taking advantage of Miss Christine in any way. She is a friend, nothing more, and I have been assisting her as a friend."

"Nothing more," she added with a skeptical raise of her eyebrow. "Assisting her. In what way? Had she a sudden, terrible need to understand the workings of a greenhouse? Hm?"

"Not at all." Thomas finally sunk into the chair across from her, slowly, exhaustion settling in his bones. "Miss Christine approached me with a business arrangement. It seems she heard of my desire to start a horse farm; she requested that I provide a service to her, and, in return, I will be given the rights to use both her prized stallions as stud horses."

"Well!" His mother looked both disbelieving and perplexed. "I cannot say I have ever heard of a young woman granting breeding rights of her horses as a way to catch a husband, but I suppose I do not mingle enough in society to have learned of such tales."

Thomas gaped at her, surprised by her tone. "Mother!"

"What on earth do you mean, a business arrangement? Service to her? It makes no sense, Thomas. No young lady of gentle breeding goes about doing *business* of any kind with bachelors, unless it is the sort that ends in a wedding or disgrace." Her eyes went to the door behind him, assuring herself it remained shut, and then back to Thomas. "And suppose I was not the only one to see the two of you leaving the greenhouse together? What on earth are you about, meeting secretly, on our property? What is this terribly clandestine business?"

"It is nothing so sinister as you imagine," he insisted, a headache pulsing at his temple. "Indeed, it is absolutely ridiculous."

"Pray, enlighten me." Her tone remained firm and her gaze hardened. "Because what you might call ridiculous, others could call scandalous. I do not want you ruining the reputation of that poor girl."

"So it is Christine you are worried for?" he asked, looking up at her through his fingers as he massaged his forehead. "Not your well-behaved son?"

She waved that comment away impatiently. "Tell me what you were up to, Thomas, or I will go report to the girl's father myself of your skulking about."

"You will not believe it," he cautioned, letting his hand fall to the arm of the chair. Her unrelenting glare did nothing but demand he continue, and with greater speed.

With nothing for it, Thomas tried to explain.

"Miss Christine Devon has found, in planning for her first season in London, that she is woefully ill-prepared to move about in society in a way that would attract potential suitors." His mother's imperious eyebrows hastened him on.

"Knowing that I was raised a gentleman, yet I find myself now in less than favorable circumstances, she offered me the rights to her horses if I would do her the kindness of tutoring her in social graces." He shut his mouth over the final word and dared his mother, with raised eyebrows and his most serious expression, to doubt him.

For a long moment she stared at Thomas, then opened her mouth as if to ask a question. She closed it again without a sound, and her eyebrows drew down in a tight V. At last she managed to say, "That is unbelievable. Tutoring a girl in social graces? What does that even mean?"

"It means," he said, slowly and with his tone carefully measured, "that she believes her education in terms of what is and is not appropriate behavior in mixed company is inadequate. I happened to witness, firsthand, her strained attempts at conversation with Mr. Ames and a group of young people. It seems no one ever taught Miss Christine to politely curb her tongue."

"Is that all?" his mother asked, her tone faint. "You met with her today in the greenhouse to teach her how to carry on a conversation?"

He reached up to rub the bridge of his nose, pinching his eyes shut. "Because of the rain. And today, we were actually working on appropriate ways to gain a gentleman's attention when one has not been introduced." He offered her a tentative smile when she gaped at him. "Normally, we meet by the brook. Away from where anyone might see. For precisely this reason. People jump to the most absurd conclusions."

"And well they might, when a handsome young bachelor and a beautiful miss exit a secluded greenhouse," she said, barely keeping her voice down. "Thomas, this is terrible. You have been meeting in secret to teach her how to catch a husband."

"You could put it like that," he conceded. "But I much prefer to say that I have been tutoring her in social customs." He risked the smile that saved him from many a reprimand in his youth. "It is not too terrible, Mother."

"It is positively ghastly," she countered, pulling her shawl tighter about her. "And were you any younger I might take you straight to your father."

"Really?" He raised his eyebrows. "It is that bad, is it?" Perhaps if he kept making light of the situation, she might lesson her level of concern.

One hand whipped out, index finger pointed directly at him the way a soldier might brandish a saber to intimidate underlings. "Do not toy with me, young man. I am still your mother and I can still ring a peel over you for getting into a terrible scrape. This must stop. At once. You will give the young lady your regrets, forget about her horses or breeding rights or whatever the arrangement was, and start behaving like a gentleman again."

"That will not do, Mother," he said. "A gentleman does not go back on his agreements. Especially with young ladies. And I have no wish to do so. I need her stallions, Mother, or I must give up my own horses, and all my dreams with them."

A mother's heart, he well knew, would not be entirely immune to such an argument as that. Indeed, she did pause and regard him solemnly for several long moments.

"If anyone should catch you, Tom," she said softly, "then both of you might have to forgo your dreams. You could be forced to marry. Your reputation and hers would be ruined."

"We are careful. Today is the single time we have been in a location where we might be caught." He sighed and looked toward the fire. "It was a touch of bad luck. Or carelessness, on my part."

"Tom," she whispered and he looked to see her eyes pleading with him, her expression worried. "Swear to me you are conducting yourself as a complete gentleman. Please."

"I swear, Mother. Miss Christine is safe in my company and always will be," he stated, eyes level, tone sincere. "I hold her in great respect and I would never do a thing to harm her person or her reputation. But in this way, as I give her the guidance she has requested, I will also have the means to save our family from the shame of selling lands or harming our tenants."

"I do not like it, Tom." She shook her head. "But I trust you to behave yourself. Oh, dear." She sighed deeply. "I have so often worried over those girls, and now it seems those worries were well founded."

This sounded like an interesting revelation. He relaxed more fully into his chair and regarded his mother with raised eyebrows. "Whatever do you mean?"

"Their mother, dying so young, leaving them at such a critical age. They have had positively no feminine guidance except what their father provided through governesses. I doubt he ever took the time to ensure those dreary women were doing a fair job. The man is never at home and he keeps his daughters terribly cloistered. It is rare the young ladies attend any community functions. I see them at private events, from time to time, but the young people always keep to themselves. Oh, if I would have paid more attention to them."

"Mother," he said, amused at the way she wrung her hands. "It was hardly your place to intervene in their upbringing."

"I could have been a better neighbor. Dear me. I wonder if this is why poor Julia never married? I have never been one for gossip, but no one really talked of why she had the one season and did not marry. She entered into society and society pushed her out again."

Thomas shifted in his seat, his mind going down that path as well. "That is not our concern or business, Mother. I have been asked to help a young woman who is the daughter of your friend. Let us leave it at that and know I will do my best to prepare her for London."

She shook her head slightly, her eyes still distant. "I should invite them to dinner. All three of the girls. It would be a kindness." Her gaze came back to him. "And I could evaluate whether you know what you are doing. How could a man ever truly understand what a lady must inherently know?"

He snorted. "Very well. You can assure yourself that there is nothing terribly scandalous in our behavior and enjoy an evening with lovely young ladies at the same time."

"Indeed. Or I may find everything is as I fear and I will have your father take a strap to you," she threatened, though her fond smile took all the sting from her words. Thomas could not help but chuckle as he agreed to see his mother's invitation delivered to the Devon household as soon as possible.

With Father away on business, this time to Bedfordshire, Christine felt more at ease in her comings and goings. Apparently, the others did as well, as both her sisters were more talkative and willing to forget their disastrous conversation on the subject of romance.

They were sitting in the music room when the invitation to dinner from Mrs. Gilbert arrived. Julia was surprised and delighted. "We have not been to the Gilbert home in an age. Not since their son left for Italy. I used to love visiting there."

"Wasn't she a friend of Mother's?" Rebecca asked, turning over a piece of new music and examining the notes with a studious frown.

"Yes, though Mrs. Gilbert is considerably older," Julia said, looking the invitation over again. "Dear me. Christine, do you think this a matchmaking scheme? It occurs to me that we may be invited because her son is in residence once more."

Christine, having remained quiet as she contemplated the invitation, shook her head. "No, likely not. Father has made certain the whole county knows his daughters are too fine to marry anyone from here. It is likely she thought of us because of her son. She may wish to entertain him with the company of other young people."

That line of thought was reasonable, but Christine knew Thomas had something to do with the invitation being extended. Maybe he was giving her a chance to show all that she had learned in a private setting, where he could observe her without anyone making suppositions as to why. Or perhaps he simply wanted to afford her the opportunity to view his mares.

"They have asked us for this evening," Julia said, "or the next evening we are available, yet I sense no urgency in the note. Friendliness, a touch of informality."

Christine was itching to read the note for herself but did not wish to appear too eager, lest she draw attention to her thoughts on the matter. "That would suggest it is a friendly, neighborly meal. Nothing more."

Rebecca rose and went to stand behind Julia's seat on the piano bench, reading the note over her eldest sister's shoulder. "I am glad she specifically asked for me. I do not like it when the two of you go off and I am left here alone, like a little girl fit for nothing except the nursery."

"You are sixteen," Julia reminded her, tilting her head back to look at Rebecca. "And not out yet."

"I know." Rebecca sighed, much put upon, and went back to her chair and her music sheets. "But it's nice to be treated like a person who enjoys dinner invitations."

Christine bit back a laugh. "And how does one treat such a person?"

"By issuing dinner invitations with great frequency," Rebecca quipped saucily. "We are going tonight, yes?"

"Yes, I think we shall." Julia stood and went to the door. "I will let Cook know not to worry about us this evening."

"Should we send a note around to the stables?" Christine ventured to ask, coming to her feet as well. "To prepare a carriage?"

"Mrs. Gilbert is sending hers for us, complete with a footman for our perilous journey, three miles to her estate," Julia answered, eyes alight. "She thought of everything. Rebecca. Transportation. *Dinner.*"

"I have always liked Mrs. Gilbert." Christine leaned back, trying not to feel nervous. This felt like a test of some sort. She steeled her nerves. Surely she could hold her own in such a small, private setting as a family dinner.

⬥

CHRISTINE ALIGHTED FROM THE CARRIAGE AFTER HER SISTERS, with the aid of a young footman. The butler held open the door at the top of the steps to admit them to the house. All three of the sisters were dressed with care for an evening away from home, but wore nothing too daring. Julia's hair was pulled up and back with a thin pink ribbon twined through it to lend her light brown ringlets elegance. Christine wore her darker hair up with a handful of pearl-tipped pins as decoration. Rebecca's hair was half down, as was becoming for one her age, and all three wore coats and gloves against the chilly night air.

They were led into a small room with mirrors to adjust their clothing and pull on their evening gloves; a maid waited upon them patiently before they were taken in to greet the family.

Mr. Gilbert, Mrs. Gilbert, Thomas, and Mrs. Brody with her husband, all stood when the sisters entered the room. Christine held her breath and kept her place behind Julia, who was acting as the leader of their party. She did, however, allow her eyes to wander as Julia thanked their hostess for the invitation.

The room in which they stood was a parlor, well-appointed with westward-facing windows to give the room warmth in the evening hours. A large hearth crackled with a toasty and welcoming fire. The decor was tasteful, yet simple, with a few pieces of art that were likely done by members of the family. The comfortable room did not in any way appear to boast of its owners' wealth or position in the world.

Mrs. Gilbert came forward to take Julia's hands and offer words of welcome and kindness, then she acknowledged Rebecca, similarly, before coming to take Christine's hands as well.

"Miss Christine," she said kindly, her eyes as green as Thomas's. "It is wonderful to have you here. I am delighted you accepted my invitation along with your sisters. I understand you are to go to London for the season?"

"Yes, Ma'am," Christine answered in what she hoped was a demure tone of voice. "I am excited for the adventure."

"Aren't we all, in those first years?" Mrs. Gilbert said with a little sigh. "It is an adventure, to be certain. I enjoyed taking my own daughters to London immensely, but I must confess," she said, lowering her voice in a conspiratorial manner, "I am quite relieved I have no need to go through that experience again."

"Oh, Mama," her daughter protested, "it was not a terrible thing."

"I quite agree with your mother," Mr. Gilbert announced from his place near the fire. "It was a relief I had only two girls go through the perils of the social jungle. There was forever some new drama in the drawing room of our townhouse, or upon a ballroom floor, or at afternoon tea."

Julia actually smiled and surprised her sisters by adding her own thoughts on the subject. "The London atmosphere certainly calls for tantrums, handkerchiefs, smelling salts, and of course, the odd headache to appear. And people were forever complaining of the crowds and crushes, yet continued to seek them out night after night."

"Seeking after torture," Mr. Brody said blithely.

His wife shot daggers at him with her eyes. "I seem to recall you came to your fair share of torturous events."

"Had to," he answered evenly, reaching across the settee to take her hand. "It was the only way I could ever hope to catch your eye, braving the untold horrors of a ballroom."

Several of them laughed, but Christine's eyes sought out Thomas with a mixture of amusement and confusion. She could not tell how much of their words were said in jest and how much were truthful. She had forever imagined her season as one of endless pleasures, but that did not seem to be the general consensus in this household. It also quite amazed her that Julia would offer a single word about London seasons.

"Come now," Thomas said, catching her look before turning to give his brother-in-law a smile. "You are frightening Miss Christine. She has nothing to base her expectations on except the conversations of others. We must not make her dread her first season."

"Indeed," Mrs. Gilbert added with a nod. "You will be fine, dear girl." She gave Christine's arm a pat and glanced about the room, as if in search of another topic for conversation.

"Where might your father be this evening? I heard he was not at home," Mr. Gilbert noted with a differential nod. "We certainly would have included him if he were."

"He is away on business," Julia answered.

"As is nearly always the case," Christine added lightly, half-smiling. "So we are especially glad to have an invitation to join such pleasant company." She glanced at Thomas from the corner of her eye to ascertain whether or not the comment was appropriate. He gave the barest of nods.

"Sweet girl." Mrs. Gilbert looked as though she would say more, then the butler appeared to inform them that dinner was ready to be served. Mr. Gilbert took his wife's arm, Mr. Brody his wife's, and Thomas offered his arm to Julia, the eldest of the sisters.

Rebecca and Christine made up the rear of the party, walking alongside each other. Rebecca looked about her with barely concealed curiosity and Christine could not help but do the same. For all that the family was known to be in a difficult financial state, their home was neat and clean, and very comfortable. It was not as old as the Devon estate, which neared eighty years, but that meant the layout was much more the thing. Christine liked it a great deal, from the polished wooden floors to the sweeping staircase. The house was slightly smaller than the Devon home, but that made it more comfortable, more inviting.

She found herself seated next to Thomas at the table, much to her surprise.

"Please excuse the informality of the table arrangements," Mrs. Gilbert said as they took their places. "I was not so much concerned with numbers and balancing the table as I was that we all be comfortable and enjoy our evening."

Mr. Gilbert sat at one end of the table, Mrs. Gilbert at the other, with Mr. Brody, his wife, and Julia on one side and Thomas, Christine, and Rebecca on the other.

"I believe the arrangements are perfect, Mrs. Gilbert," Julia commented warmly.

As the first course was served, Christine did her best to be nothing but civil and so spoke very little. Yet every time she glanced up at Mrs. Gilbert's end of the table, the matron was watching her, lips pursed and eyebrows raised.

Could she be conducting herself in a manner that displeased her hostess? She sincerely hoped not. Occasionally she would look to Thomas; each time, he offered her a reassuring smile.

They spoke casually of the weather, the book Mr. Gilbert was reading at present, and whether or not they could expect snow in the near future. Each topic was safe and Christine did her part in asking thoughtful questions and agreeing with what the gentlemen had to say. Nevertheless, the conversation did not fulfill Christine's ideals.

Julia and Thomas exchanged several comments about the changes in the neighborhood since his absence, and Christine wondered, for the barest instant, if Julia and Thomas would make a good match.

Immediately, she banished the idea. Julia, the spinster who cared so little for outdoor pursuits, and Thomas, the sportsman who wished to start a horse farm? No, they were far too dissimilar. Besides that, Julia had never expressed any wish to marry, not after her season. She never spoke of gentlemen that way.

Christine set aside the absurd and irritating notion, trying to bring her attention back to the conversation taking place on her side of the table, but caught Mrs. Gilbert looking at her again, her eyebrows drawn together and her lips pursed, as she were studying her.

Christine would have to ask Thomas about it later. For the time being, she did her best to enjoy the meal and practice all the tricks he had taught her by the brook. Her only disappointment was that she would yet have to wait to see his mares, but one simply did not leave a pleasant table to walk through the stables on a cold night, at least not without drawing unnecessary and undesired attention.

THE DOOR CLOSED ON THEIR GUESTS, INCLUDING HIS SISTER AND her husband, and Thomas let out a relieved moan which he quickly disguised as a yawn when his mother turned to him, eyebrows arched.

"Thomas," she said, "would you have the time to speak with me?"

"Is this a conversation I should be part of?" his father asked, sounding amused. "It sounds serious."

"Not at all, Harold," she answered, leaning in to kiss his cheek. "I will meet you in the library after I speak with our boy."

Father chuckled and gave his son a little shrug. "I have my marching orders. I suspect you are about to receive yours. Good night, Tom."

"Good night, Father." Thomas offered his arm to his mother and led her back into the parlor, where the fire was still lit and giving off a comfortable heat. He guided her to her favorite chair. Once she was seated, positioned himself in front of the fire, leaning against the mantel.

"Very well, Mother. You have seen Miss Christine for yourself and spent most of the evening unnerving her with your stare."

"Oh, do you think she noticed my study of her?" Mrs. Gilbert asked, tilting her head to one side. "I thought she caught me at it once or twice, but I did not think it too pointed."

"Perhaps not. I certainly noticed, because I was looking for it." Thomas sighed and put his elbow on the mantel, pushing his hand through his hair. "What did you think of her overall? Are you still concerned that she is after my entirely ineligible hand?"

She waved that comment aside impatiently. "You are highly eligible for the right woman, Tom. A woman who will love you and help you face whatever the future brings. To answer your question, no. I do not believe she has designs on you, though her trust in you is quite obvious. As often as I was watching her, she was looking to you."

"To ascertain if I approved of her speech and conduct. Not surprising, given my odd position as tutor."

"Indeed." Yet still his mother appeared troubled. "She trusts you too much."

"What do you mean?" he asked, narrowing his eyes. "I thought you wanted me to be a trustworthy sort of person."

"It is not that, Tom. It is more to do with the other things I observed this evening. Miss Christine is not at all a flighty young woman. She seems quite genuine in her words and personality. However, she is also incredibly trusting, naive, and without guile. Even while smiling and agreeing with every word dear George said, you could tell by her expression she wished to say more or felt differently. She took everything we said to her at face value, including our teasing about the social season. I am terribly concerned for her." The verdict, stated openly and honestly with a quiet fervor, alarmed Thomas.

"Why?"

"While we both know that you are completely trustworthy, and behaving honorably, I worry at how quick she was to enlist your help in her endeavor and how much she has come to rely upon you. You cannot help her in London, Thomas, but there may be many eager gentlemen ready to assume the role of mentor, to take advantage of her inexperience."

Thomas considered her words, his heart dropping as he realized the truth of them. "You are concerned that men take advantage of her."

"Yes. And not only men. You know as well as I do that there are plenty of women in London who will delight in eating her alive," his mother said slowly. "Saying one thing to her face and another when her back is turned, seemingly paying a compliment that is really an insult, drawing her out to later use her own words against her in gossip. There are many who will see her innocence as weakness and prey upon it."

The dire predictions of his mother sent a chill through Thomas, leaving him ill. "What can be done to avert such disasters?" he asked at last, voice soft. "Surely her aunt will chaperone her well, averting such problems?"

"Perhaps, but perhaps not. Think on Julia. We know she returned from her season as something of a disappointment to her family, yet no one has ever said why. Can the aunt truly care any more about Christine's success than Julia's? We do not know what happened, but if Julia was as naive as Christine, we can guess. And we can also suppose that Christine's season will end in much the same way." She gestured helplessly with her hands. "Yet what can we do? Christine will have to learn the hard way, for I can think of no way for you to impart to her a keener sense of judgement, not at this late stage."

"Yet that is precisely what I must try to do," he murmured,

looking down into the fire. "Thank you, Mother. You have given me a great deal to think upon."

She stood and came to his side, offering a kiss on the cheek. "My dear boy, be careful. I still believe this is an ill-advised scheme to spend so much time in private with a young lady. It endangers the both of you."

"It will be all right, Mother. Christmas is not long in coming now." He heaved a sigh. "And I assure you again, I am behaving as a perfect gentleman. Our reputations are safe."

Her expression remained concerned, though she attempted a smile. "I was not speaking entirely of reputations. But...well. Never mind. Good night, Tom." She patted his arm and left him to his own worrisome thoughts.

Chapter Thirteen

Thomas waited beneath a tree, going over his mother's words. He recounted all he knew of Christine: her trusting nature, her lack of experience with men, her innocence and naivete to the ways of the world.

She had asked him, a near stranger, to meet with her in private in order to be taught how to flirt.

His mother was right. This foolish endeavor was only giving her tools that would lead her into trouble, making *him* responsible for her downfall. There was no doubt in his mind that a rake of the ton would recognize her at once for what she was: an innocent maiden with very few protectors. Christine could easily fall prey to the flattering advances of a man whose intentions were anything but honorable.

How could he teach her the dangers of trusting just anyone? Or how to recognize a man of ill repute? How would she recognize trouble when it came to call? She likely wouldn't even understand the danger until it became too late. The very thought of Christine, so young and kind and well-intentioned, ruined by a cad, set his teeth to grinding.

Thomas's temper rose slowly. He was angry at Christine, but also at himself. How could he have been so foolish? To take on a role of such import and responsibility should never have been his place. His clumsy attempts had likely done nothing but prepare the victim for the sacrifice.

Yet he could not abandon her now. Maybe enough time remained to give her a lesson in care. Though perhaps, he did not give her enough credit. She could not completely unaware of the dangers facing young ladies, could she? Surely someone, even her pugnacious father, had already warned her against wolves in sheep's clothing?

Christine arrived precisely on time, as she always did, on her side of the brook.

"Mr. Gilbert," she said brightly. "Good afternoon! Isn't it lovely to have the sun back?" Without even a by-your-leave, she crossed the water on her stunning horse.

She did not even blink. Did not even question the appropriateness of the move.

But then, the last time they were together had been in the greenhouse. A very confined space.

Circumstances forced that, he told himself, wishing she had gone back to the boundaries they had deemed appropriate when they first started meeting. But then, they hadn't agreed, had they? He had appreciated the barrier the brook created, but he'd never instructed her not to cross.

Christine dismounted while he debated what to say, whether or not to reprimand her. She tethered her horse next to his near a scraggly patch of late autumn weeds, then approached with a confident grin.

"I have some very particular questions today. Shall we begin, Mr. Gilbert?"

All at once the idea came to him and his plan of action, only half-formed, was launched with all the subtlety of an English warship.

"Thomas. Please, call me Thomas. After all, we have been meeting in secret long enough to become friends." He smiled in what he hoped was a charming manner, though he would not be surprised if she caught a hint of his frustration.

She hesitated, narrowing her eyes at him. "I thought you wanted to follow all the proper forms?"

He lifted one shoulder in a shrug and turned to fully face her, hands clasped behind his back. "I know. It seems foolish, given that we have met these many times and no one has ever come to eavesdrop or spy. I was overly cautious. You are right that we have known each other for a long time. In private, there is no reason to be so formal."

Much to his horror, her smile brightened. "Oh, I am glad you see it that way! I do feel we are becoming such good friends. I believe you know more about me than my own sisters, at present. You will call me Christine, please."

"Christine." He tried to relax and plan his next move, all the while clenching a fist behind his back. "It is a lovely name." Having never been a man of loose morals, acting as one in the moment should have been difficult.

Surprisingly, Thomas found it all too easy.

"Come, that rock will be much too cold to sit upon for the lesson. There is a fallen tree here." He nodded his head to indicate a place a few feet into the thicket, away from the open area in which they usually met.

"An excellent idea," she said, her chipper tone grating further on his frustration. She led the way to the log. She sat down, bringing her riding cape tight about her. "It is more wintry today, isn't it? I am not certain how much longer I will be able to go for rides in the weather without taking ill. But I suppose there is always the greenhouse to use again, isn't there?"

"If you think we should risk it," he said, sitting next to her more closely than necessary. Their thighs nearly brushed.

He watched her rub her gloved hands together and she raised them to her lips to blow on them. "My fingers will turn blue before long."

His horrible plan continued to produce equally awful ideas.

"Here, let me see your hands." He stripped his gloves off and put them on the log and when she gave him hers, eyes curious, he unbuttoned the glove of her left wrist.

"What are you doing?" she questioned, sounding more amused than offended. She did not withdraw her hand.

"Warming you," he said, trying to affect a light tone of voice while his pulse slammed against his temple. His anger, still present, simmered beneath the surface. How could she be so trusting?

He unbuttoned the first glove and took it off as though it were an everyday, ordinary act. He held her hand between his and chafed it, briskly.

"That does help," she admitted. "My fingers were positively frigid from holding the reins. One cannot carry a muff on horseback."

"Indeed." He finished with that hand. "Tuck it there, under your other arm." She followed his instructions and carried on conversation about the lovely blue sky and the pleasant ride she had enjoyed on her way to their meeting.

His temper mounted, though he tamped it down, lest he give himself away. He unbuttoned her other glove at her wrist, but moved more slowly. Now, instead of simply peeling the glove off, he ran a fingertip gently across the wrist beneath her glove. He cupped her hand carefully, slowly removing the article of clothing. He concentrated on making the movement last as long as possible, allowing his touch to glide against each exposed inch of skin.

Her raptures over the cloudless day trailed off to silence.

Finally. A reaction.

Once the glove was off, he took her bare hand in both of his and proceeded in warming it, this time with deliberately slow strokes. Then he raised her hand up to his lips and placed a kiss upon the inside of her wrist.

Christine's sharp intake of breath indicated he was getting through to her, at least on some level. He raised his eyes at last, meeting hers to find them wide in shock, her lips parted to form a perfect 'o' of surprise. Yet she said nothing. Did nothing. She should have pulled away. Slapped him. Said something cutting. Screamed.

The devil inside him prodded him further while his anger mounted. How could she be so helpless in the face of such a blatant onslaught?

"You are no longer cold?" he asked, barely keeping his voice controlled when he so desperately wanted to grab her and shake some sense into her.

"I am—I am warm enough," she near-whispered, her voice low and strangled. "Th-thank you." At last she acted, withdrawing her hand, but the gesture was far too slow to show she felt any real affront.

Thomas moved closer and put his arm deliberately behind her, his hand on the log and his forearm brushing her waist. "Are you certain? As you said, the days grow colder. I would not wish you to catch a chill."

Her face flamed red. "I am f-fine." Her spine stiffened and she leaned away slightly. "Are *you* feeling quite the thing today?"

"Yes. I am very well. Thank you." He put all the heat and desire he could into his gaze and turned his lips up slowly in a smile. "Better than ever. I am glad you are here."

"I come every third day," she said. Her eyes dropped from his. "And I think we ought to begin our lesson."

"Certainly." Her discomfort still wasn't enough to have him believe her truly secure. "Have we ever discussed what you are to do when you are alone with a gentleman?" he asked, reaching with his free hand to tilt her chin up. When his eyes met hers, he could see she still felt bewildered by his sudden change in attitude.

"Alone? No. We-we haven't." Her deep brown eyes met his with uncertainty, then darted down to look at his mouth.

"No? Now would be a good time to explain." He leaned closer, watching her eyes widen in momentary confusion and then—inexplicably—her lashes lowered as she lifted her face to his.

He leaned nearer, so close he could feel her warm breath upon his lips.

"Some gentlemen will have expectations of you, should they find themselves alone with you. Like this. Unguarded." His words whispered softly against her skin. She made it all too easy, and her loveliness, her trust, enticed him.

What would it be like to kiss her? His eyes went to her lips.

"Expectations?" she asked, barely breathing. "Of what, Thomas?"

It was her use of his name that snapped him out of his act, which may not have been an act for much longer, as surely as a bucket of the brook's water would have done. He jerked back, putting his hands on her shoulders and holding her away.

"Christine, you brainless little chit!" he said between his teeth. "What are you playing at?" He gave her one little shake.

Her eyes nearly leaped from their sockets and her face went white, then red. "Me?" she gasped out. "What are *you* playing at? I thought you might kiss me!"

"And I nearly did. You certainly would not have stopped me." He leaped up from his place on the log and marched away, nearly trembling in his anger. "Of all the fool-headed, naive, witless things to do. I gave you every opportunity to run, to scream, to slap me, even to tell me off. How far would you have let it go, Christine?" he demanded, whirling on her.

She sat, looking positively flabbergasted, and rose slowly to her feet. "What are you saying? Was this all some sort of—sort of test?" Her face paled again. "It was. Of all the horrid, mean things to do." She looked mortified, then incensed.

"It is a good thing I did. This throws a whole new light onto your tutoring sessions. Has no one taught you to leave scoundrels alone? To stay away from rakes? From those who would hold your reputation cheaply?" he demanded, striding quickly toward her. He stopped barely a foot away from her and glared down into her eyes. "Never, ever let a man lead you to a secluded place, and never, ever let him divest you of even a glove. And kissing you? As soon as my lips touched your wrist, you should have slapped me soundly."

"First," she snarled up at him, with real heat in her voice, "I was not aware that you were a scoundrel or a rake. I thought you were my friend. How many times have we been in company that we have behaved ourselves? I did not expect that you would be—"

She broke off, then growled. "I *could* slap you. How dare you? How dare you touch me and make me think you wished to *kiss* me?" She tossed her head back, eyes blazing. "How cruel and monstrous. I would never let another man get so close. I am not an idiot. But I *trusted* you." She placed both ungloved hands on his chest and shoved, taking him by surprise enough that he took a step back.

He reached up and caught her wrists, the bare skin against his fingertips hot, her pulse thrumming against his thumb.

"Trust or not," he argued, his glare unabated, "no man should get that close to you unless he has made his intentions clear with you and your father. Even then it would be questionable."

She yanked her arms away and took a step back. "You took me by surprise. Here you were being my friend, caring for me." Her tone changed from hurt to angry. "You were only trying to trick me. I was confused." She closed her eyes and took a deep breath. "I thought you were going to kiss me."

"And why didn't you run? Right then?" he demanded. He shoved both hands through his hair, knocking his hat off. "*Zeus*, Christine."

"*Miss* Christine," she corrected quietly. "The ruse is over, Mr. Gilbert." She took another step, backing away from him. Then another. "I think I have learned all I care to learn today." She turned on her heel and moved briskly to where the horses were waiting.

He watched her go, still angry, then rapidly moved to catch up to her. "Never," he said from behind her, "be in a secluded place, alone, with a man of any kind. No alcoves, no shaded trees, or walled-in gardens."

"I believe you made that lesson quite clear," she shouted, not even looking as she turned her mount to lead him to the stone.

Thomas stopped and knelt before her, offering his cupped hands to throw her up into the saddle. "Good."

She took his help without a word. The moment she sat properly, she urged her horse forward across the brook. Once on the other side she turned, glaring at him.

"You could have spoken to me about it, Mr. Gilbert. I hardly needed a demonstration of what a rake looks like."

"You are too trusting," he argued back, folding his arms before him and sending her the sternest of glares. "What do you really know of me? What if I was no better than a common rake?"

"You are a Gilbert," she said, her words biting. "I know your father, your mother, your sisters. I followed you around while you learned from my mother. You have always behaved as a gentleman. Why would I ever have reason to doubt you? To distrust you? I never did. Not until today, when you behaved like a perfect ruffian. You made your point, Mr. Gilbert." She pulled her horse around, turning her back to him. "Good day."

His anger receded as he watched her, straight-backed and furious, ride away. His breathing slowed, as did the blood pounding through his veins, but it was not until he turned to see her gloves upon the log and his hat on the ground that he realized his misgivings about how he'd chosen to teach her.

What *had* he been thinking?

Chapter Fourteen

Three days of rain kept Christine indoors and away from the brook. She highly doubted that Thomas would come and wait for her during a deluge, but she considered with great satisfaction how he might look, waiting for her in the pouring rain. After their last session, Providence gave them a reprieve from each other. She wanted to forgive him for his actions, but the way he had chosen to teach her, treating her as though she were a fool, hurt her pride.

She never would have allowed a man she barely knew to take such liberties with her gloves, her hand, or come so near to kissing her. She was not a complete fool. She read novels and knew to look out for villains seeking to take advantage. A woman's reputation was all she had. No woman could afford to risk herself. Christine *knew* that.

But the question remained, niggling at the back of her mind, why *did* she trust Thomas so completely? Trust him enough that when he moved toward her as though to kiss her, she didn't lean away but instead waited with bated breath?

Her reaction was obviously due to the fact that she had never been kissed. Ever. It was only curiosity that had caused her hesitation. Truly, who could help but wonder if the sensation was marvelous or strange? Practically speaking, she'd always thought it an odd way to show affection, but when Thomas leaned in closely, she suddenly understood the appeal.

She dropped her shoulders and stood to pace the room. Rebecca was curled up on her favorite chair, scowling down at her gardening book. Julia sat at the piano bench, playing a melancholy air.

"Confound the weather," Christine muttered.

"Hm?" Julia looked away from her music, though her fingers continued on the keys. "Did you say something, Christine?"

"She made a crude statement about the weather," Rebecca answered for her, turning a page. "And I quite agree with her. I am tired of the rain. I wish it would be fine and sunny or else soft and snowy."

"Rain must come sometimes," Julia said with an arched brow and. "You both do look bored and in need of exercise. You ought to take a walk indoors, to stretch."

Christine scoffed. "Don't be silly." She flung herself back into her chair and glared at the window. "I am in need of an occupation, not exercise. Something to keep my mind busy."

"Borrow my horrid horticulture book," Rebecca suggested, snapping the book closed. "You may learn the difference between peonies and pansies and when to plant them."

Julia laughed, still plunking at her piano keys but without as much dedication as before. "You know, Mother loved flowers. She always brought them into the house. But she claimed the moment she tried her hand at gardening, everything wilted away. She had no talent for growing things."

"Except daughters," Rebecca quipped. "I didn't know that. We have such beautiful gardens. I thought Mama must have loved to garden."

"Not at all. She loved to walk there though, when she was not indoors with us or out riding." Julia shifted on the piano bench and dropped her hands to her lap. "Do you remember the picnics we took out amongst the flowers? Late spring, when the ground was dry enough to lay a blanket down."

Rebecca nodded, appearing eager. "I do remember. We used to take tea cakes and sandwiches to eat."

"I loved those picnics," Christine said quietly, picturing her mother's face as she doled out biscuits. "We would spend all afternoon outside, and Mother never once lectured us on freckling."

"She used to say that sunshine must be good for growing girls if it was good for the flowers," Julia said, sounding wistful. "When the weather turned, we still took walks on the garden paths until our noses were pink with cold and our fingers numb. Then we would come inside and sit before the fire."

"And drink chocolate," Rebecca burst in. "Oh, I do remember. Mama would tell us stories. Or teach us a game."

Christine shared a smile with Julia. "I sometimes forget how much time she spent with the three of us together. I normally think on the timed just the two of spent together, out riding mostly."

Julia nodded and rose to come around the instrument. "I think she took special time with each of us. I remember Mother showing me how to knit and then taking me on visits around the parish to see friends and give the blankets out as gifts. She was always so kind. I wanted to be like that."

"But you are," Rebecca said, offering her assurance. "Everyone knows you are the kind one." She sighed. "I can barely remember Mama some days, though she is never far from my thoughts. I cannot think if there was anything special we did together, just her and me."

"Mother read to you," Christine hastened to remind her, lest her sister grew sad. "All the time. And she taught you your letters when you were very little."

"You were only eleven when she passed," Julia said, tenderness in her voice. "But she loved spending time with you. I remember you were forever following her about the house as she worked with Mrs.

North to keep things in order. Or in the kitchens when she planned menus. I think she must have enjoyed your company."

Rebecca smiled and leaned back into her chair. "I like to think the two of you do as well."

The elder two laughed and agreed.

"Among the three of us, we can keep her memory and her kindness alive." Julia spoke softly. "If we try, and do our best not to bicker with each other, we will make her very proud."

"I hope so," Christine whispered while Rebecca nodded. "We are all that is left of her."

"And Horrible Horace," Rebecca added with a laugh, lightening the mood.

"You promised to stop calling him that when he went away to school," Julia reminded her, eyebrows raised. "He prefers to go by Harry now."

"Which is not really an acceptable substitute," Rebecca countered. "I feel most sorry for him. He was so little when Mama died. I can at least remember some things about her. And then he went away for school."

"At least he has her kind disposition," Julia said. "Harry is forever thinking of us when he comes home to visit."

Christine nodded. "True. And he looks the most like her, with his coloring."

"Red hair and freckles," Rebecca said. "I do not envy him that." She hesitated, biting her lip for a moment before pressing forward with her next question. "What do you think Mother would say to Christine about her upcoming season?"

Christine waited and watched, wondering what Julia might say. When she finally answered, her voice was near a whisper. "She would want her to be happy. I think all she would advise for any of us is to look for the events, the friendships, and the gentleman who will bring us the most happiness." Julia reached out and squeezed Christine's hand, meeting her eyes.

Christine looked away and sighed. "I'm sure you are right.

Mother would want our happiness. I must confess, I am not always certain what that will look like."

The rain filled the silence following that remark, though Christine, Julia, and Rebecca remained sitting close. Christine felt certain they shared more in that moment than they had in a long time, even if they did not utter their thoughts aloud.

CHRISTINE PREPARED FOR HER AFTERNOON EXCURSION EARLY; she needed a good long ride before facing Thomas again. Reflecting on his behavior during their last meeting still left her with a strange ache, much like she had a rock settled in the pit of her stomach. Simply ignoring him wouldn't do. She rarely saw him outside of their scheduled meetings, so such a punishment would likely be lost on him. No, she wanted to go to the brook and tell him, in very clear terms, that she thought him a complete cad and wanted nothing further to do with him. That would get her message across.

Truly, she no longer even wished to *think* of Thomas.

Except for that perfect, single, awe-inspiring moment that she could not forget, when he might have wanted to kiss her.

A blush crept up her neck as she relived the minutes leading up to that one, pivotal moment. How could she not have realized what he was doing? He had drawn her in expertly, in such a friendly manner. One moment he was the tutor, the neighbor and friend, and then, quite suddenly, the world shifted.

She had *wanted* him to kiss her.

That was the moment she continued to think on, pick apart, put back together, and relive in her mind. His lips close, his eyes looking deeply into hers. He had beautiful eyes. But before their lips actually met, it all ended.

Christine wanted to understand why she had been perfectly content—even happy—in that short breadth of time. Was it truly curiosity? A consequence of her inexperience and desire to give it a try? Or was it something else? Something far more dangerous? Was she actually attracted to Thomas?

She adjusted her hat in the mirror while her maid, Sarah, stood back, examining every line of her to make certain all was well with her wardrobe.

"Have a lovely ride, miss. It's been so wet out, I hope the paths are clear enough for you."

"Thank you, Sarah. I know of a few places that tend to remain firm." She smiled her gratitude and prepared to leave.

A knock at the door stalled her plans. Sarah opened the door to a footman who handed her a note, then disappeared.

The maid brought the note, eyebrows raised. "It is your father's card, Miss Christine."

Christine's father had only just returned that morning. She had expected a summons eventually, but she had hoped to avoid him a while longer. Christine turned the card over to see her father's firm handwriting. "Come to the study at once."

She sighed and tucked the card into her waistband. "It seems I may be delayed at the stables. Please send a message to the groom. Let him know to keep my horse ready, but I do not know how soon I will be out."

"Of course, miss."

Christine nodded her thanks and left the room at a brisk pace. To keep her father waiting overly long would be a supremely bad idea.

Mentally, Christine went over all her expenditures for the season. She remained within her budget, she well knew, so that couldn't be the reason for her summons. She went over her recent behavior at the events she had attended with her family and without. She could think of nothing she had done to upset her father.

She arrived at his study door still agitated and perplexed. Taking a deep breath, she raised her hand and knocked. As tempted as she was to analyze his call to enter, she squared her shoulders and lifted her chin, breezing into the room.

"You sent for me, Father?"

"Christine. Sit." He did not rise from his desk nor look up immediately from his papers. Only after she sat, perched on the edge of the chair, did he look up. He did not offer her a reassuring smile as she so wished he would. Surely, before her mother passed, he had been happier.

But then, in those days, Christine rarely saw him. He spent much of his time on business in London, and their mother preferred the country life where she could raise children and horses in the sunshine and fresh air—or so she had always said. For the first time, Christine wondered if her father's frowns were the real reason her mother had stayed at home when her father went into the city.

"We are now two weeks away from Christmas. Will you be sufficiently prepared by that point?"

This was a planning meeting? That she could handle. She could even smile. "Yes, Father. Everything will be prepared and packed before that date. I am certain all will be ready."

"Excellent." He sat back in his chair and steepled his fingers before him, regarding her with the same flat expression. "You are more realistic and level-headed about your foray into society than your sister. She was too young. Immature. But you see this opportunity for what it is, a chance to advance in society and raise your family with you."

Christine swallowed and nodded once. "I hope to make you very proud, Father."

"So long as you remember your duty to your family, and your obligation to see a return on my investment in you these many years, I believe you will."

Having heard this same lecture many times before, why did this time make her feel as though a stone sat in her stomach?

"Your duty to the family goes beyond the day I give your hand to another. Once the marriage contract is made, your obligations double. You will be responsible for keeping your husband in good standing with society and his associates. You will also continue to be a representative of this household and our family name."

She knew his expectations, yet they had never sounded this pointed before.

He stood and came around the desk, paper in hand. "I have taken the liberty of making a list of the families I find most suitable for you to join. The eldest eligible male in each family would be best." He held the sheet out to her.

Christine stared at the paper in his hand, her confusion mounting even as that stone sunk deeper into her core. "You have a list of families you would like me to marry into?" Her eyes darted up to his, hoping she misunderstood somehow or that there was a better explanation forthcoming.

"Indeed." He raised both eyebrows at her. "I need not tell you, with your extensive knowledge of horse breeding, how important the right bloodlines and connections are?"

She felt a chill run through her and then all the heat returned in her cheeks as she accepted the sheet of paper. "Bloodlines?" she whispered, her eyes turning to the page, though she found herself unable to take in a single name.

"Yes. Pedigrees. I went through a great deal of work to approve each name on this list. I looked into finances, social status, and titles. I have ranked my preference from top to bottom. There are fifteen families listed. Any of them will do, but you should begin at the top." He tapped a name at the corresponding space on the paper. "The Earl of Darbinger's family. He has two sons. Both will inherit titles, one from the mother's side. If you can manage to snare either of them, I would be pleasantly surprised. The sooner we form a marriage contract, the better."

"What of gentlemen not on the list?" she asked, voice softer than she liked. Her eyes darted up to meet his, to find them cold and hard upon her.

"Adhere to the list, Christine. If another option presents itself, we can discuss the matter, but I'd prefer it not be an issue. With the money I will spend on you this season, and have already spent on your upbringing, I expect a very advantageous match. You are the only one among my daughters to never be foolish enough to dwell upon the idea of romance."

That smote her, though it was true. Never had Christine spoken to her father of romance, of novels, or of love. She spoke of the things which would please him, parroting his opinions to him, behaving in exactly the manner he demanded.

Father never spoke of love, so she did not. He never spoke of his hopes for her future happiness, so she did not. He spoke of the connections he wished her marriage to make, and she pledged herself to finding the perfect match, the son-in-law who would make him pleased.

Now she had fifteen options to choose from.

While she struggled through this mental avalanche, her father went back to his place behind the desk. "Study the list carefully. Your aunt has been sent a copy, in order to arrange introductions. If we plan accordingly, we will have you engaged by February."

She started at that. "February?"

"It would be better to snatch up a promising subject before anyone else has a chance at him," he said, eyes back on his desk. "There is little time to waste in the business world, Christine."

"Business world? But it is my first season—"

The look he gave her, icy in its formality, cut her off. "It is your only season. I will not throw money away on a bad investment." He rose slowly and narrowed his eyes at her. "That was Julia's mistake, and you see how she regrets it. I gave her everything a girl could desire for her season, including a wide variety of gentlemen I approved of. She chose to ignore my wishes. Now she is no better than a housekeeper. What of you, Christine? With Julia fulfilling that role here, what do you hope to become if you fail to marry?"

He paused, lifting his chin and looking down his nose at her. "Your mother understood her duty too little. She married me and when her eyes were opened to the realities of the world and our place in it, she withdrew from society and buried herself here, caring for nothing but those horses she would not even breed or sell. Of what use was she to me? The one thing your mother did correctly was give me an heir." A lesser man would have snorted, he only exhaled forcefully. "Do not shame me as she did."

Her whole body felt as though she had been carved from marble, so stiff she became when he spoke of her mother.

Her mother, who she recalled with love and fondness. The mother who was always there with a smile and encouragement, warmth radiating from her every expression and word. How could he speak of her so carelessly?

She tamped down a shudder at his demanding expectations. There was nothing she could think to say except what was expected. "Yes, Father."

"You are dismissed." He flicked a hand toward the door, his eyes already back on his desk.

She stood, but hesitated, wondering why the meeting felt as though it had gone horribly wrong. Not wishing to further irritate her father, she turned and left as quietly as she had entered, only this time with her head much lower.

When the study door closed behind her, she looked down at the list and swallowed back tears.

"I am no better than a broodmare."

Chapter Fifteen

Thomas paced on his side of the brook, his coat billowing out behind him, Christine's gloves in his pocket. He checked his watch again and scowled at the infuriating piece of machinery. She was nearly half an hour late, leaving him and his horse to stand long in the cold. If she wished to cancel their agreement after their last meeting, she should have sent a note. She had ample opportunity, with the storm three days past interrupting their usual meeting time.

For the first two days after that disastrous lesson, he berated himself for upsetting her so greatly. Christine, innocent as she was, surely did not deserve such harsh censure and inappropriate treatment. But he still felt overwhelmed with frustration whenever he thought of her nearly allowing him such liberties.

He was angry that she would fall into such a trap without a second thought. Angry that he took advantage of the situation. Angry that he was tutoring her at all. How touched in the head did one have to be to agree to her confusing, madcap scheme? Thomas also felt a great deal of frustration toward any and all people in her life who had failed to prepare her for her entrance into society. How could a girl go so long, even moving in such a small society as theirs, without learning when a man meant trouble?

Christine trusted him completely. She surely never expected to be on the defensive in his company. But then, shouldn't his change of character, abrupt as it was, have sent her fleeing? Why did she draw closer instead of away? And, blast it, why did she raise her face to him and look so much as though she wanted to be kissed?

His self-abasement did not last long as he argued with himself, again and again. He did his duty, as promised, to prepare her for whatever *civilized* society threw at her when she arrived in London. There would doubtless be men present capable of gaining her trust, even her friendship, before attempting to take liberties with such a sweet, guileless woman.

The very idea of anyone attempting what he had, abusing her trust in such a vile way, outraged Thomas. He felt a yearning deep in his gut to stay with her, to protect her and help guide her through London. But it wasn't possible. He could not be there to watch over her, no matter how much he wished it so. Even if he could, it wasn't his place.

His fists closed and opened several times as he imagined the would-be suitors closing in upon her as she innocently flirted her way into their clutches, like a lamb to the slaughter.

No. Thomas could not allow it to happen. Today, he would drive home the point. He would give her a lecture, sparing her no detail of what such men could do to her reputation, to her heart. He glanced again across the brook. That is, if she ever bothered to show up.

He was reaching for his watch again when he finally heard her coming, heard the horse's hooves upon the ground and the rustling of the branches across the way.

He planted his feet apart and stood, shoulders back, ready to turn the full force of his glare upon her. Thomas would not apologize. He would stand his ground and show her the folly of her trust.

Christine did not stop on her side of the brook but rode straight across to his. His desire to ring a peel over her head dissolved the moment he took in her expression.

Her face was pale and streaked with tears, her eyes telling of great distress, even grief. She looked as if she had lost a loved one, as though doom had been pronounced upon her.

Dread pooled in his stomach and he reached up for her before she could dismount on her own. She slid down, the least graceful he had ever seen her move, and took one stumbling step into his arms. She buried her face into his coat front; without a word, her sobs began anew.

As a man with sisters whom he loved, he told himself it was completely natural to wrap his arms around her and rest his cheek upon her head. Though he did not think his sisters, either of them, ever fit so nicely in that place.

It did not escape him how entirely inappropriate their position was, but he could not find it in himself to rebuke her or put her away as her broken-hearted sobs, quiet as they were, shook them both.

After a time, her body stilled and a few last, stuttering breaths were taken before she inhaled deeply. She lifted her head from his shoulder, her eyes swollen and red, her cheeks pale.

"Thomas," she said, and his heart lurched forward suddenly. Had she asked him in that moment to run through whatever blackguard caused those tears, he would have done it. "I am sorry." She put her hands flat upon his chest and gently pushed away. He released her from the embrace but moved his hands to hers.

"Come." He pulled her gently toward that log, that place where all the trouble of their last meeting began. "Something terrible has happened. Tell me. What can I do?"

She shook her head, yet followed him docilely. "It is not so terrible." She wilted when she sat, folding her gloved hands in her lap. "I do not know what has come over me. I just—" She shuddered and wrapped her arms about herself. "I do not know who to talk to or how to explain what has happened."

"Is your family well?" he asked softly, still standing before her.

He did not want to sit next to her and risk her thinking he had any intention of repeating his actions from their last meeting.

"Y-yes. Everyone is well. Healthy." She smiled weakly. "I suppose I did rather act as though someone had d-died." Her liquid brown eyes met his, nothing at all in them to smile about. "I had something of a shock today, I suppose. A dreadful shock."

"What happened?" he asked. When she hesitated to speak, he hastily added, "Not that you need tell me. It is none of my affair. I—"

"Are you my friend, Mr. Gilbert?" she asked softly, interrupting him.

The answer came without him having to think on it. "Yes. Undoubtedly."

"Then I believe I can tell you." Her shoulders slumped and she lowered her eyes to the ground. "I spoke to my father today. He wanted to remind me of my prospects this season and make certain I understood what he expects of me." Again, that smile, devoid of happiness appeared. It was a rueful, sad smile. "He presented me with a list of families of whose pedigree he approves. A stud list, if you will."

Thomas blinked, his mind processing what she said, and then he felt his ire begin to build. "A list of appropriate mates?" His jaw clenched over the word.

"Yes. The approved families which I am permitted to entertain thoughts of marrying into. I am not to deviate from that list."

"You knew he wished you to marry well. I thought it was your intention to please him," he said darkly, crossing his arms before him. "Why would it be shocking he has a particular idea of who would be best for his daughter?" But a list? It sounded unbelievable and insulting.

A humorless laugh escaped her. "I suppose it isn't too shocking, when you say it that way. But the list is not of those who are best for me. They are the list of those who are best for him. Business and society connections he wishes to strengthen or begin—to receive a return on his investment." At his narrowed eyes, she clarified. "*I am* an *investment*. That is all a daughter is. Or did you not know?" A trace of bitter humor underscored her words.

"He said something along those lines to me once," Thomas conceded. "I thought little of it. It is true that a woman's marriage can benefit her family, after all."

"That is all my marriage is meant to do." Her tone sounded as though she was weary of the thought. "He also made sure I knew, quite clearly, that I would have no place in the family at the end of the season unless I married. He doesn't want another failure, like Julia, to care for into spinsterhood."

Thomas raised his eyebrows. "You must have misunderstood. One season to make such a spectacular connection? It has been done, but to expect it is completely unreasonable."

"My father *expects* results in his business dealings."

"You are his daughter. Not a business associate."

"More like an employee," she said, "meant to do my master's bidding and be dismissed if I am unable to fulfill my contracted requirements."

Thomas sat next to her, turned sideways on the log, and reached out to take up one of her hands. "Christine, you must have misunderstood. No one could be so callous."

"He said my mother was useless to him, and to their marriage," she whispered, eyes glimmering with tears again. "*Useless*."

Now Thomas understood the heartbroken sobs. While Devon's words about his daughter's worth were cruel, they did not seem to be the true surprise as she had long been preparing for her grand entrance into society. She had long understood his expectations and though they put pressure and anxiety upon her, it was his words about her mother that had truly shattered her heart. Thomas took up her hands and held them in his, his eyes meeting hers.

"Your mother," he said softly, "was one of the kindest women I have ever known. She was happy. She loved her life. She loved her children. She enjoyed her horses. She liked helping others. My mother adored her. Spoke of her the other day, in fact, as a light that went out far too soon. If your father did not know what a precious gift he had in marrying such a lady, that is his loss. Not yours."

She sniffled and smiled, the most honest smile he had seen that day. "I miss her. I miss her so much it hurts. I wish she were here. I wish she could help me." She bit her lip as the tears started to spill again.

Thomas reached into his coat for a handkerchief and dried beneath her eyes. "None of that. Your nose is turning red. If you keep crying, and stay out in this weather, you will catch a terrible cold. I must warn you, as your tutor, it is nearly impossible to flirt with a stuffy head."

A startled laugh burst from her and she covered her mouth with one hand.

"See now? The world isn't such a bad place. You have had a rough time of it, but your faithful tutor will see you through." He gave her hand a squeeze and then pressed the handkerchief into it. "Keep that. In case you need it again."

Though he very much wished to tell her exactly what sort of person he thought her father to be, he thought it better to change the subject and help her move forward. He could hardly do anything about her father's decisions regarding her future. But he could give her whatever tools she needed to find her own happiness.

"Now. What is it you wish to learn today?"

⚜

CHRISTINE WORRIED THE HANDKERCHIEF IN HER HANDS FOR A few moments, eyes lowered to her lap. "I am tired of learning. It seems my list of appropriate and eligible husbands has grown quite short. I am not sure general flirting would be advisable. I feel I need more specific help. If I want to be the sort of lady who captures interest and retains it, I need to immediately be seen as the sort that would make a good wife."

Christine darted a glance at him from under her lashes. She

couldn't be sure, but she thought his eyes darkened at her words. "Would that not be advisable? Up until this point, we have talked of how I might gain a man's interest or at least avoid making a complete fool of myself. But what of appearing to be a fine wife?"

"I believe different men have different opinions on what that would entail," he told her, turning away to face the brook again. "For instance, I believe that your father and I have vastly different ideas of what makes a good wife."

"Truly?" The idea intrigued her when she thought on what she knew of her father, and she found she could believe it. "Father says a woman is to represent him well in society. Do you agree with that?"

"Yes," he answered slowly, drawing out the word. "But I also believe a man ought to do his wife the same honor."

She tipped her head to one side, taking in the firm set of his shoulders, the tilt of his head while he studied the water. "Whatever do you mean?"

"A man should act honorably in his business dealings and social activities, bringing no shame to his wife or family. He should be faithful to the woman he marries, and I believe that means more than convention would say." He looked down into her eyes, his eyebrows drawing together, perhaps uncertain as to how much detail he should share on the subject. "Being faithful means never giving her a moment's doubt as to his regard for her or his desire to see her happy, and it means supporting her efforts in their family."

"I like the sound of that," Christine said. "A true partnership." She looked toward the brook and their horses, standing side by side to share their body heat. She felt grateful the weather was mild today, allowing for this conversation to take place. She sniffled softly and took a deep breath, wondering if she ought to ask the most impertinent question of all. "What would a woman be like to attract a gentleman such as you?"

His expression turned curious, his eyebrows raised. "What do you mean?"

Christine swallowed and hoped any blush that escaped could be excused by her recent bout of crying, or the cold breeze. She could not tell him the truth, ever, about her curiosity over him. She could not tell him she wished to know if he could see himself ever marrying someone like her.

During their lessons together, Christine had come to admire Thomas's kindness, his resolve, and intelligence. The more time they spent in one another's company, the more she came to know him and his expressions. When she teased him and he half-smiled, then rolled his eyes and tried to return them to more serious conversation, she always wished to bring his smile back. Thomas's smile elevated him from merely pleasant looking to handsome.

"I suppose what I really mean is what sort of woman do you hope to find when you take a wife?"

There. She said it, and in general enough terms he could not possibly know what she truly meant. She kept her shoulders back and her eyes forward, trying not to notice his scrutiny in the long moment of silence which followed her question. Christine lost her nerve and decided to retract the inquiry.

"That is entirely too personal a question. Forgive me." At least she did not sound too disappointed. She looked down at her lap and pretended to adjust her gloves, tugging them up at the wrists.

"Not at all. I suppose with your limited experience," he said with a hint of amusement in his voice, "you would wish to understand how a man different than your father might feel about matrimony."

Christine's eyes came back up to his and she relaxed, smiling. "Yes. Please." They sat close, though they did not touch, and he looked down into her eyes for a long moment before turning away, clearing his throat.

Thomas stood abruptly and brushed off the back of his breeches. He started pacing before her, his expression thoughtful. "I hope there are many such men, different from your father." He stopped and turned to face her. "Very well. I will tell you about my ideal woman. Would that suit you?"

"Yes," Christine answered, more than a touch eager. She leaned forward. "Please. I would like very much to know."

"To start," he said, half-smiling at her, likely amused by the turn in conversation. "I would hope she would be a woman of understanding. It would be difficult to spend the rest of my life listening to a woman who spoke only of local gossip, or the weather, as if that were all there is of value in the world. I would much prefer conversations about our life, our common concerns. To speak of business and politics on occasion, to talk of books. My parents speak of all things together, sharing each other's worries and amusements, enjoying one another's company as friends. I would like that."

"A friendly relationship," she said, "as well as a partnership." She allowed herself to reflect on this new thought. To be more than an asset, but actually be valued as a person with thoughts of her own would be incredible. The people who treated her as though she was of value now were her sisters and Thomas. They often spoke of things with true substance. Thomas never censured her for sharing her opinion or speaking her mind. Being with him always made her more hopeful for the future and what it held.

"What else?" she asked, bringing her attention back to him. He stared down at her, lost in his thoughts as she had been in hers, but dragged himself back to the present.

"I should like it if we shared similar interests," he added, resuming his pacing. "I cannot hope to necessarily find someone as mad about horses as I am, but it would be a credit to her if she understood why I feel as I do about them and why I would like to begin a horse farm."

"That is reasonable. A woman who thought you daft could hardly be supportive of your work." Christine tried to picture the sort of lady of which he spoke. Kind, caring, interested in every word he had to say about horses. "What if she is not as fond of them?"

Christine knew *she* felt a similar passion for the animals, but she could not think of a single lady of her acquaintance with half as much interest.

"I think so long as she is mad about me, she would be interested in what I like, at least enough to make intelligent conversation. Offer encouragement." He shrugged, eyes meeting hers before darting away again.

"That would be of benefit to the relationship." Christine's heart picked up at the idea of finding a man who would not resent her attention to her prized horses or merely indulge her in her interest of them. Most gentlemen did not think it entirely proper for women to spend such a great deal of time in the saddle. She could not imagine Thomas would ever mind.

His next words confirmed her thoughts.

"I hope she will like the countryside. I am not overly fond of London and would prefer to remain near my horses and my home. Take bruising rides every day instead of sedate walks through the parks of the city." Thomas shrugged, one side of his mouth inching upward. "I prefer the open air to the crowded streets of London."

"I certainly understand that," she said with sympathy. "I am not overly excited about that aspect of town. How am I or my horses to get any exercise when we must walk slowly everywhere?" She sighed and adjusted her seat on the log, not minding the cold. She usually forgot all about the weather when she and Thomas met. "What else?"

He chuckled and turned to face her. "What else? I would like a woman of feeling, of passion. Someone who is kind to others. A woman who loves children and wants to be a mother to ours." His cheeks went pink and he stuttered to a stop. He cleared his throat. "My family is very close. We care greatly for one another. I want my future family to be the same."

"What about appearance?" she asked softly. "What should she look like?" Christine held her breath, waiting for an answer she knew he should not give.

He glanced away too swiftly for her to see his expression, though she gathered from the stiffening of his shoulders that this was where he might wish to stop the line of questioning. But why? Could his thoughts have turned like hers had?

He surprised her by continuing instead of waving off the question. "I think so long as she cares for me and I for her, I have no opinion whether her hair is brown or red or yellow. Whether she is tall or short. Fair or dark."

Christine bit her bottom lip and rose slowly, disappointed and unable to admit why. She knew enough now and it was time to end this line of discussion.

"It seems you know what you wish to find in a wife. I..." She swallowed. "I wish you luck." It did not escape her notice that much of what he said could easily apply to her and their relationship thus far. Did he realize how much of what he said reflected her personality and desires? Could he know how she felt when they stood here, in the cold, laughing and talking of the inconsequential and the important aspects of their lives?

"Thank you." He looked away still, across the brook. "What sort of man is it you wish to marry?"

She laughed, though it was without any true humor. "If I can find someone who will treat me as a friend instead of an acquired asset, I believe I will be content enough." And there was nothing further she wished to say on the subject, knowing that her father's expectations put her desires far out of reach. "I am afraid I should not allow myself to dream since my father will have the last say on the matter."

"That sounds dreary," he said, his head turning back so that she could see the lines of his profile, including the bump on his nose where it must have once been broken. She wondered how that had happened. "Perhaps one of the gentlemen on his list might turn out to be exactly the sort of man you wish for."

"Perhaps," she said, sighing. "But I dare not get my hopes up. It would be very difficult to find a man who wishes to marry a woman who is horse-mad, with very little experience in society, and a father who is determined to use every resource available, including his own family, to further his aspirations." She looked at the graying sky and found a reason to withdraw from what had become a difficult conversation. "The weather seems to be turning. I should get home."

"Yes. The clouds insist upon it." He walked her to the horses in silence. She wished she could reach out to him and speak her mind again, tell him something that would make him smile. But her tongue was learning its place. What she most wanted to say, and what she certainly could not say, was that she wished he was on that list of bachelors. Then at least, if he wished it, they could marry as friends.

Except she knew, Thomas would only marry someone he loved.

As she rode home along the familiar path, Christine could not put their conversation from her mind. Her reaction to his description of the woman he hoped to marry touched every inch of her person, from her physical body, all the way to her mind and heart. It confirmed the niggling suspicion that had been eating at her since that blasted almost-kiss.

Christine cared for Thomas Gilbert. Deeply.

It made her heart ache to think of him marrying. She hoped he found great happiness, but knowing it would be with another, and she would marry as her father wished, made it difficult to feel anything except dreary and alone.

Chapter Sixteen

The week wore on, but Christine's melancholy lingered. She sat silently in the window seat of her room, staring out at the now cloudless sky, reliving her conversation with Thomas again and again. Though it began in tears, it had ended on such a different, odd note. Her melancholy lingered, but her loneliness abated after speaking with him. She turned his description of his ideal woman over in her mind. She fit the qualifications almost perfectly. She believed they could be happy together if given the chance.

Even if her father would allow such a match, which he never would, Thomas would likely think her absurd. He would never want to marry a woman whom he had taught how to flirt. The very idea was laughable.

Yet here she sat, imagining what such a marriage might be like.

A quiet knock sounded and Christine looked to the door. "Yes?"

The door opened and Julia slipped in, smiling. "I finished your shawl," she said, coming forward with the material in her hands. "With the weather turning, I thought you might like it now instead of at Christmas, when I usually give you new pieces."

Christine gestured for her sister to join her on the window seat. "You always give me such lovely things." She took the knitted material her sister handed her and examined the deep green wool, soft to the touch, with real appreciation. "It's beautiful, Julia! Thank you. I love the color." It was close to that of Thomas's eyes, which was such a silly thought that Christine pushed it away fiercely, wrapping the shawl around her shoulders.

"I thought it might suit you. Makes your eyes look darker, full of mystery," Julia said teasingly, pulling her legs beneath her on the cushioned seat. "Have you been hiding up here all day? I haven't seen you since breakfast and it is nearly tea time."

With a shrug, Christine allowed her eyes to slip back to the window. "I have been thinking."

"Hm. More like avoiding Father," Julia said, lips pursed and eyebrows up.

Christine laughed, though little humor colored the sound. "How did you know?"

Her sister half shrugged and leaned against the windowpane, looking out into the world beyond. "I have become adept at avoiding him. I recognize all the attempts. With him home, it is rather difficult to predict where he will be and when. Bedrooms are generally the safest place. Or the attics."

"Is it terrible?" Christine asked. "Hiding like this?"

"It is not terrible to hide. It *is* terrible to cause people to hide from you." She took a deep breath and let it out slowly. "I must say, it is strange not to hear you defending him as you usually do. By now you have usually told me if we do as he wishes, all will be peace and harmony in the home."

Christine shook her head and pulled her new shawl tighter about her. "I am sorry. That was stupid of me to say." She looked to her older sister, taking in her tired eyes and drooping shoulders. "I should have stood up for you more, or at least helped you make the best of things, instead of lecture."

"Oh, Chrissy," Julia said softly, using a pet name long ago put aside for lace and ribbons. "I am actually sorry it has come time for you to see him more as I do."

"See the reality of the situation, you mean," Christine stated, shaking her head. "That we will never fit into the mold he made for us. Never make him proud, because we are worthless until we marry men of worth."

"We are only as good as our connections." Julia nodded, reaching out to squeeze Christine's hand. "It is a hard thing to learn. I knew, after you came home from your ride the other day, that something happened. You did not say a single word about the upcoming season, or the Christmas ball, or anything that has made you excited for so long. Then I did not see you at all yesterday, and most of today."

"So you gave me a very early Christmas present, to cheer me up." Christine smiled, truly touched by her sister's thoughtfulness. "You are too good, Julia." Then, without thinking, she rested her head against the glass and whispered, "Why has no good man come to rescue you?"

Julia's eyes widened, but then she released one quick laugh. "What a picture. I immediately imagined a knight in shining armor, riding down the garden path to save me from an ogre."

Christine laughed as well, though it was brief. "It is a fitting picture. We do have an ogre in our midst."

Julia shook her head. "I am not all good, Christine. And there are precious few knights in the world who would come to this part of the kingdom looking for maidens to rescue." She took a deep breath, then let it out slowly. "Though once I thought there was a man who might make a try for it." Julia watched her closely, Christine saw, and so she fought to control her reaction.

"Julia," she said, nearly whispering. "You had a gentleman suitor?" Christine would much rather take her sister by the shoulders and shake her for keeping a secret of that magnitude for so long.

The way Julia's mouth turned up in a smile made the sadness in her eyes all the more heartbreaking.

"The second son of a lowly baron was what I thought I had." Julia looked down at her hands, now clasped together in her lap. "I met him during the first week of my season. Quite by accident. Aunt Jacqueline stopped the carriage to speak to a friend of hers, and I was looking around like a girl fresh from the schoolroom, a regular country bumpkin." Julia's eyes grew soft and distant with the memory. "And there he was, across the street. I looked and caught him staring at me. He tipped his hat and grinned, cheekily as you can imagine, and came to the carriage. Which isn't done, you know. We had not been introduced. Aunt Jacqueline had not entered yet, talking to someone on the walkway. She could not have even seen him there." Julia chuckled at the memory.

"He made a flower appear from nowhere and held it up to me. 'Did you drop this, Miss?' he asked, when he knew very well I did not. I said as much, as politely as I could. 'But you must keep it,' he said, pressing it into my hand. 'You look as though you might give it a good home.' As if the flower were a kitten to care for. He was so handsome, and bold as you please, and he looked at me with kindness and admiration. He tipped his hat again and he was gone."

Christine shook her head, leaning closer, placing her hand on Julia's arm. "Did you see him again? You must have, to form an attachment."

"Indeed. I saw him the very next evening and he arranged for an introduction." She looked down and sighed. "His name was Nathaniel Hastings. The second son of a minor baron."

"Ah. No title. An 'Honorable,'" Christine said. "Yet you do not seem to have been disappointed in him."

"I was not. Not at all." Julia tilted her head back against the window, her eyes staring straight ahead at nothing. "He inquired after my calendar and turned up just about everywhere, always coming upon me with a flower, or a ribbon, or a penny. He made them appear from nowhere and gave them to me as gifts."

She sighed and closed her eyes tightly, her cheeks turned pale. "But Father was vastly disappointed when he learned of Mr. Hastings. Aunt Jacqueline told him how much time I spent speaking with him, ignoring nearly everyone else. She said it needed to stop, if I was to have more promising suitors. I did try, Chrissy. I met every young and old man I was introduced to by our aunt, at our father's wishes. I danced. I conversed. I attended teas and concerts and balls. But I could not find it in me to encourage them when all I did, at every event, was hope for a glimpse or a word with Mr. Hastings."

"Did he care for you greatly?" Christine asked, her voice hushed in the quiet room.

"I thought so. But I will never know. Father told me one day that he had met with Mr. Hastings." She shuddered at the recollection. "And he said that I would never see him again. Father said other things, too. Terrible things. I was hurt and discouraged. A part of me hoped that Nath—Mr. Hastings would ignore Father and continue to seek out my company. He came to me once more, but that meeting did not end well. Soon after, he left London. I never saw him, or heard from him, again. Now here I am, years later, a spinster."

Christine's heart ached for her sister, and she reached out to touch her hand, gaining her attention. "I am sorry, Julia. Why did you not tell me? I am your sister."

"At first, it hurt too much," Julia answered, her whispered tone matching Christine's, as though they spoke of something sacred rather than painful. "And I wanted to try to forget. Then, you were quite firmly upset at me for making Father set your season for later and before long you were lecturing me on how to appease him." She shrugged. "It was easier to keep it to myself. I did not want to tell you in order to hear a lecture or have my hurts dismissed. But lately, as I have watched you these last weeks, I felt like it was time for you to know. For better or worse. To better prepare for your season."

Christine moved closer and put her arm around her elder sister, her head on her shoulder. "Please Julia, forgive me. I was terrible and unkind. I should have known better than to treat you as I did. It is only that—only that—oh, I do not know how to explain!" She shook her head against Julia's shoulder.

"I understand," Julia said for her, embracing her tightly. "You wanted very much to make Father proud. To be a good daughter. And you wanted your season to be as all girls dream of it being."

"See?" Christine said with a nudge. "You are terribly good. You give my excuses better than I do." They both laughed, and after a moment, Christine continued. "I am truly sorry. I see so much better now than I did before, and I understand. I will never make Father happy. What about you, Julia? Could I make you happy?" Her voice sounded meeker than she wished. Timid.

"I am already quite proud of you for holding on to those horses of yours all these years. Father has always wanted them to be under his control. But you've forever been the expert on bringing up Mother's bequest at the right moments." Julia nudged her shoulder back, a crooked grin in place.

Christine squirmed, ashamed that she put her horses above all else. "I wish I had protected my sisters as well as my horses."

"Unfortunately," Julia said, with an eye roll, "one cannot bequeath their daughters to others while their father is alive. I belong to Father so long as I am unmarried. As do you. If we protected each other from his terrible censure, he likely would find another way to ensure we stayed in line."

"Indeed," Christine said, shaking her head. "He is terribly manipulative."

"As are you, sister," Julia reminded her teasingly. "You find the strangest ways to turn one's own words against them. You have won many a sisterly argument that way." She shook a finger at Christine. "It is most unfair." She stood with a stretch, putting on a more cheerful countenance.

"Now. I have sorely neglected you as you prepare for your season. I was nursing my hurt a little too much, I think. It is past time to take you in hand and teach you some things every girl should know before going to London."

Christine's cheeks, she well knew, immediately turned bright red, causing Julia to laugh.

"Oh, it is not as terrible as that," Julia said, still laughing.

"It isn't terrible," Christine squeaked. "That is—I mean—it really isn't necessary."

Julia appeared suspicious. "What isn't necessary?"

"Lessons."

"Lessons?" Her elder sister's voice rang with perplexity.

"On flirting and social behavior." Christine bit her bottom lip.

Her sister's eyes widened. "Who said anything about that? I was going to discuss the cafes and libraries!"

Immediately feeling like an imbecile, Christine nodded violently. "Oh. Yes. Cafes. Libraries. Go on?"

Julia's eyes narrowed again. "Christine. You are terrible at keeping secrets. Why did you think I wished to discuss flirting? That is supposed to come naturally. And why in heavens—if you thought I was—would you say it isn't necessary? Dear me! Have you been reading more scandalous novels than Rebecca?" Julia looked oddly pleased by the notion.

"No! Me? Absolutely not." But her cheeks reddened further. "But since you told me your secret, maybe it is time I tell you mine?" She said it like a question to which Julia promptly nodded her answer. "Oh, dear. Julia. First promise you will not laugh at me or tell anyone else."

After giving her most solemn oath to both stipulations, Julia sat back down on the window seat and Christine shared her story, haltingly at first, but finally spilling each and every detail to her elder sister, including the terrible lesson on recognizing a rake. Julia bit her lip to keep from laughing at points in the telling, and at others, she appeared downright shocked; in the end she shook her head in wonder.

"By far, this is the strangest situation I have ever heard of," she said at last. "Dear me. And I think you have not even realized the worst part yet."

Christine blinked and frowned. "The worst part is having to admit I needed such lessons in the first place."

"No, Chrissy, darling," Julia said with a consoling pat on the hand. "The worst part is that you seem to have fallen in love with Mr. Gilbert."

Christine felt sudden warmth rush through her. "In love? Absolutely not. What an incredible thing to say. We are friends."

Julia shook her head once, then sighed. "I hope so or else you and I will have a great deal in common very soon."

Christine forced aside the concern Julia's words caused and insisted to her sister, and to herself, that she could *not* be in love with Thomas Gilbert.

In the end, she wasn't sure who remained less convinced: Julia or herself.

Chapter Seventeen

Thomas waited for her arrival, this time on Christine's side of the brook, his breath turning to fog in the cold air. He smoothed a blanket over his horse, trying to distract himself from the thoughts coursing through his mind. They had not been far from Christine since their last meeting, when she had questioned him on his ideal woman. Although a strange conversation to have at first, he'd felt comfortable confiding in her. He could not help but wonder, if Christine did not have such fantastic social ambitions, if they might not be something *more* than friends.

Today he had a different sort of lesson in mind. One which he felt would be of benefit to Christine, though he had other motives for suggesting it. When she arrived, he would propose that they dance.

This lesson might lead to his undoing. But impropriety notwithstanding, he greatly desired to dance with her, to see what it would be like. This could be his chance to glide with her, to hold her close in a way acceptable to society. More importantly, it would provide the opportunity for him to test his heart and see if what he felt for Christine was what he suspected.

The very idea of taking her hand in his caused him both joy and misery, as he knew Christine could never be his. It made the whole idea sound like folly that would only end in his own heartache, but he had to try anyway. He had to ascertain his feelings.

Giving his horse a gentle pat, Thomas began pacing around the small clearing, anxious for Christine's arrival. Though he'd well exhausted the subject, his mind turned again to her father. He demanded she marry for wealth and status, and now he stipulated that she marry within the confines of a preposterous list. Even given the financial straits his own family faced, Thomas could not imagine his father ever forcing any child of his into an unwanted union. Such heartless behavior could never be attributed to one who loved their family. Every time Thomas thought of it, it soured his stomach and nearly spoiled his mood. It simply wasn't fair that Christine, after all she had endured in losing her mother, be forced into an unhappy life to appease an already unhappy man.

Hearing Christine approach, Thomas shook away the unpleasant thoughts, composing his face before she came into view. Quite suddenly, a strangeness filled him, his heart beating out an unsteady rhythm. He was *nervous*. After their last interaction, how would they greet one another?

When Christine appeared, her usual bright grin in place, it did much to reassure him. Dismounting with her usual ease, she tethered her horse to an obliging bush. Christine adjusted her riding cap, and after she tucked a stray dark curl behind her ear, she turned to him and raised both arms in a shrug. "What shall it be today, Mr. Gilbert?"

The formal use of his name made him smile. "Thomas will do. Or Tom. If you like." They moved beyond that formality with their last meeting, after all. Crying into someone's shoulder, sharing their deepest hopes, left little room for conventionalism.

"I do," she answered, her eyes fairly twinkling. Her cheerful character, her accepting nature, would earn her nothing but scorn in society for showing so much emotion in one expression. Yet he did not correct her, returning the grin.

"Would you call me Christine?" she asked.

"It would be an honor." He bowed, most formally, earning a laugh which lightened his heart.

Relax, he told himself sternly.

Clearly she had recovered from her father's unkindness and so too should he. "I thought today we would practice dancing."

"Dancing?" Her eyebrows came together and her smile turned crooked. "I've had a dancing instructor, Tom."

Her use of his family's nickname made it easier to tease her. "I know old Mr. Crowley taught you as he did half the people in our hamlet. But did he teach you how to use a dance to build interest in a potential suitor? To make them curious? To leave them wanting more with the touch of a hand?" He raised his eyebrows at her skeptical look. "You doubt me? Come. We will begin with a simple step."

"There is no music!" she countered, gesturing around to the tree-lined clearing.

"You shall have to hum while I instruct," he said, brooking no argument. "Come. The gentleman asks for you to dance and you gracefully accept." He bowed. "Would you do me the honor of standing up with me for the next set, Miss Christine?"

She sighed and swept up her riding habit as she would a gown. "It would be my pleasure, Mr. Gilbert." Her curtsy was perfect, though her eyebrows remained most skeptically raised.

He took her gloved hand in his and led her a few steps into the middle of the cleared ground. "Music, please." She dutifully began to hum as he made his bow and she, her curtsy. They came together, clasping hands briefly before releasing each other and stepping to the side.

He spoke, she hummed.

"As you dance with your gentleman of choice, you can let him know much of your thoughts by your expression alone. If you are bold, you maintain eye contact as often as possible. I do not entirely recommend that unless you are already assured of his interest in you. Boldness can scare gentlemen away. It would be far more to your advantage to make eye contact briefly, smile slightly, then look down and away."

"Why not up and away?" she questioned most studiously, then went right back to humming.

"Try it. Both ways. See which you think communicates being coy."

She shook her head at him, but continued her humming. They stepped toward each other, with the briefest of hand clasps, then she looked up and away. "Oh. It seems dismissive. I think."

"Indeed." She stepped in again, then around him as the figure they had chosen demanded. She looked up and held his gaze, then looked down and away.

"See? You are being shy, or charming and uncertain, instead of dismissive. That is my perception."

"The details you come up with astonish me," she said, shaking her head in wonder.

"All from observation of what works and what does not when ladies attempt to flirt," he said with a shrug, never missing a step. "Now. That is the look. Let us go on with the hand clasp. When next we hold hands, pay attention."

They passed each other again, his hand taking hers for a brief promenade. Instead of holding onto the tips of her fingers, as was the usual manner, he held more of her hand and offered the gentlest of squeezes before they let go.

"What does that communicate to you?" he asked, smiling over his shoulder as they stepped away, meeting with invisible partners before coming to the center again.

"Affection," she remarked. "But is it right for me to do the same? Or would it be too bold?"

"I would not risk it more than once in a dance," he answered evenly, smiling at her dutiful commentary. "After a particularly kind smile shared or witty remark made, I believe you could well use such a simple movement to communicate pleasure in the dance and the company. Try it."

She did, and he nodded, ignoring the way his heart stuttered in his chest. "Your conversation during a dance need not be too witty, so long as you offer those shy glances, the slight encouragement of a hand clasp, and a very small smile. Too much smiling and your partner will not be able to tell whether you are laughing at him or enjoying yourself."

"Do ladies not smile much in public?" she asked, blinking up at him in surprise. "Oh, dear. I thought it was my sour old governess who did not appreciate pleasant expressions. She was forever telling me to keep a more serious countenance."

He chuckled. "I am afraid it is more than your sour old governess." He offered another gentle squeeze of her hand and she smiled softly, looking right into his eyes. His heart turned over in his chest. "Yes, just like that."

She blinked. "Like what?"

"Smile. Like that."

"Was I smiling?" she asked, and her cheeks went pink.

"Yes. As though you were enjoying yourself."

"Oh. I meant that one, I'm afraid. I wasn't practicing."

He stopped dancing, looking down at her, uncertain as to what he should say. "Then you do not need to practice. You seem to come by the right expression naturally." Her lips curled upward again and her eyes brightened with pleasure. "Yes. Exactly." He cleared his throat and took a step back. "Very well. That is that."

"What about a waltz?" she asked. "I have barely learned it, but my aunt assures me that the waltz is done at private balls all the time now. She's had word it will be permitted at Almack's assembly rooms. Are there different ways to converse or act during a waltz?"

The alarming sensation of heat rushing into his cheeks made him turn away, pretending to cough into his hand.

Christine's brows drew together in concern. "Thomas, are you catching cold? Your throat is giving you great difficulty today."

"Not at all." He straightened his shoulders and attempted to sound indifferent. "I understand the waltz has gained popularity here in England. But are you certain your father will approve of the dance?"

"Of course," she answered, seemingly unconcerned. "Anything Aunt Jacqueline approves, he will approve. I am left to her stewardship during my time in London."

He hesitated, uncertain as to whether he should proceed. The waltz made its way into England during his time away, but he understood the dance well. While his logical mind said there was nothing to dancing a waltz with Christine, a part of him whispered this would not be a good idea. But why? They were alone, undisturbed, as they had been all along.

Besides, Thomas *wanted* to dance with her, to test the limits of his affections.

Very well. He would waltz with her. Even if it proved his undoing.

CHRISTINE CURTSIED AND HUMMED THE WALTZ SHE KNEW BEST, a melody Julia played often. Thomas approached, one hand taking hers in his, while he placed the other at the middle of her back. He drew her in as she slid her free hand to his shoulder. The empty air between them became charged with warmth, despite the cool autumn weather. Christine swallowed, her cheeks warming as she met his eyes. "Should I look away during the waltz?"

"Yes. But spend more time looking at your partner," he instructed, his voice softer than before. "The waltz is an intimate dance. You will not change companions, but will spend the entirety of the dance with one man, traveling about the room. His hands alone will guide you with the lightest touch upon your shoulder or movement of your hands." He demonstrated, leading her through the steps in a way that felt so natural, she hardly had to think about the movements.

"We stand close," she said as he changed positions, switching their form, raising their left arms to form an arch above them while their right hands went to each other's waists.

"And even in a crowded ballroom, it is unlikely for anyone nearby to hear what you say. This makes it possible—" he broke off to clear his throat, sounding slightly hoarse. "This makes it possible to say things of a more personal nature without being overheard. Imagine you particularly like the gentleman you dance with."

She lowered her eyes, glancing away, willing her cheeks to cool. "That is not too difficult a thing."

"Excellent," he said, his voice low. Her eyes darted up to his again, realizing he thought she had already begun her "practice" flirtation. "Now, a gentleman who is waltzing with you will be tempted to pay a compliment, I am certain. Something such as, 'You look lovely this evening, Miss Christine.'"

She and tilted her head to the side. "Surely you can do better than that, Tom," she teased. "If a gentleman wishes me to dance in an *intimate* manner, I should hope he would converse at a more intimate level as well."

He looked disconcerted as they shifted positions once again, his arm back around her, and her hand in his. "We are practicing. Imagine a more outrageous compliment, then."

Although she felt a trifle disappointed that he would not venture his own, she nodded. "Then I shall say, with my littlest of smiles, 'Thank you, Mr. Gilbert. I am pleased you noticed.'" He turned her at that instant, hand brushing her waist, and her heart skipped a beat. Somehow, with the dance instructor, she never felt how truly close and personal a dance this was. With Thomas, her dear friend, her heart skipped ahead of each movement with excitement. How would it be to dance this way with a man who had every intention of courting her? Marrying her?

She could not imagine it would be much better than this, as she met Thomas's warm green eyes.

"What else?" she asked, voice low, as though there might truly be others dancing nearby to hear. Her heart hammered so loudly she wondered if he could hear it above her words.

He gulped and it was his turn to look down and away. "The movements themselves are flirtation enough, would you not agree?" His hand, holding hers as he led, squeezed hers gently while the other hand, though gloved, radiated with heat at her back.

Her stomach dropped in a strange manner and she had to swallow before speaking. "Yes. Yes, obviously, you are right."

It had been some time since she hummed their dance music, yet he continued the movements with perfect time, effortlessly gliding her over the uneven ground, his eyes meeting hers again.

We are made to dance together this way, she thought, *I have never felt so at ease, so graceful, as I do now. In his arms.*

"If you dance this beautifully in London," he told her, "any one of your suitors is likely to be half in love with you before the music ends."

Her eyes widened and heat rushed up her neck, into her cheeks. Her lips parted, but Christine could not think what to say until she noticed his eyes lower to her mouth. Slowly, he stopped moving, his gaze alternating between her eyes and her lips; the green of his eyes darkened and his breathing became shallow, matching hers as she realized how difficult it suddenly felt to draw in air.

"Tom," she whispered, still standing with one arm about his shoulders as he released her hand. Would he kiss her now? Her heart ached to be kissed while her mind rebelled, fearing the very idea of becoming more closely attached to the man before her, knowing a romance between them could never be.

His hand lifted to her cheek, lightly touching her skin, and—in the time it took her to blink—he released her and stepped backward, dropping his hand from her waist while hers fell from his shoulder.

"I think you will do well at the balls," he said, hands going behind him as he turned. He did not look at her, but moved away toward the bank. "Remember to smile, drop your eyes now and again, and offer quiet encouragement to any fellow you particularly admire." He went all the way to the edge of the water, as though unable to put enough distance between them. "I think that is enough for this lesson."

Christine watched his back, saw the stiff set of his shoulders, and could not help the confusion which overtook her. She wanted him back at her side, at once, at all costs, even as her more rational side new it was better, safer this way.

"Thomas, have I done something wrong?" She could not help asking. "You are upset with me."

He turned quickly, looking at her with a strained smile. "Upset? Not at all. You did very well today."

"Oh." She brought her hands together and pretended she felt pleased. She doubted she succeeded as well as he did. "Thank you. I enjoyed the lesson."

One side of his mouth quirked upward. "As did I."

Afraid that he might leave her if she said nothing else, she grasped on the first topic that popped into her head. "How are your mares?" Though a particularly inane comment, he nodded readily enough to indicate acceptance of the change in topic.

"Fine. Very fine. Well exercised and in good health."

"Good. Excellent. Um. I was thinking that I might send my groom over this afternoon to discuss arrangements with you." This was madness, discussing their horses as if they had not come very near to kissing. Or had they? Would he have kissed her if her father's wishes did not stand in their way?

"Oh?" He nodded, his smile looking more forced. "Yes. I suppose we are nearing the end of our agreement. Only two more weeks until Christmas and then you depart for London."

"I am a lady of my word." She tried to make the statement light and airy, uncaring, yet the words came out far heavier than she intended. "Your help has been invaluable. I cannot imagine what more you could have to teach me. I think I will be a great success in London."

"Yes. The toast of the season. You can begin at Lord Annesbury's ball." Thomas's half-hearted agreement did not make her feel any better. He looked away, across the bank. "We should both probably be going. To make arrangements."

"All right." She went to her horse and turned to speak another word on the matter, if only to prolong their time together, but stopped abruptly, seeing Thomas coming toward her.

"Allow me, Christine." His hands went to her waist and in one fluid movement, with seemingly no effort, he lifted her onto her saddle. Not once, in all the time they met together, had he helped her to mount except to cup his hands to offer a lift. But today, after dancing, his hands clasping her waist felt like the most natural thing in the world. When he released her, he put a hand on either side of her saddle and looked up at her. Her breath caught. Looking into his eyes did wholly unnatural things to her heart.

"Until next time," he said, eyes still upon her, the look in them causing both happiness to spark inside and her mind to feel terribly muddled.

"Next time," she echoed, reaching for the reins. "Good day, Tom."

"And to you, Christine." He stepped away, but she felt that his eyes never left her as she headed down the path toward home.

Christine sighed and urged her horse forward. She would be dreaming of that waltz by the stream for a very long time.

Chapter Eighteen

Julia would not let Christine wave away the events of her outing. No sooner had she changed out of her riding habit than her elder sister knocked on her bedroom door.

"Julia, there is nothing to tell," Christine said. Still, she opened her bedroom door wide, inviting her sister in.

"The pink in your cheeks suggests otherwise." The normally staid young woman practically bounced on her toes, her eyes bright. "I am incredibly curious as to what went on today, and you must tell me so that I am certain you are both behaving yourselves. This is already a very compromising situation for you both."

Christine sat down at her window seat and crossed her arms, holding herself tight and willing her cheeks to stop blushing. "Nothing of importance happened."

"Then tell me the unimportant things." Julia leaned against the bedpost and crossed her arms as well, fixing Christine with a sterner expression. "I will not let you alone until you do."

Christine looked down at the floor and ran her slipper over the carpet, tracing a swirling pattern. "We practiced waltzing."

Julia's entire body jolted and she stood straighter. "You did what?

All alone? In the middle of the woods?" She hurried to Christine's side and sat, appearing more gleeful than concerned. "Christine, that dance is barely considered civilized. What in Heaven's name were you thinking, to agree to such a thing?"

"It was my suggestion, actually," Christine admitted, watching Julia from the corner of her eye.

In the space of just a few moments, Julia's face showed more emotion than Christine had seen from her in years. Her jaw completely dropped and her eyes widened near to the size of saucers. "You? Oh, Chrissy. And he agreed?" Julia reached out and put her hands on Christine's shoulders, holding her tightly. "What were you thinking?"

Her words spoke outrage, but her tone indicated she was actually delighted by the idea.

Christine closed her eyes and shook her head. "I don't know. I told him I wanted to practice flirting and waltzing. I could hardly believe he agreed, but when he did, when he took my hand—" She could not finish the thought; she felt her cheeks grow warm again.

"You really are in love with him," Julia whispered. "And now you are playing with fire. What if he loves you, too? Is this fair to either of you?"

Christine stood, pulling away from her sister, and walked to the other side of the room. But she could not outrun the truth of her sister's words.

"No. I cannot love him. It can never, ever be. His family is unsuitable. They have no title, no wealth or consequence. Father would never hear of such a match. Plus, I am sure Thomas does not love me."

Her sister spoke quietly enough that Christine could barely hear her over the sound of her own rapid heartbeat. "You could elope. Make a dash to Gretna Green."

Christine whirled, finding it her turn to stand with mouth agape and stare at Julia. "Elope? How could you even suggest such a thing? The scandal would ruin us both. Thomas needs to be well respected if he is to be successful. You cannot worry about a waltz in the woods on one hand and suggest eloping with the other."

Julia continued to stare at her, though all her delight had been replaced with sorrow. "But you love him, Chrissy."

Christine turned her gaze to the ceiling before closing her eyes tightly, a vain attempt to block the pain Julia's words caused. She could not admit such a thing out loud, not when it could never be.

"This is not one of Rebecca's novels. There cannot be an elopement. Father will not give his permission. I cannot, and will not, love Thomas Gilbert and that must be an end to it. He is my friend and nothing more."

She heard Julia's sigh. "Then you had better not see him again."

The words sounded as a death knell in her head, echoing into her heart until it ached. "You are right, Julia. I will tell Thomas —I mean, Mr. Gilbert—I will tell Mr. Gilbert that his lessons are no longer necessary, and he has fulfilled our agreement. Then he can go about his business, and I can finish preparing for the season. You will help me prepare now, won't you?" She opened her eyes at last and looked to Julia, desperation welling inside her.

She had to say goodbye to Thomas, to let go of him. But she would do so in person. She owed him that, at least. She would go to their brook and explain things, as best she could, without revealing her feelings for him. That would be the best way, she felt certain, to end their time together.

Julia watched her, eyes shining with sympathy and unshed tears. "Yes, Christine. I am sorry. I should have been helping you long before." A tremulous smile turned her lips upward. "All will be well. And you will have the chance to practice a little more before London."

"The Christmas ball," Christine said, walking toward the small hearth in her room, feeling a sudden need for its warmth. Her body felt strangely chilled.

"I am afraid that is not all." Julia came to stand beside her. "While you were away, we received an invitation to attend the Whitsons' evening party, and Mrs. Gilbert has offered to chaperone us, since it is a more formal occasion."

Christine felt as though she'd been slapped and she turned to her sister with what must be a stricken expression, as Julia immediately put her arm around her waist. "We are to attend with the Gilberts?"

"Yes. I already sent our acceptance. But...Christine, you don't really have to go."

"No. I must." Her mind started whirling. If Thomas *did* love her, the longer they allowed their feelings to grow, the harder it would be to end things. She had to do more than just say goodbye. She needed to let him know she did not care for him in that way. "If I go, I might be able to show Thomas that he has taught me well, but that I am only his pupil—his *friend*, she amended—but nothing more. I don't know if he has entertained feelings for me, but if he has, it would be better if he go back to seeing me the little girl that followed him about in Mother's stables." Christine forced a smile, hoping it would convince Julia of her ability to see this through.

Julia frowned. "But you will be kind, Christine. Don't injure him with your indifference."

"Of course not," Christine said. "I will be all grace and kindness."

Julia nodded and offered a final, gentle hug. "Then it will be a delightful evening." She sighed. "All will be well, Christine. Somehow, all will be well."

THOMAS SAT BETWEEN HIS MOTHER AND FATHER IN THE carriage, hardly believing his mother's maneuverings to arrange playing chaperone for the Devon sisters. Julia and Christine both entered the carriage with assistance from a footman. The Whitsons' party was to be the last social activity for the neighborhood until Lord Annesbury's Christmas ball. The moment the idea came to his mother to invite the "dear, poor girls" to attend with their family, she had talked of little else. Except when she was alone with Thomas. In those instances, she plied him for all the details on his tutoring sessions with Miss Christine.

It took careful wording to say enough to his mother about their lessons to appease her without breaking Christine's trust. Although Thomas wished to tell his mother everything Christine said about her father and his expectations, he held back. Truly, their family business was not his to spread about to anyone. Even he should not know so much about what went on behind their closed doors. But as Christine's friend, he had also become her confidant.

Now, watching her sit across from him, speaking in an animated manner with his mother, he felt relieved to see her doing so well. Their waltzing by the stream had ended their last lesson on strange ground. He was happy to see there were no lingering effects. Well, mostly happy.

The thought alternately relieved and irritated him.

"I am very much looking forward to this evening," Julia said, tugging her wrap more tightly around her shoulders. "The weather keeps threatening to turn. We will have snow by Christmas, I am certain."

"I quite agree," Thomas's father added. "Which will be a great boon to the children and a great headache to the rest of us."

"Oh, not me," Christine chirped from her seat. "I love the snow. I love how silent the woods become when it falls, as if the whole of creation is holding its breath to watch."

In the dark, he had to imagine her expression, though he thought it must be one of eagerness, likely with one of her larger smiles curving her pink lips upward. Her eyes would be dancing at the very thought of a winter snowfall.

"I love it until I must go out in it," Julia added, much more practically. "I quite tire of slogging through mounds of the stuff when it seems it's only purpose is to make me cold and damp."

They all laughed and agreed, the conversation flowing easily between his parents and the young ladies for the duration of the ride.

Thomas had little to say, content as he was to listen. But his mind wandered, frequently turning to his waltz with Christine.

When he had learned that the evening's festivities would not include dancing, due to the small size of the gathering and other entertainments, he could not tell whether the information had pleased or perturbed him. The conflicting emotions had made him take steady stock of his emotions.

Thomas tried to convince himself he regretted the lack of dancing only because it would have been an excellent opportunity for Christine to utilize her lessons about the ballroom. It was a good reason, and the only one he'd give credence to in his mind. It would not be a good idea to dance with Christine again. Even a simple country tune where they would bow and promenade down a line of other dancers might bring him too close to her.

Best to keep his distance.

For both their sakes.

The carriage drew to a stop in front of the Whitsons' home. Thomas left the vehicle first, then his father, and they both assisted each of the ladies down to the path. When Christine came to step out, the light from the house bathing her face in a warm yellow glow; their eyes met. Before Thomas could offer so much as a reassuring smile, she ducked her head and reached for his father's hand instead of his own.

Once past him and his outstretched hand, she shivered and pulled her cloak tighter about her. "Oh, let's hurry! It is freezing!" She grabbed her sister's arm and darted up the steps with great speed and impressive agility for one encumbered by a winter cloak and skirts.

Thomas stood, gaping after her, knowing at that moment her pretended oversight was a purposeful move.

"Coming, Tom?" his father asked, already halfway up the walk with Thomas's mother on his arm.

Thomas closed his mouth and hurried to follow, his mind churning over the reasons Christine would have to avoid him in such a manner. Had he offended her? While their last parting felt strained, he did not think it ended entirely unpleasantly. She did, after all, send over her head groom to discuss moving her fine stallions into his stables the week of Christmas.

His puzzlement continued as they greeted their host, removed their coats and hats, and found warm cider and refreshments waiting in a parlor.

Christine stayed on the opposite side of the parlor from him. It shouldn't have rankled; he'd determined the very thing—distance—would be best for them both. And yet, to have her be the instigator felt like a sting. Wanting to test just how much she wished to keep out of his way, he slowly walked around the room, greeting others, keeping an eye on his pupil.

She moved counter to each of his movements until they were once again on opposite sides of the room.

Thomas huffed, but determined to give her the space she apparently desired. He would stand back and observe; but if the opportunity presented itself, he would most assuredly find out why she was acting as skittish as an unbroken filly.

⚜

How is it possible, Christine wondered, to feel Thomas watching me?

It did not matter whether she stood with her back to him or in a place where she could see him out of the corner of her eye; she simply knew his eyes were upon her. The sensation left her unnerved.

Her decision to ignore him, to completely push him out of her circle, had felt reasonable and wise at the time she had made it. But that they occupied the same space, she had half a mind to turn to him and ask why he continued to stare at her so.

But she wouldn't do it. If Julia was right, if Christine truly was falling in love with Thomas Gilbert, she must do all in her power to stop. At once. And she must keep him from doing the same. Their waltz at the stream, beautiful as it was, gave her every indication that Julia knew what she was talking about.

To love Thomas put her in a situation both dangerous and hopeless. She could never marry him. Her father would withdraw all support from her, she would never obtain his favor, and he would denounce her as a disappointment. Thomas came from a well-respected family, but their means and their connections were modest, at best. He could not even afford stud fees to begin his horse farm; how could he ever afford to take a wife?

Christine continuously pushed this question from her mind. It was not her place to wonder about his matrimonial hopes or ambitions. She *had* to focus on her own goals.

She scoffed at the thought. Her goals had narrowed to fifteen family names on a piece of paper shoved to the bottom of the trunk awaiting her London trip.

She did not like thinking on that list. She liked it less than thinking on Thomas's marriage prospects.

Not that he had any, that she knew of, because he never mentioned having a particular lady's attention. Indeed, if their conversation about his ideal woman was any indication, he had yet to meet a woman who would fulfill his dreams of a love match.

She admired his desire to find such a match, but was it even possible? In her circle, it seemed Thomas's parents were a rare exception. In any case, to marry for love was well beyond her reach and a silly thing for anyone to hope for. It was more important to marry for comfort and security.

Wasn't it?

Decidedly muddled, Christine lost several hands of cards before realizing she'd better give her spot at the table to someone more focused on the game at hand. She made her way to the refreshment table, looking for another cup of spiced cider.

Her mind remained distracted enough that she did not realize Thomas himself stood next to the table until he refilled her cup. She blinked up at him, lost in her musings, and tried to clear her thoughts.

"Enjoying your evening, Miss Christine?" he asked, his deep voice low and quiet, his dark green eyes searching hers.

"Immensely," she squeaked, then cleared her throat. "Very much, Mr. Gilbert. Thank you for asking. How are you enjoying the games?"

"I haven't played any of them yet," he said, crossing his arms and looking down at her with a raised brow. "You do not seem to be doing well, however."

She swallowed. "I find I am not suited for cards tonight."

He leaned slightly closer, though the distance between them remained completely respectable. "That is not the game I meant."

She felt her cheeks heat and she brought a hand up to grasp her pearl necklace, if only to have something to do. "Oh? I have not tried any other game this evening."

"I have noticed." His tone was amused. "I would think this would be an excellent opportunity for you to practice that other game you and I have spoken of so often."

That got her attention and she focused on him in great surprise. "The other game—?" She blinked, unable to believe he would bring up their tutoring in public even in such a disguised way. "I see."

Captain Markham appeared at the table, shaking his head ruefully. "It is a lucky thing we gamble with pennies tonight, or I would have lost a fortune! I must try my hand at something else. What of you, Miss Christine? Have you any winnings to speak of?"

Her eyes still on Thomas, Christine answered plainly. "No. None at all."

But then her resolve hardened. If he wished her to begin a flirtation, to practice the games between men and women, she would. Immediately.

"Captain," she said brightly, turning to him with the perfectly polite smile of society, one which barely turned up her lips. "Would you care to try your hand at something besides cards?"

"I'm game," he answered amiably. "There is a draughts board. Do you play draughts?"

"Indeed. It is a favorite of my younger brother." She moved to slip her hand through his arm, though he had yet to offer it. "I would be most delighted to play against you, Captain."

The young officer turned absolutely pink, but beamed down at her in a most gratifying manner. "Of course. Wonderful. Yes." He led the way to the table and Christine resisted the urge to look over her shoulder and send a triumphant smile to her erstwhile tutor.

Yet she knew, without a doubt, that he would continue watching her.

Very well. Back straight and shoulders square enough to please any general, Christine knew what she must do. High time for her to prove both that she could maneuver about in society and that she could push her growing affection for Thomas Gilbert to the back of her mind and heart.

"Captain," she said, tone light, "tell me how you have enjoyed your stay in our sleepy little part of England. How does it compare to the life of a soldier?"

The young man looked incredibly pleased with himself as he set up the draught board at a table for two. He launched right in to describing his great enjoyment of the country and the society of his uncle and cousins. The food, apparently, tasted much better, and the company he found fine and diverting.

"I particularly enjoy the time we have spent visiting all the neighbors, and tonight's entertainment. The best thing about small neighborhoods," he said, "is how friendly and inviting everyone can be."

"We do try," she said, reminding herself not to smile too broadly. "Ah, I am white. I will move first." She played the game, keeping her chin lowered enough to make it possible to glance up at him through her eyelashes. She kept that little half-smile on her face, though it felt rather absurd, like playing a part in a theatrical. "Tell me more about being an officer. You must see and do the most interesting things. Where will you go after Christmas?"

He needed very little encouragement to talk of himself and his men, though there was no arrogance to his words. But talking and strategizing were obviously difficult for him as he continually blundered his draughts to set up jumps for her. She pretended not to see them, for the most part, and kept the game going longer than necessary. She smiled at the right moments, allowed a soft laugh at one point, and even managed to lose the game.

All in all, a splendid effort, she thought.

Except after their game finished, he gave every indication of wishing to speak to someone on the other side of the room.

Desperate not to be left behind, she spoke hastily. "I do wish I had been available to spend more time with you and your brother. You are both delightful company. I hope we will see much of each other in London."

Captain Markham's eyes met hers and he hesitated the barest instant before offering his arm. "Would you like to enjoy our company a little more? Archie would be delighted, I am certain."

She slipped her arm through his, pleased with her quick thinking. "Thank you."

He led her across the room where they struck up a conversation with his elder brother, their cousin Hannah, and the vicar's eldest daughter.

Christine dutifully let the men guide the conversation and noted with some admiration that Hannah knew exactly how to encourage the gentlemen to converse while remaining complimentary herself.

At this rate, however, with both of them acting as accessories, Christine would hardly stand out in a crowd. Frustrated, she bit her lip and automatically looked in Thomas's direction.

Thomas stood, tall and handsome, against a wall across the room. Arms crossed, eyes on her, when he saw her watching, he smirked. *Smirked.* As though amused by her attempts to engage the interests in either of the young men to whom she spoke.

Her cheeks burned.

Julia was wrong. She must be wrong. Thomas was not in love with her. He fulfilled their arrangement to get what he really wanted —her horses—and now he stood laughing at her ineptitude.

Her heart hammered against her chest as she attempted to bring her focus back to the young men on either side of her. Fine, then. She put on a gentle smile, threaded her arm through that of the elder brother, and asked in a soft voice, "Do you still intend to come to the Christmas ball?"

"I wouldn't miss it," he said, sounding friendly though somewhat puzzled.

Had she spoken dreadfully out of turn? But there was nothing for it. She pressed onward, aware that all standing in their little group now watched her. "Delightful. It seems we are forever short on gentlemen when it comes time to dance. I do hope you enjoy dancing."

"We have been known to attempt it," Mr. Markham said. "What of you, Miss Christine? Do you enjoy dancing?"

"When my partners are handsome and agreeable, I do," she said lightly, casting an admiring glance up at him before looking down and away. The trick apparently worked in company as well as on the dance floor, as the gentleman drew himself up taller.

Captain Markham chuckled. "Then you had better forgo dancing with my brother. He is far too unhandsome and disagreeable. But I would be pleased to stand up with you, Miss Christine."

Archibald Markham bristled. "But my younger brother is far more used to marching in time than dancing with young ladies. You ought to avoid standing up with him. With the captain as your partner, it will end up looking more like a military parade than the graceful movement to which you are doubtless accustomed. Would you allow me the honor of your first dance of the evening?"

In that moment, Christine discovered the delightful possibilities of stirring up a competitive match between gentlemen. Why had that tactic never occurred to her before? Feeling clever, and wicked, she shot a quick look toward Thomas, where he was watching with less amusement now.

"Certainly, Mr. Markham. I would be most delighted."

"I would ask of you the next dance," Captain Markham added,

half-bowing. "Then I might help you recover from the company of my brother." Although he grinned as he spoke, she detected a level of challenge in his tone.

"Now, gentlemen," she said, pulling her arm from them in order to fold her hands before her. "You are both so kind. I am certain you each dance beautifully. But tell me, how do you ride? I so love to go riding and I was thinking that tomorrow, if the weather is fine, I will ride into the village. I am in need of ribbon, you see, for the ball. I should like some company."

They both volunteered at the same moment, and Christine looked to Hannah, who had grown rather quiet and wide eyed as she watched her cousins behave nonsensically. "Miss Hannah, will you join us? I would very much like your opinion. The exercise will be lovely, and you sit a horse so well, I think you would enjoy it."

Hannah looked gratified to be invited and nodded. "I would happily come. Shall we make a regular party out of the afternoon?"

"Indeed." Christine looked up at Mr. Markham, coyly tipping her head to one side. "Do you have any particular friends we should invite, Mr. Markham?"

Obviously delighted with the attention he was receiving, he answered gallantly. "I do not, so long as you are present with my cousin."

"How very kind of you. But we have the four of us. It would hardly be wise to make that sojourn in such a small company. Suppose we were set upon by brigands?"

"I think we could defend you admirably from the sort of scoundrels this part of the country would produce," the Captain countered with raised chin. "Rest assured, dear lady, I would defend you."

"As would I," Mr. Markham added, chest puffing out.

Christine touched each of them on the arm, simultaneously. "What wonderful protectors we have, Miss Hannah. Truly, it is a great shame that you gentlemen have not been about more often. We would have grand adventures, I am certain."

The handsome young captain nodded, his eyes resting on hers in a familiar manner she did not find comfortable. "Undoubtedly. I really must visit my uncle more often. Knowing there is such splendid company in his neighborhood gives greater encouragement, you see."

Not to be outdone or ignored, Mr. Markham launched into planning their ride for the next day. By alternating her attention between the two, stroking the ego of each with smiles and well-placed compliments, Christine surprised herself at how easily she had them both eating out of her hand. When she moved to the refreshment table, they followed. Hannah excused herself to try another hand of cards, but Christine managed to keep the brothers with her through a cup of cider, a sandwich each, and then manipulated them into playing a game of backgammon to determine who the cleverer brother could be. They agreed, most amiably, and she sat to watch with seemingly rapt attention.

Brothers appeared to be a naturally competitive sort as the two traded a good many jabs, insulting each other's intelligence, strategy, luck, and general appearance, and all this done with a smile. Christine played the flirt, asking them a question here or there, and generally keeping their good-natured feud going for the duration of the evening.

Through it all, she tried very hard not to look at Thomas Gilbert.

Chapter Nineteen

Thomas, his thoughts on the evening before, waited quietly by their brook. He could not forget the many society-perfect, simpering smiles Christine shared with the Markham brothers throughout the course of the party, or even the sound of the soft, polite laugh she emitted when one or the other brother said something they thought witty.

She maneuvered perfectly, all evening long, engaging multiple people in conversation, not putting a word or foot out of place, and the few single men present had cast their eyes at her for longer than a passing glance. Without exception, everyone at that party knew of her father's snobbish expectations, so while no one could possibly harbor a serious interest in her, they certainly puffed out their chests when she gave them her attention.

But he did not think she had enjoyed herself. As he watched, he saw the facade slip a time or two. Thomas noted a brief sag of her shoulders, or a slight turndown of her mouth, and once, he thought for certain she rolled her eyes when the young captain's back was turned.

He saw these things, he well knew, because he looked for them.

Thomas watched her closely, attentively, nearly holding his breath for her all night.

His mother took the time to let him know, before she went on to bed, that she believed Christine behaved very well. "Though I must say, Tom," she said in parting, "she seems to have lost all of that vivacious personality I liked so much."

He could not help agreeing.

The most difficult part of the evening was that Christine did not speak to him after their brief conversation by the refreshments. She barely looked his way again, completely ignoring him.

Thomas told himself such a thing did not matter; she had practiced her lessons on others, which she must do to be successful. She had no reason to acknowledge him in public and he must count it a good thing for people not to see them together too often. Or at all.

Yet as he waited, his eyes continually going to the path from her family estate, he looked forward to seeing her. Spending time in Christine's company left him refreshed, his burdens lighter. Her conversation revived his interest in the world around him.

He put from his mind, as best he could, the memory of their waltz and instead focused on their growing friendship. She understood him and his enthusiastic dreams. She conversed well on a variety of subjects. Her affection for her sisters and brother was easily felt.

Thomas also enjoyed watching her speak, gesturing animatedly with her hands, eyes lit, smile bright. Christine found joy and amusement in nearly everything. When she found the hypocrisies in society's ways, she delighted in pointing them out and laughing over them.

Christine, he felt, was the person out of all, that he got on with the best.

He heard movement in the brush, jolting him from his thoughts. Christine emerged from the foliage into the clearing, her head ducked to avoid a branch. The moment his eyes fell upon her, he felt his cares grow lighter. Indeed, the sight of her made his very heart lift.

Thomas ruthlessly hushed the whisper of doubt in his mind, a little voice that warned him, saying he felt too much, that he ought to walk away now or it would be too late.

But he held his ground, sweeping his hat off and smiling brightly.

Until he saw the look on her face.

Christine looked pale, her expression downcast, and she dismounted without her usual cheery greeting.

"Christine," he said, tension returning to his shoulders. Could her father have caused yet more damage to her joyful heart? "What is wrong?" He glanced down at the brook separating them and hurried to step on the least-submerged rocks, picking his way across to her.

"Thomas, please don't trouble yourself," she said, but he was halfway across the stream by then.

"Nonsense." He approached, not caring that his boots would need a good polishing, which he must do himself for his valet had sought another position with better pay. "You are distressed." He well remembered the last time she came to their meeting upset, and while he did not wish her to be in such a state, he found he would not at all mind offering the comfort of his arms once more.

"A little," she stated, folding her arms before her and looking up with a furrow between her brow. "I have a great deal on my mind."

"Would you like to talk about it?" he offered, tone soft. "We can forgo the lesson, if you wish."

She shook her head. "Thank you, no. I am quite able to get through this one on my own." Her hand came up to tuck a loose strand of hair behind her ear, then her eyes fell to the ground. "But I do wish to speak to you about my lessons. You see, I have told Julia about them."

He sucked in a quick breath, a creeping sense of panic tightening his lungs. "What did she say?"

"She said it sounded rather ridiculous and then she gave me some very dire warnings," Christine answered, a humorless smile turning her lips upward for a brief moment. "She said other things, too, which made me stop to reconsider our arrangement."

The surprise he felt must have been evident for she went on in a rush.

"The horses are certainly still to come to your stables, tomorrow in fact, but I think we ought to forgo any further lessons." She shrugged, keeping her shoulders pulled tightly upward. "We have two more left. I feel that I have learned a great deal and I will do well enough, now that Julia is speaking to me on the subject. She will help prepare me, and you will be free to see to more important business." Christine dropped her gaze to the cold ground between them.

A long moment stretched wherein the only sound made came from the brook, as the water tumbled and crashed into the rocks.

He realized Christine peered up at him again, looking uncertain. He must be the one to speak, to agree to her new terms.

He managed two words. "I see." But he did not. He told himself it was for the best. Had he not seen these sessions as pure folly in the beginning? A person with any sense would warn against their bargain as indecent, or at least an ill-advised scheme. Now, at last, Christine felt the same way.

But the thought of not seeing her again at their little brook made panic rise in his throat.

Strange how things had changed; once he had needed persuasion to meet with Christine, now he was terribly disappointed to have those meetings come to an end.

"I will take my leave of you, Mr. Gilbert, and use no more of your valuable time."

"I thought it time well spent." He spoke quietly, watching her take a step back. "And please. It is Thomas."

Christine shook her head, darting another glance up at him, refusing to meet his eyes as squarely as she had previously. "No, it had better be Mr. Gilbert again. In case we are in company, I would hate to forget and cause a scene."

He stared at the top of her riding hat, uncertain as to why he felt the sudden urge to reach out and take her hand, to stop or at least slow her withdrawal. To lose the time with her, days he thought were yet theirs, left him uncertain and empty. The chill in the air finally sunk into his skin.

"If you think it best, Miss Christine. Though I hope you will always think of me as a friend."

Her brief nod did nothing to reassure him and she turned away. "Thank you, Mr. Gilbert. Good day."

She did not even raise her head after she mounted, did not glance at him one more time, but disappeared into the foliage, gracefully as ever, upon her horse. "Good day," he whispered, though in his heart he wished to call her back.

※

CHRISTINE WALKED SLOWLY DOWN THE HALLWAY ON THE FIRST floor, her beautiful green shawl wrapped tight around her shoulders against the chill in the air. Occasionally, she would stop to look at the artwork which lined the walls of her home, standing before them as if she had never seen them before. It felt better to walk about, contemplating works of art, than to sit still with her sisters in their cozy room to talk of inconsequential things. Rebecca kept asking about her plans for her London wardrobe. Julia kept looking at her with concern and tenderness. Despite her sisters' best intentions, she did not feel comfortable with them at present.

Being alone gave her a much better avenue for contemplation. It allowed her time to organize her thoughts in relative peace.

The painting before her now was a winter garden scene, a strange subject devoid of any movement, of true life. A fountain not running but dusted with snow, bushes trimmed back, evergreen trees along the back of the scene. Though the painting did not show exceptional skill, it imparted an air of loneliness that she could certainly understand.

"Who would paint a garden in winter?" she said out loud. The tidiness of the garden, the barren and cold paths, made her heart shudder.

"I miss him," she whispered to the quiet garden. "But that is foolishness." Indeed, it felt like the very height of madness to find herself longing for a ride to the brook, to stand out in the cold for an hour or more, to be told how to go about catching a husband.

But not all their lessons had gone that way. The moments her mind lingered on most were those when they had done very little tutoring, such as their time in the greenhouse, talking of his parents and his horses. Remembering the day he had told her of his ideal woman, speaking as though he was already half in love with someone he had never met, made her heart ache. She recalled his actions when she came to him in tears, after speaking with her father, giving her leave to believe him to be the very best of men. He was kind, a gentleman, he offered her comfort, and he acted the part of a true friend.

But it was their waltz in the fall sunshine, the sky cerulean blue above them, his warm hands on hers, that made her heart thump faster and her cheeks turn warm. The way he gazed at her as they danced, his green eyes never leaving hers, looking into her as though he knew her through and through, left her knees weak.

In that moment, she should have realized how deeply she had come to care for him.

Christine loved him.

She bit her bottom lip and blinked away the tears that blurred her view of the painting. It would do her no good to dwell upon these thoughts, as she well knew, for her life lay out before her, fully planned by her father. She would marry a man of wealth or with a title, preferably both, and spend the remainder of her days providing offspring for her future husband, and business contacts for her father. Her life would never be her own, her destiny never hers to control.

As a woman, she was left to the care of the men in her life and forever would be.

Thinking about Thomas would only leave her more broken and dissatisfied with life. Christine would give herself today to grieve, but no longer. She must put him firmly behind her by the time the

Christmas ball arrived. More importantly, she could not carry Thomas's memory with her to London.

A door opened down the hall, causing her to jump and hastily wipe at her eyes.

"Christine," her father said, stepping out of the doorway. He came down the hall in several long, leisurely strides. "You look unwell." His statement contained no warmth, only observation, without concern for her health.

"Merely a slight cold, Father," she said, straightening her shoulders and withdrawing a handkerchief from her sleeve. "It is nothing, I am certain."

He lifted his chin, studying her as he might an underperforming hound. "Good. We cannot have you ill when it is time to depart. I wish for no delays."

Of course not. A sick daughter would be terribly inconvenient. "I will be well soon enough. I am never ill long. Strong constitution."

"It had better be." His tight-lipped smile appeared. "I am looking forward to overseeing your entrance into society. While we are not titled, our name commands enough respect that you should have invitations into the best of circles. Your aunt will see to it."

"Yes, Father," she answered dutifully, tone soft.

"I expect we will spend the first days paying monumental bills for your trousseau. I hope you are worth the investment. I would hate to throw money away."

"Yes, Father. I will do my best to see your investment gives you a good return." She could not help the way her tongue turned the words, making them sound more flippant than she normally would have dared had her emotions not been so close to the surface. Christine thought he did not notice, but then his smirk disappeared.

"Is that cheek you are giving me, Christine?" he asked, expression darkening. "I warn you, child, to show respect when you speak to me. I have fed and clothed you these many years, but should you prove to be a disappointment, I will cut my losses. You will spend your days wandering this estate alone, without pin money, and I will cut off my funding of your useless horses. I will not have another failure of a daughter draining my coffers for her foolishness."

Her spine stiffened. Normally, she would wither beneath his words. Today, they made her angry. Was it not every father's duty to provide for his children? And Christine never asked for much. She did not demand the latest fashions every season, or spend large sums on trifles and trimmings.

Indeed, only his payment of her groom and the upkeep of her horses could be construed as an expense, and she knew he could spare it.

"I understand, Father," she said softly, though her voice remained steady. "I am well aware of what my season means to you." After all, he had drilled it into her since Julia's *failure*. For so very long, she had wished to fulfill his demands and so gain her place in his affections. Now, after her time with Thomas, she realized she should never have been required to earn her way into her father's heart.

"Good. I will see you at dinner." He turned and went back to his office, shutting the door firmly behind him and cutting off any further conversation between them.

Christine turned and went back the way she had come, turning a corner in time to see someone else duck into a room. She hesitated, wondering if she and her father had been overheard. Then she shrugged. It did not matter. It was likely a servant anyway, judging by the dark fabric she had barely glimpsed. They knew well enough what sort of person her father was, and she refused to be shamed by him. She tried to maintain her poise, but after a few steps down the hallway her shoulders sagged again. Weary, Christine made her way to her room, deciding it might be best to spend a few hours curled up in bed.

After all, today she allowed herself to mourn.

Chapter Twenty

"A letter for you, son," Harold Gilbert said from across the desk where they both worked. Thomas brought his thoughts back to the present, surprised to see a footman standing next to his father with the silver tray used to deliver notes. Having buried his consciousness as deeply as possible in estate business, he was incapable of perceiving anything going on about him.

"Thank you, Father. Peters." He nodded to the footman and took the folded letter, sealed with blue wax. He did not recognize the hand but thought it looked feminine.

He stamped down the swell of hope that rose in him at the thought.

Thomas sat back further in his chair and broke the seal, knowing if he left the letter waiting it would distract him from his work. Christine's horses had arrived yesterday, so this letter may detail some of the arrangements she wished for their stay. It might only be business she wished to settle.

Mr. Thomas Gilbert, it began. *Please do not think me too forward in writing to you. My sister has told me of your meetings and all the*

*assistance you have given her. She claims you are her friend. I must
say, I hope you are more.*

Thomas stood and paced away from the desk, frowning deeply at
the letter. His eyes darted to the end to see it signed "J. D." Julia
Devon. He went back to where he had left off reading, his heart
pounding.

*My sister has been forlorn for days, wandering about our home as if
lost. I have attempted to comfort her, but I can see she is beyond my
help. She is hurting, deeply, and as the days before her departure to
London go by, I find I am fearful for her. Our father has brought a
great deal of pressure to bear on her. Today I witnessed a disturbing
conversation between them both. He has threatened Christine with
destitution and the loss of her beloved horses should she not bend to
his wishes. As Christine believes herself without a place to turn for
shelter or help, reliant as we women are upon our male relatives for
our livelihood, I fear she will put herself into a situation where she
will be unhappy the rest of her days.*

*Mr. Gilbert, I love my sister deeply. I cannot help feeling if she
had a place to go she would gladly give up London and all the plans
made for her by others.*

Can you do anything to help?

Thomas raised his eyes from the letter, not seeing the room
around him.

"Tom?" his father said, coming to stand beside him. "Is it bad
news? You are as pale as a ghost, lad."

Thomas folded the letter carefully and turned to look at his
father. "How much has Mother told you about where I go on my
rides?"

Harold smiled, his eyes twinkling. "You know we keep no secrets
from each other."

Despite the seriousness of his thoughts, Thomas could not help returning the smile. "This letter is from Miss Julia Devon in regards to her sister, Christine."

"Ah." Harold tucked his hands behind him. "Intriguing. You look as though you aren't pleased with what she had to say. Warning you off, is she?"

Thomas shook his head. "Calling me back, rather. Here." He handed the folded letter to his father and paced the study while it was read. Thoughts whirled about in his mind, too chaotic for him to make sense of any of them.

The days which had passed since their parting had crawled slowly by, each longer than the last. Thomas knew, instinctively, that should he wish to preserve his heart and mind he must bury himself in the work of the estate. If he kept his mind on facts and figures, on writing letters to prospective horsemen interested in the offspring of his horse farm, he would have little time to acknowledge just how heartbroken he was.

Thinking of her now, the agony he'd been trying to outrun came back full force. Watching Christine ride away had left him empty and bereft; knowing he would not speak to her in private again made his chest ache. Still, Thomas could not give words to the way he felt, he would not describe his state of emotion, even to himself. That path would lead to a dark place.

Christine Devon had made it quite clear, from the beginning of their arrangement, that she could never wed one such as him. His social standing was too low for her family, his finances in too much uncertainty to take a wife, and though their families were friends, friendship would never be enough to change those facts when Mr. Devon's expectations were set on loftier climbs.

But here, spelled out at last by her sister, were his concerns for her happiness. There was also a strong hint as to what it might take, or what he could do, to save her from such a fate.

"Tom," his father said, interrupting his thoughts. Thomas looked to his father to find the man regarding him with a steady gaze. "What can you do to help?"

Thomas let out a puff of air in a near laugh. "I can offer for her." The moment the words left his lips, his heart felt lighter. He stood straighter, hope filling him as he took in a deeper breath. "I cannot give her the social standing or connections her father wishes, but those are his desires. Not hers. It may very well be..." His voice trailed off as he saw his father's look turn thoughtful. "What is it?"

"Are you in love with her?" the elder Gilbert asked, his eyes steady. "Is that it, son?"

The word Thomas refused to use, though gently spoken, crashed through the barriers around his heart and his breath hitched. Looking into the open expression of his father, a man he respected and loved dearly, Thomas nodded.

"Yes." He felt immensely better the moment the admission escaped his lips. "I am very much in love with her."

Harold Gilbert looked more concerned than comforted by the admission. "Everyone knows of Mr. Devon's expectations for his daughter's season. He has made no secret of his desires for a future son-in-law. I do not think he will look well upon your suit. Not at all. Especially if he comes to know how you have been meeting in secret all this time."

The weight settled on his shoulders again, yet now Thomas felt more able to bare it. "We must have his permission. I fear he will never give it willingly."

His father launched another unexpected question. "Does Miss Christine love you, Tom? I would not see you marry someone who is only fond of you."

Thomas considered the question, allowing his mind to linger on the memories built at the side of the brook. Her laugh, her smile, her touch. Even the way in which she leaned into him when she thought he might kiss her. Their waltz.

He answered his father honestly. "I do not know for certain, as she has never told me of her heart. But I have every reason to hope she returns my regard."

"Then you must speak to Miss Christine without delay. Once

you know her thoughts on the matter, we can find a way to appease her father." Harold sighed deeply and looked toward the desk of paperwork. "We are not in the best position to elevate Christine Devon or her father in society, but we are a respected family. Perhaps it will be enough." The elder Gilbert did not sound overly hopeful, but Thomas did not allow himself to dwell on that.

"I will go call on Christine now," Thomas stated, already moving to the door. "Wish me well."

"With all my heart, Tom," his father said as he disappeared out the door.

His heart full, his hopes high, Thomas called out instructions for the preparation of his horse. He would not delay another moment in speaking to Christine. His hopes for saving her from unhappiness combined with his recognition of his love for her gave him no room for doubt.

He hoped his suit would be enough for her. That *he* would be enough for her.

Thomas traveled to the Devon home at a breakneck speed, grateful for a mount that could easily match the frenzied pace of his thoughts. Yet he knew to feel confident at this point would not be advisable. He needed to speak to Christine to ascertain whether or not his suit would be welcome and then he would ask Devon for permission to court and marry his daughter. The man could not act heartlessly if he knew that Thomas cared for her.

When Thomas asked the footman at the door for Miss Christine, he was shown into Devon's office. He knew at once this was not where he should be, and Devon's disinterested greeting made his heart sink.

"What can I do for you, Mr. Gilbert?" Devon asked after rising from his seat behind the desk.

"I hoped to see your daughter, Miss Christine," Thomas informed him, trying to keep a neutral tone.

"All my daughters' visitors must see me first." Devon did not sit and did not offer for Thomas to do so. He meant to keep the interview short. "It is my way of protecting them. I would not allow them to keep low company, after all." The level of control this man exerted on his children struck Thomas as unusual, not merely overprotective.

"I understand," Thomas said slowly, caution creeping into his manner. "May I see her now?"

Devon regarded him silently for several long moments. "I think not. It has come to my attention that you and my daughter have entered into some sort of agreement regarding her horses. An agreement that I should have been consulted about, prior to the removal of her stallions. Those are very expensive animals you are currently housing."

It struck Thomas in that moment how Christine refrained from mentioning her father's opinion of her use of the animals, except to clarify that they were legally her property.

"Yes. Miss Christine has agreed to take part in my horse farm. I hope to give her a return on her investment, in time," Thomas said slowly, using the business term that Christine so often applied to herself when she spoke of her father.

"A foolish investment." Devon waived his hand dismissively. "And one which should have been made through me or my man of business. Not my daughter."

Thomas refused to be cowed. "I apologize, sir. Your daughter gave me every reason to believe she was within her rights to arrange for the removal of her animals to my property."

Devon sat without allowing Thomas to do the same, a blatant and rude slight. "Legally. However, the world of business is best left to men. I would never have countenanced the free use of those animals without some deposit or promissory note from you for their time. What *are* the arrangements behind the deal? What does Christine get from you having her stallions?" Devon leaned forward, his eyes piercing and cold, taking Thomas's measure without blinking.

The ground on which Thomas stood he knew to be treacherous.

"As I said, my use of the horses is an investment. Should the foals sired by the stallions sell well, I hope to give your daughter a percentage of the profits." Although they never discussed as much, he wanted to do more to show his gratitude for her help.

Devon smirked. "It sounds like a risky venture, given your family's current financial state."

Thomas's hopes sunk more and more drastically by the second. "I have spent many years studying horses and their markets. I feel my success is a certainty."

"You feel that way, do you? But all the risk is being taken by my daughter. Foolish girl." Devon sighed deeply and continued to sort through the papers on his desk, no longer granting Thomas his full attention. "Is that why you wished to speak to her? To talk of your supposed business?" His disinterest in the idea could not be made clearer.

Thomas did his best to remain calm and collected, though he bristled at the man's condescension. "No. I came on a more personal matter. I wished to determine your daughter's interest in courtship. Should she indicate she finds it favorable, I would then apply to you for permission."

Devon paused in his movement and looked up, slowly, the calculating look back in his eyes. His expression remained neutral, his posture relaxed. "Regardless of her preferences, if you are the one applying to court her, my answer is no."

Thomas straightened, his hands balling into fists at his side. "No? Just like that?" He fought to control his tone, to refrain from shouting.

"Exactly."

Thomas unclenched his jaw long enough to ask, "On what grounds am I to be denied?"

Devon sighed deeply and sat back in his chair. At his ease, fingers steepled before him, he spoke calmly. "On the grounds that you are far inferior to the type of person I hope to secure her to. You have no title, no social standing worth speaking of, and every land owner in the vicinity is aware of the mismanagement of your family's small estate. What would I have to gain marrying her off to the likes of you?" Now Devon's smile curled his lips up in a manner that looked far too sly for a man speaking of his child's future. "I am about to spend a small fortune launching her into society. I intend to make back every farthing. Christine is meant for a better circle than you could hope to give her."

Thomas stood stock still, highly aware of how little power he held in this situation. He would not even be permitted an audience with Christine to learn if she regarded him as more than a friend. He could not tell her his feelings. Devon would not give permission for them to wed, his ambition too great for the connections his daughter could bring him.

Thomas jerked his head down in a brief nod. "Then I have nothing more to say to you, Mr. Devon. Goodbye."

The man had the gall to look pleased. "Goodbye, Mr. Gilbert."

Thomas ignored the footman outside the study and went straight to the door on his own. He wished to fly through the house calling her name, but he would not make a spectacle of himself or put her in the difficult position of watching him being thrown out by her father.

He mounted his horse and was soon riding back the way he had come, angry and hurt, all too aware that, while he viewed Devon's reasons for keeping them apart as cold and heartless, they were valid. But what could he do? If he knew Christine's true feelings on the matter, he might find a better way to act, even if it meant taking her to Scotland to elope.

He sighed and slowed his mount when his home came into view. His best course of action at present would be to take his parents more fully into his confidence. Together, the three of them might come up with a plan.

He would not give up, though Devon gave him a thorough set down.

He loved Christine. He was not prepared to let her go to London without telling her so.

Chapter Twenty-One

DECEMBER 25, 1811

Thomas arrived at the Earl of Annesbury's residence before the ball, a sheaf of papers tucked under his arm. The earl, Lord Annesbury, wished to discuss Thomas's proposal of an investment in his horse farm. Although Thomas's mind did not cease to turn over the situation with Christine, he knew he must continue to labor for his dream. Thomas retained hope that speaking with Christine at the ball would be possible and he could at least determine where her heart lay.

The butler showed him to Lord Annesbury's study and the nobleman stood when he entered. "Ah, Gilbert. I am glad you made it. I am terribly sorry for the inconvenience of meeting on the same night as the ball."

Thomas shook his head. "Not at all, my lord."

"Call me Annesbury, or Lucas," the other man said with a wave of his hand. "We practically grew up together, after all. I can clearly recall racing you across the village green during a fair or two."

Thomas relaxed and shook hands with the earl, a man not much older than himself, but with much more prestige and wealth. He was taller than Thomas, too, and looked the part of a nobleman with lighter hair and eyes. If he had been in love with Christine, Lord Annesbury could easily have had her.

He pulled his mind back to the task at hand. "Thank you for seeing me. I hope you will find this meeting a good use of your time. I have brought a fair number of things for you to look through, but I think you will be most interested in the pedigree charts." Thomas took a sheet from the top of the stack and held it out to the earl.

"I have always thought this land fine enough, though not entirely suited to the farms enriching other parts of England." Lucas sat down and offered Thomas a seat as he perused the document. After his eyes went down the whole page, he sucked in a deep breath. "This is most impressive. The Devon stables are providing the sires for your first crop of foals?"

"Yes, they are." Many knew the stallions in those stables were priceless, but none had ever gained the right to match mares to them. "And my mares are from the finest stables in Italy."

"They are, and rare lines at that. How involved is Devon in this business?" Lucas looked up, his forehead wrinkled. "I have known the man for years. I do not do business with him by choice, I am afraid."

At least Thomas could reassure him on that front. "The horses do not belong to Devon, but to his second daughter, Miss Christine. I negotiated with her for the rights to her stallions." He could not help the twitch of his lips as he thought on those circumstances. "They have been in the paddocks with my mares for over a week, getting to know one another."

The earl nodded and put the paper down. "What are your projected expenses? You will forgive me for saying this, Gilbert, but I am not unaware of your family's current financial situation. I am assuming you will need a large investment to begin your work."

Thomas nodded and handed the earl the next sheet of paper. "That is why I've sought you out, my lord. I know you have an interest in hunters and I intend to produce a top line of them. It will take a few years and, at present, my resources are slim. Apart from the horses, there is little I can offer by way of collateral. My estimations are modest and the return I offer for the investment is generous."

"Should you succeed it will be," Lucas told him, going over the document carefully. "What does Miss Devon get for her part in starting your stables?"

Thomas froze and the earl chuckled.

"I did not miss the smile her name conjured," the earl admitted, raising one sandy eyebrow. "The young woman knows horses, they tell me, as well as her mother knew them. She must have driven a hard bargain, considering those stallions of hers have rarely ever been bred."

Thomas reflected on his lessons with Christine, remembering how the suggestion disturbed him when first she proposed their arrangement, and he sighed. "It was a hard bargain, but it will not undercut your income in the slightest. Miss Christine did not ask for a monetary return."

Lucas reached for the next sheet of paper, glancing briefly across the proposed improvements to the Gilbert stables before turning his attention back to Thomas. "I see a great deal of promise here, Gilbert. I have asked after your time in Italy, learned who you spent all your time with, and I must say that I am impressed. The fact that you enticed Miss Devon to invest her horses in the venture further reassures me that you know what you are about. I must go over the figures with my man of business, but I believe this would be a sound investment for me."

Thomas's hopes rose and some of the burden fell from his shoulders. "You would agree to the mares as collateral, should the venture fail?"

"They are valuable horses, and the foals they will produce will be more so, against good English stock." The earl rose and extended his hand. "Consider me a partner. I will invest what you ask the moment the papers are in order and signed."

"Thank you, my lord." Thomas grinned and firmly shook on the deal, amazed at how simple the matter had been, though he had known of Lord Annesbury's reputation for quick business decisions. "I appreciate your faith in me and my animals."

"As I said, I looked into you and I know you are a sound investment." The earl gestured to the windows. "Would you mind stepping outside? We have a short time until the ball begins. I should like to show you my stables and get your opinion on a few matters."

"Will that not upset your preparations for the ball?" Thomas asked, knowing how frenzied his household became when they prepared to entertain guests.

Lucas chuckled and shook his head. "Not at all. My mother does all the work. She lives for balls and parties and comes all the way from London to make sure I keep up tradition every Christmas." He led the way through the house, only stopping so Thomas could retrieve his overcoat from the front hall.

They spent a quarter of an hour inspecting the earl's prized hunters, the stables, the feed, and discussing improvements Lucas had implemented and whether Thomas might try the same. But try as he would to focus, Thomas's mind kept going back to Christine. With the earl's investment assured, he still would not be a man of great means or connections, but perhaps it would be good enough to approach Devon again.

"I can see your mind is already spinning ahead to the future of your stables," Lucas said, bringing Thomas back to the present.

"Only a little." Thomas glanced around them, taking in a deep breath, enjoying the warmth and scents of the stables. These were smells which never changed, whether he found himself in England or Italy. "I apologize for my distraction."

"Not at all, not at all." The earl reached out and gave Thomas a friendly slap on the shoulder. "You have a great many plans to make, especially if you are to marry Miss Christine Devon."

Thomas jerked completely out of his thoughts and froze on the spot, turning wide eyes to the earl. "What?" he gasped out. "How did you know—no one knows."

The earl did not smile, yet good humor glittered in his eyes. "I was in love once. I know the look a man gets when he is thinking of his lady. I made a calculated guess, based on our conversation, and you confirmed it. Congratulations. Do you have a wedding date at present?"

Thomas continued to gape for a moment before he shook his head. "No, Annesbury. I am afraid that there is no understanding at present between myself and Miss Christine."

The earl raised an eyebrow. "The loan of her horses was not part of that understanding?"

"No." Thomas hesitated, wondering what he ought to tell this man he barely knew. The earl held Thomas's future in his hands and could yet withdraw his support if he did not understand that all had been arranged in an honorable manner.

"Miss Christine's horses are part of a private arrangement between ourselves, and I have come to care for her a great deal since my return from Italy. Nothing would please me more than to take her as my wife. However, circumstances do not, at present, allow me to approach her with an offer of marriage."

The earl's curiosity was replaced with sudden understanding. "Ah. Miss Devon is the one about to make her debut into London society. I have heard of her father's hopes for her future. I must surmise that it is he who stands in the way of your offer?" The taller gentleman shook his head, lips pursed. "How unfortunate."

Thomas relaxed and reached up to run a hand through his hair, not caring if he ruined it before the ball. "Very. But please do not trouble yourself thinking on it."

"I apologize for prying, Gilbert. As I said, I loved a young woman once very deeply. I cannot imagine what I would have done had her hand been denied me." His expression took on a more wistful look and he turned away, eyes toward the stable doors. "I lost my wife too soon. I am forever grateful for the time we had together. I would not wish such loss on anyone."

"Thank you, my lord." Thomas nodded and took a step toward the exit. "Should we go inside, my lord, before we begin to smell of horse?"

"I suppose most people do not find such a scent pleasant in the ballroom." Lucas led the way out, turning the conversation back to horses, and Thomas kept his thoughts to himself.

CHRISTINE SAT NEXT TO JULIA IN THE CARRIAGE, WARM BRICKS at her feet, staring out the window at the earl's beautiful estate. Torches lit his drive as it was already dark, and carriages even grander than the Devon equipage lined the drive ahead of them. Their father sat across from them, in the forward-facing seat.

What should have been the most exciting night of her year only filled her with anxiety and sorrow. Tonight would be her last chance to see Thomas before leaving for London to experience a season she no longer found any pleasure anticipating. After their last meeting, she hadn't heard a single word from him, which she expected. An unmarried woman could never exchange letters with a gentleman; she did not even dare to drop him a note to ask after her horses.

"I love the Christmas ball," Julia spoke suddenly, breaking the uneasy silence of the carriage. She reached over and took Christine's gloved hand in hers. "You will see, Christine. The earl's home is absolutely breathtaking, but when evergreen boughs decorate the ballroom, with gold and silver ribbons everywhere, it is magical."

Their father snorted before Christine could respond to such an obvious effort to cheer her. "Nonsense. Annesbury spends a fortune on these events. I suppose it is worth it, given the number of important people who attend."

"I understand the earl's brother will be here this evening, though his betrothed will not be able to make the celebration. Such a shame. I met her in Bath, when I visited Cousin Virginia."

"Before your attempt at a season," their father muttered, staring out the window. "What I truly find a shame is the Earl's inability to move beyond the loss of his wife. I have heard he enjoys horses. You could have had a chance with him, Christine." He shook his head.

Christine repressed a sigh and exchanged a frustrated glance with Julia. "Indeed. He would be a magnificent catch." It was usually easier to agree with him and move on. Christine had enough experience with such conversations.

Devon made a sound of agreement, then turned from the window to fix Christine with a hard stare. "I am suddenly reminded, Christine, that I need to express my disapproval of you speaking with Mr. Gilbert this evening. I would prefer you to keep your distance from him."

Taken aback, Christine tightened her hold on Julia's hand. How could her father know to make such an edict?

"I am certain you need not worry about that, Father," Christine said hastily, grateful the shadows in the carriage concealed her blush.

"I meant to speak to you sooner, but I have been busy with an important business arrangement." He leaned forward, his eyes and expression hard. "You should not have acted without my consent, giving him access to your horses. The man is an upstart and believed such an action gave him the right to request permission to court you."

Julia gasped and Christine's heart lifted for an instant, then plummeted downward.

"The Gilberts have been our neighbors for generations," Julia said, her voice shaky. "You cannot call him an upstart."

"His father has completely mismanaged their estate and now the boy harbors some ridiculous notion of beginning a horse farm. But with what capital? He has nothing to recommend him except his ability to negotiate with young women." He shook his head dismissively. "Keep away from him, Christine. We leave for London tomorrow and I do not want him getting any ideas in his head about you."

Christine gaped at her father, disbelieving the situation. Thomas had gone to her father, the most close-minded man in the county, and requested permission to court her. Thomas *did* have feelings for her. How deep did they go?

And how could she discover them?

The carriage halted again, but this time the door was opened by a liveried footman who assisted the ladies from the carriage ahead of their father. Once aground, he did not wait for them but went for the large front steps of Annesbury's home immediately.

Julia took Christine's arm and leaned in close, whispering. "I sent a note to Thomas. I asked him to rescue you," she admitted.

Christine's breath hitched. "You did what?"

"I did not think he acted on it. He must've gone to Father." Julia shook her head and chewed her lower lip.

Christine's poor heart fell again, cracked this time. "Then he only acted because of your note."

Julia shook her head, her breath creating a fog before them in the winter air. "He would not have asked unless he meant to have you as a wife, Christine. I am convinced he loves you. I can see how you feel for him and he would be an idiot not to return your regard. We must find him at once."

Christine pulled away from her sister as they entered the house, shaking her head in denial. "I cannot," she whispered. "I won't." She hurried away from Julia, forgoing a visit to the lady's withdrawing room. What did she care if a curl remained out of place or a wrinkle appeared in her skirts? It did not matter whether or not she impressed anyone.

How could Julia do such a thing? Why would she send a note, obliging Thomas to answer with an offer of courtship? And her father must have humiliated him, given his words in the carriage. Christine hurt to think of Thomas being subjected to such abuse. Thomas, a man of honor and compassion, could never hope to be treated with respect when all her father valued was a large wallet and long titles.

"Ah, Miss Christine Devon, isn't it?" The deep voice startled her out of her thoughts and she looked up, finding herself at the edge of the ballroom, standing before the tall, handsome Earl of Annesbury.

She dropped a hasty curtsy. "My lord. Thank you for inviting me." When she raised her eyes to his, the intensity in his gaze startled her.

"You are most welcome." He gestured to the floor where couples were already dancing. "Might I have a dance with you, Miss Christine?"

Her mind went blank of every lesson Thomas had given her and she could not fathom why the most powerful man in their county would suddenly show such a pointed interest in her. "Yes. I would be honored. My first two are spoken for, but after that—"

He nodded sharply. "Splendid. I will return for you shortly." He offered a bow and strode away, disappearing into the crowd. She watched as a few ladies with fans gazed after him as he moved away, only to turn and take *her* in, standing there stupidly staring after Lord Annesbury.

Fans snapped up to cover faces, and the sounds of murmured words and whispers reached her ears, causing warmth to creep up her neck and into her cheeks. She turned away from the stares, wondering why anyone would wish to be the subject of such talk.

Is this what London will be like?

Why would Lord Annesbury single her out? They had only been introduced years ago, when she was still in the schoolroom, and seen each other in passing. Christine did not understand. Everyone knew he yet mourned his wife and he had not sought the company of any young ladies for years. She was not so vain as to think one look at her could change his mind about courtship. Could this only be the mark of his famous eccentricity? Perhaps he always spoke to people with such abruptness.

"Ah, Miss Christine you have arrived at last." Captain Markham appeared beside her, his elder brother just behind him.

"I have come to claim my dance," Mr. Markham said, extending his hand to her.

Christine forced her mind to stop spinning and turned her full attention to her dancing partner. "Yes. Thank you. Shall we?"

Recalling Thomas's lessons, Christine did her best to give Mr. Markham her undivided attention. The ballroom was full to bursting with people she recognized and strangers alike. While tempted to look about for friends, for Thomas, she decided it best not to. Thinking on Thomas only hurt and, considering the earl's odd interest, would only confuse her further. She turned her eyes to Mr. Markham and her mind to the steps of the dance.

"I hope we see each other in London," Markham said when the dance brought them together. "If we do, I promise to stand up with you. You are a very fine dancer."

"Thank you, Mr. Markham. You are very kind." She gave him her tiniest of polite smiles but could not bring herself to do more. It felt wrong to flirt and lead this gentleman on. He had been nothing except kind to her since their introduction, but she had no interest in him beyond their acquaintance, and her father had even less than that.

The dance with Captain Markham was accomplished with equal politeness and conversation on the weather.

"I am certain it will snow tonight," he announced when they drew close enough to speak. "You can taste it in the air."

"I enjoy snow," Christine said politely. "Especially at Christmas."

When he returned her from the dance floor, the earl stood waiting, hands clasped behind his back, unsmiling. He bowed. "Our dance, Miss Christine."

She curtsied and allowed him to lead her to form the next set. "I hope you do not think me too forward," he said when they met the first time, stepping delicately around each other before reforming the lines. "I have a need to speak with you on a matter of some importance."

"With me, my lord?" As confused as she was by his approach, this statement made even less sense. She slipped back into old habits and spoke her mind, without even a hint of flirtation. "I cannot understand why that would be necessary."

He blinked at her and his lips twitched. "Ah, a forthright young lady. How refreshing. I expected you to play coy."

Christine nearly said something unladylike but stopped herself. What would Thomas think of her complete disregard for all his hard work?

"I ought to have," she said with a toss of her head. "I find I am not in the mood and I am thoroughly flummoxed by your behavior."

He was separated from her for several moments to complete the necessary steps of the dance, but as soon as he returned they stood close again.

"I apologize," he said calmly. "I wish to ask after your investment with Gilbert's horse farm."

Had he announced a sudden fancy for wearing straw bonnets, she could not have been more surprised, and it must have shown, because he took her elbow and removed them from the floor. "Forgive me, Miss Christine; you are tired."

As it was only her third dance, she was nothing of the sort, but she allowed him to lead her to a row of chairs along the wall. He gestured for her to sit near an especially large column, concealing her from half the room easily.

"Again, I offer my sincerest apologies for my actions tonight, Miss Christine."

"I would accept if I knew what on earth you are talking about," she said, peering up at him, her eyebrows pinched together. "My lord, whatever are you about? I barely know you, and here you ask to dance, then question me about Mr. Gilbert, and—"

"I questioned you about your investment," he corrected, interrupting her smoothly. He took the seat next to her, his eyes moving to look over the crowd before them. "Smile so no one thinks I hold you here against your will."

"Heaven forbid," she muttered, following his instructions and hoping she was convincing. "Is something wrong with Mr. Gilbert's horses?"

"I merely wished to ask if you thought his farm a sound investment, since you know so much about the beasts yourself." He turned his eyes to her again, his expression still made of stone.

Christine lowered her gaze and looked away, not liking his frank study of her. What would he see if she spoke of Thomas? Could he know of their meetings somehow? What did he hope to gain through this line of questioning?

"I have invested my horses with Mr. Gilbert. That ought to tell you my opinion of the matter."

He nodded, she saw from the corner of her eye. "Good. Now, what can you tell me about the man? I am not well acquainted with him and you are his nearest neighbor."

"My lord." Her cheeks flooded with heat, but she pressed on. "He is an honorable man and very knowledgeable of horses. His family is kind and good to their tenants. They are well liked throughout the neighborhood. Is that all?"

"No, but it is an excellent start." He leaned in slightly closer than usually permissible in polite company. "Do you love him?"

Christine's head snapped up and her eyes flew to his. The heat that coursed through her moments before evaporated, leaving her chilled. "How could you know to ask that?" she whispered, then turned to look around them, certain the whole room must be watching this exchange. Yet no one batted an eye in their direction.

"I have a knack for these things," he said, tone as solemn as his expression. "You did not answer the question."

"It is a most impertinent question," she responded hotly, wishing she could get up and move away without causing a scene. "No matter who you are, my lord."

The earl shrugged and hummed an agreement. "I think you would have denied it at once if it were not true."

Christine turned to look at him, still shocked, and began to shake her head. "You ought to take lessons, my lord, in polite conversation. You asked if the stables were a good investment. I believe they are. I trust Mr. Gilbert implicitly." She raised her eyebrows and took a deep breath. "As to your other question, I care for Mr. Gilbert a very great deal."

He leaned back in his chair and crossed his arms before him. "Miss Christine, I will risk shocking you with yet greater impertinence. If you are in love with him, I can help you, whatever your father may say on the matter." With one last calculating look, he examined her face. He nodded to himself, then stood and reached for her hand. "Let me escort you back to a friend."

She allowed him to lead her along the walls of the ballroom, staring at him with complete consternation. He continued to nod and smile at other guests they passed.

When she took her eyes away from his to find some manner of escape, she saw that they were making a direct path to Thomas himself. He stood at ease beside his sister, Mrs. Brody, completely unaware of their approach.

She froze, bringing both of them to a halt. "My lord, why are you doing this?" she asked quietly, her eyes suddenly filling with tears. "I am forbidden to speak to him."

The earl leaned down, meeting her eyes squarely. "Miss Christine, I outrank your father. And, as it is my home, I may do whatever I wish." He gave her arm a gentle tug and she continued walking toward Thomas.

Though he did not smile, she thought she detected the air of a trickster about him. How else could one ever explain his behavior?

They were only a handful of steps away when Thomas looked up, his eyes catching hers.

Thomas did not turn away, but surprised her by moving quickly in her direction, his eyes lit from within. She swallowed her happiness and took his gloved hand as he offered it, stepping away from the eccentric nobleman without a thought.

The music began anew and Thomas, eyes only on her, spoke quietly. "Will you dance with me, Christine?"

Her father would not like it.

She did not care.

"Yes, Thomas."

Chapter Twenty-Two

The music began to play and Christine realized, belatedly, that it was a waltz. Few would dance, as many still did not approve of the intimate movements. This would put Thomas and Christine on display before everyone of importance in the county. But he did not hesitate when they reached the edge of the crowd. Her hand went to his shoulder, his to hers, and their free hands clasped as they entered the first position of the German waltz.

Christine could not keep her eyes from his, though she fought hard to keep her gaze down as directed in their lessons.

"You are most beautiful tonight, Miss Christine," he said.

"Thank you for the compliment." She looked up at him through her eyelashes and then tilted her chin up. "I am going to be in a great deal of trouble for dancing with you, Mr. Gilbert."

"Will it be worth it, I wonder?" he asked, tilting his head to the side and smiling at her, his deep green eyes drawing her in. She loved it when he smiled.

"That depends," she teased him softly when they moved to complete another turn, arms around each other's waists. "On whether your conversation is interesting enough."

"Shall we talk of the rights of kings or of the weather?" He attempted to quell his smile, though his lips continuously twitched upward. If they had not already started a scandal with their waltz, his continual smile might be just the thing to push them over the edge. Did he not care either?

"I would prefer the weightier topic, in truth, but I have it on good authority that I ought not to have opinions on such things." She glanced over his shoulder and saw Julia standing next to Mrs. Brody and her husband, all three watching them and conversing with the most serious of expressions. She sighed.

"Christine," he whispered, pulling her eyes back to him. "This may well be our last dance together, if not our last time speaking to one another. You must know, I have to tell you, that I tried to speak to your father." His eyes darkened and his eyebrows drew together, creating tiny wrinkles on his forehead, which she found rather endearing. "I asked permission to court you."

"I know." Christine followed his lead with ease, hardly thinking of each step. The feeling of being in his arms, guided by him, held as close as society would ever allow, made her steps light even if her heart remained heavy. "Thank you for that. I am grateful you would wish to protect me, as a friend, from an unwanted match."

His lips quirked upward again. "As a friend? I cannot allow you to misunderstand me to that extent, Christine. You cannot go to London thinking I only attempted to gain your father's favor because I like you." He twirled her about as the steps necessitated, but when she stilled and faced him again, he leaned close, his eyes searching hers. "I wished to court and marry you because I love you."

Her breath hitched and her feet forgot to move, though the room continued spinning about her. All sound ceased and there remained only the two of them, standing, and grasping each other's arms. Heart rising within her, Christine wished to burst into song or shout with joy, but she could somehow only manage to whisper.

"You do? Thomas, really?"

His eyes stayed on hers, his handsome smile melting her insides. "With my whole heart."

A murmur filled the room, drawing Thomas's attention, and Christine reluctantly looked away from him, her heart galloping faster than any horse could ever hope to run. She half expected everyone in the room to be staring at them, pointing and whispering, for how could they have missed such an incredible moment?

But the whole of the room faced toward the upper balcony, where the musicians had stopped their playing in the middle of the waltz.

The tall, fair-haired earl stood there, calling for attention by tapping a crystal glass.

"Honored guests, please forgive me for interrupting your evening," he said, deep voice carrying across the room.

Thomas took Christine's hand in his, his grasp warm and gentle. "And our waltz," he muttered, glancing around them, as though looking for someone.

"What is it, Thomas?" she asked, stepping closer so their arms were flush against each other, the cloth of his jacket against her bare forearm.

Before he could answer, Lord Annesbury continued. "I had to take the opportunity to make an announcement. The families involved will excuse my behavior, as I have received permission from the bridegroom."

Christine watched as Thomas's eyes snapped forward, intent now upon the earl, and his look changed to one of supreme shock.

"He wouldn't," Thomas muttered, his body tensing.

"I would like to take the opportunity, on this wonderful evening surrounded by many of our neighbors, to announce the engagement of Mr. Thomas Gilbert and Miss Christine Devon, both excellent friends of mine. Let us wish the happy couple joy." He raised his glass and others in the room did the same, while still more people began to politely clap and exclaim over the announcement, however unorthodox.

Christine turned her eyes to Thomas to find him staring down at her, his confusion melting into an amused smile.

"Your father will not like this at all," he whispered.

She shook her head and looked back up to the earl, who had somehow managed to extract himself from the balcony and now hurried in their direction, the crowd parting for him, as he presumably came to wish them well.

"He's ruined us both, I think," she muttered, threading her arm through Thomas's. "This is madness. Father will—"

A hand clasped her shoulder firmly and pulled her away from Thomas, turning her around, and she looked up into her father's eyes, finding in them more heat and fury than she had ever seen there before.

"How dare you?" he hissed at her, unheard as the people around them continued to clap and murmur among themselves, completely unaware of the true nature of the announced engagement.

"Ah, Mr. Devon," the earl said, and Christine realized he had reached them too. He raised his voice enough for it to carry, causing people nearby to hush and turn interested faces to what must be looking like quite the spectacle. Thomas reached for her wrist, her father held her arm in a tight grasp, and Lord Annesbury stood over them all, unsmiling but somehow still chipper.

"Thank you, sir, for giving in to my whim to announce the betrothal of your daughter and my most excellent friend, Mr. Gilbert." He reached out to lay a hand on Thomas's shoulder and offered his free hand to Devon. "I am especially gratified that such fine families will soon join forces on the Gilbert horse farm, as I have invested heavily in its future and I could not trust it to two people less capable than these."

With all her years of studying him, Christine understood her father's thoughts almost exactly. He did not know what to do, accosted in public by a man of high rank, his plans for her destroyed. Yet here Lord Annesbury presented as good a connection as any her father could wish. Christine watched as the angry light in his eyes warred with his shrewder nature. He looked away from the earl and into the tableaux of the crowd, people he did business with, people of rank, those he would want to think highly of him.

Christine had heard many a nursery tale about good kings or kind fairies whisking into a tale to save someone from danger, or bless them with great gifts, but she could hardly believe that a country nobleman now did the same for her.

At last, her father released her arm, looking about to see all eyes upon him; a pained smile appeared on his reddened face. "Not at all, Lord Annesbury. You do us great honor."

"Now, we ought to let everyone get back to the dance. I believe it was a waltz. Musicians? Please, begin again." Lord Annesbury waved in the direction of the balcony where instruments began to play, not entirely in harmony for several notes, but Thomas hurried to pull Christine back onto the floor.

"I am not certain what just happened," he said when he had put several couples between themselves and her father, who she saw was now in deep conversation with the earl. Lord Annesbury caught her eye and winked. "I think we are now engaged to be married."

Christine's heart fluttered and she turned to meet his eyes, when she realized she'd yet to tell him the truth of her feelings. He must know, but Christine wanted to say the words aloud, at last.

"I love you too, Thomas."

A broad, triumphant grin no member of polite society would ever wear appeared on his face.

Thomas pulled her completely off the dance floor, between people in the crowd, ignoring words of congratulations lobbed at them as they went. She followed, realizing they were hurrying to the doors of the balcony, left barely ajar to allow cool air to circulate in the warm ballroom.

In full view of anyone who might be watching, which likely included half the room, Thomas pulled her outside the doors and then around an obliging column.

"I think we ought to discuss your final lesson, Christine." He tucked them out of the breeze, his back to the night air and her gloved hands in both of his.

She stepped closer, lifting her face to his. Snowflakes were falling, brightening the night and adding to the magic of the moment. "Really? *Now?*" She felt certain this was not the time for any such conversation.

He nodded solemnly and twined his arm about her waist. "It is the most important lesson of all." His arms about her kept the cold away, but she came closer still. "You are to forget absolutely everything we ever discussed about how to behave in polite society, how to converse, catch a husband, and flirt. You are to just be who you are, because that is why I love you." Thomas's eyes glittered down at her through the shadows. They searched her face, taking her all in, before settling on her lips.

"Even if I distress the vicar at dinner?" she asked softly, her breath coming in small gasps, having nothing to do with the cold and everything to do with Thomas.

He laughed and bent closer, his breath soft upon her cheek. "Especially then."

His head tilted, and he slanted his lips across hers in a tender, gentle kiss, sealing his words and his love upon her. Though his arms remained wrapped about her, Christine felt as though they floated above the ground, and she had no intention of ever coming down again.

꧁꧂

OF COURSE, THEY COULD NOT STAY ON THE BALCONY FOREVER. Despite the warmth their kiss sparked, a Christmas snow was falling and Christine did not wear a coat. Thomas led them back inside, Christine's arm through his and her body tucked close. They found the door guarded by Miss Devon and his elder sister, Martha. The two looked for all the world like co-conspirators of a great crime, and highly pleased with themselves besides.

"If anyone asks," Martha whispered, "we were watching you the entire time."

Thomas saw Christine's cheeks turn a deeper shade of pink. "You were?" she squeaked.

Miss Devon shook her head, a mischievous smile on her face. "No, but I can well imagine what went on." She tossed a knowing look Martha's way before continuing. "Lord Annesbury and Father have disappeared, everyone is excited for you both, and I think you had better stay with the Brodys until the wedding."

Thomas gave his sister a grateful smile when she nodded. "Thank you."

"That will not be necessary," Christine said firmly, her hand squeezing his arm. "My father will allow the match now. It would be a scandal for him to contradict the Earl of Annesbury, and then lose that tenuous new opportunity and connection. He may try to make things unpleasant for me at home, but I will bear up, and I will not leave my sisters to get through it alone."

Thomas could not have been prouder of the wonderful, intelligent, and strong woman Christine truly was. What did society know of correct behavior and courtship? Christine won him by being herself, with her frank words and kind heart.

His father and mother were making their way along the wall, his mother beaming at them both, hardly turning to thank people who tried to stop her with their good wishes. Indeed, he saw the Markhams with their Littleton cousins approaching as well.

"You have had your moment alone, dear brother," his elder sister said with a smirk. "Now you must spend the rest of the evening collecting kind words and dancing with all the wallflowers."

He laughed and looked down into Christine's upturned face, her beauty washing over him again. "I will brave my way through it, if Christine will agree to marry me as soon as the banns are read the third time."

"And not a moment later," she agreed.

"I am sorry you will not have your season." He hoped that would not disappoint her later, though he could not say he minded.

She lifted one shoulder in a shrug, her eyes sparkling with joy. "Tom, I would rather have you than anything else in the world."

Only the strictest adherence to the ideals of society kept him from whisking her up in his arms to deliver another kiss, though she looked as though she would have welcomed it.

Chapter Twenty-Three

JANUARY 14, 1812

Christine waited for Thomas to dismount at their stream, giving him the opportunity to help her from the saddle. Though entirely proficient in maneuvering off the animal herself, she relished the feeling of her husband's hands upon her waist and his strong arms guiding her down. His thoughtfulness of her comfort and happiness awed her. Being cherished and loved by him was more than she had ever dreamed of in a husband.

Their marriage was yet new, only two days old, but she felt more herself than ever before. Thomas married her in the little church where their families had always attended, sitting on opposite sides and ends of the chapel; now they would sit in the Gilbert pew for the rest of her days.

"I will forever be grateful we both enjoy early morning excursions," she said, turning from him to look over their little brook, edges now frosted over in ice. "What if we would not have met here that morning?"

His arm slid around her waist and he looked across the water to what he had always referred to as *her* side of the clearing. "I do not care to think on it. Providence gave us the opportunity, and that is all that matters."

Christine nodded in agreement and looked back up at him. "I agree, with my whole heart."

He bent and kissed her cheek. "This will forever be our special place, Christine. We will come here as often as you like, especially in the spring."

"For picnics," she added. "That would be wonderful." She leaned her cheek against his chest and took in a deep, slow breath, allowing the wintry air to fill her lungs.

"We cannot linger today, however," he reminded her softly. "We must be on our way to London soon."

"Of course," she said, her heart not entirely in the agreement. "Although I would much rather stay at home with you."

Thomas laughed and pulled her into an embrace. "My beautiful wife, all you've ever dreamed of is having a season in London. I cannot give you that, but we can go for a short visit. I promise, we will not spend the entire time on business."

The Earl of Annesbury, after soothing her father's disappointments, had swiftly dispatched letters to others he thought would wish to hear of Thomas's plans. His efforts gave Thomas and Christine introductions to several of his business associates who were interested in investing in a new stable, or else in procuring a foal from the promising bloodlines. It seemed Lord Annesbury had a greater interest in their success than Thomas had ever anticipated.

Though the earl had done a great deal for them, Thomas would also be working to finalize the leasing of his family's townhouse. He was determined to do all he could to provide financial stability to his family, and the income of a lease would go a long way toward that, without having to give up the house entirely.

"I find I don't care overly much about the London season," she reminded him primly. "I care about you, and our families, and our horses." Moving her animals to his property, permanently, had been an exciting day for them both. Her entire dowry, though by no means a fortune, would soon pay for an expansion of their stables and outbuildings. Though her father had been loath to release the funds, he did so to keep up the appearance that the marriage was one he supported.

In reality, the last several weeks in his home had been difficult for Christine and her sisters. No sooner had the wedding breakfast been eaten than her sisters were whisked away, to remove them from her rebellious influence, and teach them all a lesson.

Julia had been sent to help their cousin in Bath, whose husband was very ill. Their father expected her to be treated little better than a nursemaid, minding children and the sick, but Julia and Christine both expected a better situation to be waiting for her.

It was Rebecca that Christine truly worried after. At only sixteen, she had very little experience in the wide world. She had returned to London with Aunt Jacqueline, to begin grooming for her eventual season. Christine's father had decided that his youngest daughter would do his bidding, or else; Jacqueline would ensure strict and complete obedience.

At least they had all been able to enjoy the wedding together. Even Horace came to visit, though he hated being home during the winter holidays. He preferred the company of his friends to a house full of sisters. Christine could not say she blamed him, especially since she believed he also did all he could to avoid the strictures of their father.

"I love you, Christine." Thomas's words brought her back to the present. "Or should we remain formal, Mrs. Gilbert?"

She laughed softly. "I love you, Tom. Call me whatever you wish."

"Mm. I understand Chrissy is a favorite."

Thomas kissed her cheek again, then his lips trailed down further, to her jaw. She pulled in a sharp breath, still amazed by what his kisses could do to her insides. She turned to him and lifted her lips to his, fully in his embrace, and he deepened their kiss most satisfactorily.

In the circle of his arms, Christine knew all would be well, given time, patience, and hope.

And an abundance of love.

And What of Julia?

Sneak Peek of The Gentleman Physician

Chapter One

JANUARY 10TH, 1812

NATHANIEL HASTINGS bit his bottom lip to keep from laughing while his patient, Lady Huntington, continued to spout nonsense about the reasons behind her various ailments. He knew very well nothing troubled her that a good conversation could not cure.

"You are not at all sympathetic enough to be a doctor," the septuagenarian accused, wagging a bejeweled finger at him. "Look at you. As I give you a list of my rheumatisms and poor spirits, you are laughing at me." Though her words were said with affront, her old gray eyes sparkled with mirth. "What is to become of us when young doctors like you sit and chuckle at their patients? Hardly a way to run a medical practice, if you ask me."

"I beg your pardon, my lady." He stopped trying to hide his smile. "I find it hard to believe that your aches are so dreadful when I have it on very good authority you spent last evening at a ball, dancing nearly as often as that granddaughter of yours. Rumor also has it that you turned many a head with your new turban."

Her eyes glittered playfully. She leaned forward, the scent of lavender and face powder wafting toward him as she moved, to give his hand a grandmotherly pat where it rested on the arm of the chair.

"It is not a rumor at all, dear boy. And I will show you the magnificent headpiece." She signaled her maid who disappeared briefly and returned carrying a very tall, very bright yellow turban of silk, bedecked with green and blue feathers. "You see," the old woman said triumphantly, taking in his surprised expression with glee. "Positively everyone noticed and commented upon it. They cannot decide if I am senile or too out of the world to even care about fashion. Bah." She took the hideous thing and put it on her head, the maid fluttering about to help adjust it.

Nathaniel covered his mouth with his fist, overcome with amusement and horror in equal parts. "Is that a stuffed bird at the top?"

"Indeed, it is." The dowager affected a dramatic pose, lifting her aristocratic nose in the air. "I can tell you are absolutely agog, as were all at the assembly last evening." But when she twisted her neck to allow her profile to show, she winced and raised a hand to the back of her head.

He shook his head. "I can see. I also think, my lady, that I will leave you with a tincture after all. Such a glorious headpiece likely caused you some strain due to its weight. I doubt the whole turban is as light as the feathers festooned upon it?"

"It is a taxing load," she consented, waving for her maid to remove the silk and feathered monstrosity. "What do you recommend I take to cure my suffering?"

He gave her instructions for herbal tea to ease her headache and relax her muscles, advised she rest and not wear the turban for a few days at least, and then took his leave of her. Lady Huntington always saw to it that his visits were well compensated, though he never asked a thing from her. That was the way with the wealthy. They would never stoop to paying a doctor but would give him gifts instead.

The poor insisted on paying, however meager the amount, and Nathaniel had long since decided it all evened out. He earned a respectable living, for an independent man, and he enjoyed the work.

He put his beaver atop his head, covering his dark blond hair. He would need to visit a barber soon to keep it from covering his eyes. He inhaled deeply of the afternoon air and strode down the walk, taking in the clear blue sky, half smiling. Winter usually meant gray skies and dreadful weather, but today the world remained bright.

Nathaniel liked Bath. The city, ancient and modern at the same time, appealed to him. He could visit Roman ruins or listen to the old gossips discuss the latest London scandals in the Pump Room. With the season well under way in London, Bath emptied of many of its usual citizens, to fill again with families taking leases. These families were generally not high enough in society to thrive in London, but they could command great respect in Bath.

Deciding to walk to his next appointment, Nathaniel enjoyed the brisk winter breezes. Cities were always more pleasant in the winter, the air scented by coal and wood smoke instead of animals. He missed the green trees and gardens, but the bare branches in the parks made him more restful. People stayed indoors, softening the sounds in the streets.

In spring, life returned to the parks and the noise of all the citizenry bursting out of doors bringing vibrancy back to the town. But for now, he enjoyed the peacefulness of the season.

Nathaniel turned his mind to his next patient, hoping the cold dry air would make the man's day a little easier. The Baron of Heatherton, Charles Macon, was next on his list. It would not be a light-hearted visit, as his lordship was failing with consumption. The disease had taken the man's lungs. All Nathaniel could do was alleviate the man's pain and treat the symptoms to make what time he had left meaningful.

He had tried every remedy he could find, but Lord Heatherton's case had already advanced to a point there was nothing more a doctor could do.

He arrived at the house at half past two, and Lady Heatherton greeted him. She met him at the top of the stairs, her fair hair piled upon her head in a regal manner, her dress impeccable, her countenance stoic. She bore herself like a duchess, and he nearly forgot she was younger than his own twenty-seven years.

"Doctor Hastings, welcome." She offered him her hand which he bowed over. "Your visits are most appreciated."

He smiled, having found that this family preferred a pleasant disposition over a somber one. "Thank you, my lady. I hope, with the weather drier than normal, that your husband is faring well today?"

A flicker of worry appeared in her eyes and she glanced downward. "I am afraid not. I had hoped, with the lack of rain, his cough would ease. But..." When she looked up again there were tears in her eyes. "The solicitor came earlier to go over the details of the will. His lordship does not think he has much time left."

Nathaniel frowned. "This disease is cruel in its kindness."

"Indeed. It gives us plenty of time to prepare, yet we must watch the slow progression of it take away our loved ones." She blinked away her tears and lifted her eyes, the bravery reappearing. "Thank you for coming. Please, let us see to my husband."

Lord Heatherton reclined on the fainting couch in his bedroom, sitting before a large fire. The pallor of his skin testified of his illness, and his coat hung loosely about his shoulders. The gentleman had lost a great deal of weight. He turned to the door when Nathaniel entered, the motion jarring a coughing fit. His wife hurried to his side, handing him a handkerchief and putting her hand to his shoulder in support. She offered him water when the coughing had passed but he waved it away.

The baroness gave care rivaling professional nurses and Nathaniel admired her for it.

"Perhaps he ought to have tea instead," Nathaniel suggested as he came further into the room. He always instructed soap and a basin of water be available to him, to wash his hands, before and after encountering all of his patients.

While some scoffed at what they deemed fastidious behavior, Nathaniel had seen its benefits. Having studied medicine in Scotland, Nathaniel was well read in Doctor Alexander Gordon's treatment of puerperal fever. Doctor Gordon's treatise on his findings that washing one's hands, and instruments, and airing out clothing when visiting women with child-bed fever, remained one of the most controversial topics among doctors.

Nathaniel decided to experiment with the idea in other cases of illness, to determine its veracity for himself. He came to his conclusion quickly.

A family who washed well, with sickness in their midst, did not pass the illness between themselves as often. Nathaniel and his patients enjoyed better health than his colleagues who did not take the time to wash.

"Something soothing. I imagine you have a headache, my lord?" Nathaniel asked. The baron nodded, the dark circles under his eyes more pronounced by the paleness of his face. "Willow-bark, then, with copious amounts of honey."

Lady Heatherton nodded and left the room, after washing her hands at the same basin the doctor had used. Her dedication to her husband was such that she would fetch the tea herself, rather than send for a maid. This meant Nathaniel could have a few private minutes with the baron.

"Doctor Hastings," the man said at last, his voice hoarse. "I fear you will soon lose me as a patient."

Nathaniel came forward and took a chair placed near the sick man's couch. "It is possible. But the Lord might call *me* home in the next instant. One never knows for certain." He reached out to check the man's pulse, finding the artery in the neck. He observed the dilated pupils of Lord Heatherton, took note of the thinning hair and bags under the man's eyes. "You are not sleeping well?"

"Not with this cough." The baron sat back and closed his eyes. "I have made Virginia move across the house instead of in the adjoining chamber, so I do not disturb her at night. If she insists on tending to me all day, she must have her rest. She is exhausted, spending time with the children. She moves between the nursery and my sickroom so often it is a wonder she has not worn her tracks into the floors."

Nathaniel's shoulders tensed. "She is continuing to wash, as I advised?"

"Always. I make certain she never forgets, though I do not think it necessary. She would do anything to ensure the children remain healthy." Another fit of coughing seized him and Nathaniel reached for the water glass again, insisting the man drink a few sips.

"Have you experienced any fever?" he asked, his heart heavy. Losing a patient always felt like losing a piece of himself. When a man as honorable and good as the baron succumbed, it was worse. For weeks, Nathaniel had sent letters to colleagues all across the country to try and find any new treatments for consumption, but nothing came that he had not already tried.

"It comes and goes," the baron answered. "But it is all as you told us to expect. I think the worst of it is that Virginia is angry with me."

"Angry with you?" Nathaniel shook his head, disbelieving the remark. "I have rarely seen a wife as devoted to caring for her husband."

The baron winced. "I convinced her to come to Bath with a lie. I told her I would get better here, that it wasn't consumption, but weak lungs. She wanted to stay in the country. But I knew if she was out there alone, far from people, she would not do well. My passing will already be difficult enough, but Virginia cannot be alone in that old pile of stone."

"Has she friends?" Nathaniel asked. "Or will your family come to aid her?"

"My only family is my brother. He will be of little use." The man shook his head dismissively. "And my wife's family are ridiculous people. I cannot fathom how she could've come from those lines. But I know she has a cousin, a friend from her youth, who will help with the children."

The door opened and Lady Heatherton entered, balancing a tray with a small teapot and a single cup upon it.

"I have the tea," she announced, her cheer forced, as she went directly to her husband. "And I asked Mrs. Fairchild to see that the washing water be changed." A maid came in with a new basin of water and fresh towels, efficiently replacing the old and disappearing out the door again.

"You see, Doctor?" The baron attempted a more pleasant expression. "My lady remembers all your recommendations."

"What on earth would we want a doctor for if not to heed his advice?" She poured her husband's tea and shared a smile with the doctor in question.

Nathaniel passed a few more minutes in their company, prescribing small doses of laudanum to help the baron sleep. The man protested, not wanting to deal with the effects of the drink, but his wife insisted they listen to the doctor, to allow her husband the rest his body desperately needed.

When Nathaniel took his leave, he swallowed his frustration with the case. Perhaps if the family had sought medical care earlier, something may have been done. There were cases, after all, of consumptive patients living for many years. But too often his patients, especially the wealthy, put off seeing a doctor. They would ignore symptoms as an ordinary ailment until they could no longer do so, denying for as long as possible what their bodies would succumb to. That had been the case with the baron.

He attended the remainder of his appointments with little trouble and fewer concerns for treatments. Winter brought chills and sore throats to many of Bath's residents. Nathaniel left his patients with recommendations for better care in light of the weather.

As he walked home later that evening, Nathaniel's mind returned to the baron's case. The man would leave behind a wife and two children, materially cared for, but without someone who meant the world to them. Shaking his head, Nathaniel reminded himself there was nothing he could do.

Nathaniel entered his office, a set of rooms which served as his home and place of business, thinking on the disease. At times, being a doctor felt akin to being a fraud. How could he, a man of medicine, stand to watch a patient die? Why did he not know how to cure Lord Heatherton?

He recorded his observations in his journal, as always, and tried to tuck away the guilt that came with knowing he had done all in his power, and it was not enough.

He stood and went to the window, surveying the street below, and his body stilled. A carriage sat across the way, a young woman with dark hair sitting inside, peering out at Bath with wide eyes and a hopeful smile.

Nathaniel's heart lurched inside his chest, beating an unsteady rhythm, before the girl in the carriage looked up and broke the spell. It was not her. Of course, it could not be her. The equipage moved down the street and out of sight.

After nearly five years, Nathaniel's memory continued to disconcert him. He knew the chances of seeing the woman he had loved here, in Bath, were slim. He knew even if he did see her it would not be like the first time.

The first time, he glimpsed her in a carriage in London, studying all and sundry along the street with wonder. She had captured his attention from across the crowded lane, her pleasure genuine and her face absolutely breathtaking in its fresh beauty. He'd moved without thinking to lessen the distance between them, realizing at the last moment he intended to speak to her.

When he gave her the flower he'd tucked in his pocket, having found the lovely little bud on the ground minutes before, he was also giving Julia Devon his heart.

If she had kept it, how different his life might've been.

∞∞∞∞

"This is absolutely wretched!"

Julia turned her gaze to the door, surprised by her youngest sister's outburst as she entered the bedchamber. "Father cannot do this to us. We have never been apart before, and I cannot stand the thought of being away from you." She dropped down into the chair Julia kept beside the fireplace, her lower lip protruding in a manner unseen since her nursery days.

Julia bit back both a sigh and the desire to add her complaints to Rebecca's. Bemoaning their fate would get them nowhere.

"I'm afraid it has all been decided without us. But we may write to each other as often as we wish."

"But I don't want to go to London. I'd rather go to Bath, with you."

Rebecca's body slumped further, something Julia did not think possible given the girl's already sagging form. A sixteen-year-old lady really ought to have better posture and be less prone to a fit.

"I cannot understand why we are to be banished because Christine went off and married Mr. Gilbert. They are certainly happy, and Father didn't even need to give her a season in London. I thought he would be pleased about the spared expense."

"Father did not approve of the match." Julia approved heartily, but she tried not to voice that thought too often. She brought her attention back to the open trunk beside her bed, trying to determine how many dresses she might fit in the small space. "Mr. Gilbert, though honorable, doesn't hold a high place in the world. Father desires our marriages to make connections for him in society."

The memory of a pair of blue eyes surfaced as she spoke of marriage, along with a warm smile that made her heart leap even now, many years since the last time she'd seen them. Julia thrust the memories away, unwilling to examine them when her sister needed comfort. Putting her sisters and their needs first was her best defense against her own broken heart.

"I think it terribly unfair." Rebecca cast her eyes heavenward. "I don't wish to live with Aunt Jacqueline. She will make me attend all her stuffy morning calls and meet other girls who do nothing but compare gowns, stitch samplers, and conspire to win husbands."

Rebecca Devon was to be molded into the perfect lady by Aunt Jacqueline, their father's elder sister, over the course of the next two or three years. She would be made into a fit enough wife for a duke, and married to one without her consent, if their father had his way.

Julia swallowed her anger and tried to keep her tone light.

"Think of the lovely things you will be able to do and see in London." Julia glanced up from her work to give her sister an encouraging nod. "There are lending libraries. And Aunt Jacqueline's house is near Hyde Park. You will be able to explore and have adventures, like the heroines of your favorite novels."

Rebecca's lips twitched upward. "Aunt Jacqueline does not approve of novels. I will have to read in secret if I wish to make use of the libraries."

"Which is exactly what you do now." Julia crossed to her wardrobe and opened its doors with pursed lips. "The true tragedy is that we shall be apart while you are molded into a lady and I am sent into servitude." Julia said the last dramatically, putting her hand to her forehead.

Julia was to go to the relative most in need of an extra pair of hands, her cousin, Lady Virginia Macon. They were near in age and had been good friends before Virginia's marriage, but Julia had only received a few letters since her cousin wed seven years ago.

Rebecca scoffed, wrinkling her nose. But some of the light came back into her eyes. "You are going to Bath. And Cousin Virginia adores you. She will let you do whatever you please."

Pushing a lock of dark brown hair from her eyes, Julia realized she would get nothing done in the way of packing while her sister remained sulking in the chair. Though she resented their separation as much as Rebecca, Julia had long since learned to carefully choose her battles. She was well acquainted with her father's burning censure, as like to be manifested in a callous word as it was to be in humiliating punishment. Charles Devon's cruelty was often subtle, and always carefully wielded.

According to him, Rebecca and Horace, his ten-year-old son away at Eton, would aid him in his desire to rise in society's ranks. Julia he deemed a lost cause, knowing she would not bend to his will by making an ambitious marriage, and he had little more use for her than he did a housekeeper. At twenty-three years old, he declared her a spinster.

"I will not allow you to encourage Rebecca to rebel against my wishes," he had said after informing them of his plans for their separation, his cold eyes flashing in anger.

"Oh, Rebecca." Julia went to her sister and knelt next to her chair, looking up into the freckled face of her youngest sister. "It will not be as bad as you expect. London is wonderful."

Her heart ached at being removed from her sister. Their mother died before Julia's London season, when Rebecca was but twelve years old, leaving Julia to act as mother, though she was only seven years Rebecca's senior.

Looking after her sisters in the most awkward years of youth forced Julia to mature quickly. Likewise, she had attended to their brother Horace's needs until their father sent him away to school, determined the boy not grow soft by spending extended amounts of time with his sisters. The loss of little Horace still hurt. They saw him on rare occasions when school holidays overlapped with their father's presence in the country.

"I know it cannot be helped," Rebecca said, bringing Julia back to the situation at hand and yet another loss. "Father must be obeyed. But I hate it, Julia." Her brown eyes filled with tears. "I hate that I must lose everyone I love."

Julia gathered her sister in her arms, easing the girl down to the floor next to her, holding her close and smoothing back her dark curls.

"I do too." She would not let her own tears escape as her sister cried into her shoulder. She rocked Rebecca gently, humming a lullaby from better days, until the crying slowed and finally ceased. "There now. You will feel better for letting all of it out." She set her sister back from her, gazing into her watery eyes as she spoke earnestly.

"We must be brave and promise each other that we will not allow this to be a permanent parting. We will come together again, and soon I hope. Virginia will not need me forever, and you will eventually have to make your debut in society. Either I will come to Aunt Jacqueline, or you will make a splendid match and send for me, or else we will both be completely useless to our family and end up right back here to plague our father with our failures." She smiled as brightly as she could, relieved when Rebecca started to laugh.

"That would teach all of them to meddle. Perhaps we ought to take up a cottage together and spend our days tending gardens, reading novels, and criticizing society." Rebecca rose to her feet and Julia joined her. "Promise me you will write often? I don't think I will be able to bear Aunt Jacqueline without hearing from you."

"I will write pages and pages to you," Julia promised. "And it will not be as agonizing as you think. You will see. You will have adventures, and I'll read every word you write, relieved that I am not as busy as you."

Rebecca laughed again but sobered almost at once. "I checked the maps in the library. We will be over one hundred miles apart. We have never been that far from each other."

"I know." Julia pulled her sister close in another embrace. "But all little birds must fly the nest eventually." She kissed her sister's cheek. "It's now up to you whether you soar above the clouds or go plummeting to the earth. Spread your wings, hope for the best, and I will do the same."

Rebecca nodded and forced a pleasant expression on her face. "Will you help me? I'm not sure what to take with me."

Julia called for a maid to assist her packing hours later, after soothing her sister's fears and consulting with her about what to take to London. She had to dissuade Rebecca from taking half the library in her trunks.

Though the two of them shared many common features, the same dark curls, a similar delicate build, they had plenty of differences too. While Rebecca had a fine bone structure, she had grown taller than Julia in the past year. Julia's eyes were brown with liberal dashes of green, but Rebecca's were dark as chocolate. They had the same dark hair, all curls and waves that snarled if not properly braided for bed.

But their temperaments were the most different. Julia did all things in moderation, Rebecca often kept her opinion to herself, and their sister Christine regularly threw away caution to do as she thought best.

Rebecca would leave the day after Julia climbed into her father's coach. Everything had been arranged hastily, with letters travelling from London to Kettering as Aunt Jacqueline sorted out all the details. Before their sister and Thomas Gilbert even spoke their vows, the plans were underway for Rebecca's reeducation and Julia's exile.

Julia did not know what the trip to Bath would bring for her. Aunt Jacqueline's letters informed her that Virginia and her family were in Bath for the Baron's health but included none of the details of his illness.

Resolved to handle herself with dignity, and well-schooled in hiding her thoughts and emotions, Julia could at least promise herself that none would know how her heart missed her sisters or how she would worry for them.

When morning came and Julia entered the carriage, her sister came to see her off. Their father doubtless worked in his study.

"I will write as soon as I get to London," Rebecca promised, giving her sister one last embrace.

"As will I. Take care, darling, and behave yourself for Aunt."

Rebecca nodded and sniffed back her tears, putting on a brave face. But as the coach pulled away, Julia watched from the windows and saw her sister raise a hand to dash at her eyes.

Julia felt lonelier than she had in years. As her father's home and her sister's tears fell behind her, she at last allowed herself a few moments of misery. No one was in the carriage with her to see her cry. Her father had not even given her the courtesy of a maid to guard her reputation, so little did he value her.

This last sign of rejection from him hurt, as though he'd slapped her across the cheek, leaving her bruised. Since the death of their mother, Julia had to be the comforter in the family, which left no one to soothe her own fears and sorrows.

Her heart had not been this battered since her disastrous London season, five years past, when it had been broken because of a man with intelligent blue eyes and a gentle smile.

Nathaniel.

As she gave way to her feelings, Julia allowed herself to think on those eyes and their owner.

Once, she well knew, her happiness could have been secured. If she had been brave and revealed more of what she felt—but instead, years of loneliness and heartache were her lot, both behind and ahead of her.

As the wheels tumbled over ruts and bumps in the road, Julia took a deep breath and reconstructed the careful mask she wore. She put the broken pieces of her heart back into the fortified walls she had built around it. Those walls had stood since the day she denied her love for a man her father deemed unworthy, and they must continue to protect her.

Read more of Julia's story in *The Gentleman Physician.*

Acknowledgments

I have a whole list of wonderful friends and family members who encouraged me and helped me work out all the kinks in this book. I would love to thank them all, and mention a few special people by name.

The biggest thanks must go to my husband, Skye, who encouraged and believed in me, who pushed me to complete my book, and provided me all the time I needed to get it done. I also have to thank my children, who were patient when Mommy told them to "wait just a sec" while she finished up her writing. They are the unsung heroes of all that I do.

Thank you to my mother, the woman who taught me to read, write, and do my research correctly. I owe everything I am to her.

I promised my cousin Brittany, who read all my first attempts at writing when we were very young, a sincere and public thank you for her friendship over the years. Brittany, this is it: Thank you!

My siblings, Autumn, Laura, Carri, Patrick, Molly, and Asa, thank you for accepting how much I loved to read and write and telling me I was a pretty good big sister, too.

A really huge thank you to my critique partners, Joanna Barker and Johanna Evelyn, who helped me polish this story until it shone. They are incredible.

I'm pretty sure my grandmothers deserve to know I love them and I'm grateful for all they've taught me over the years. Nanita and Wanda, thank you for being strong women with beautiful love stories.

Thanks to my friend Shaela Kay for her encouragement, the beautiful cover, and all the chats about writing.

Thank you to Jenny Proctor, an amazing editor who helped me clean up *The Social Tutor* and make it suitably reflect the rest of the series.

And a special thank you to my dear friends, Crystal, Lauren, Michayle, and Sunny, who were only a text away when I needed them.

Other Titles By Sally Britton

Heart's of Arizona Series:

Book #1, *Silver Dollar Duke*

The Inglewood Series:

Rescuing Lord Inglewood

Discovering Grace

Saving Miss Everly

Engaging Sir Isaac

Reforming Lord Neil

The Branches of Love Series:

Prequel Novella, *Martha's Patience*

The Social Tutor

The Gentleman Physician

His Bluestocking Bride

The Earl and His Lady

Miss Devon's Choice

Courting the Vicar's Daughter

Penny's Yuletide Wish (A Novella)

Stand Alone Romances:

The Captain and Miss Winter

His Unexpected Heiress

A Haunting at Havenwood

Timeless Romance Collection:

An Evening at Almack's, Regency Collection 12

About the Author

Sally Britton, along with her husband and four incredible children, now live in Oklahoma. So far, they really like it there, even if the family will always consider Texas home.

Sally started writing her first story on her mother's electric typewriter, when she was fourteen years old. Reading her way through Jane Austen, Louisa May Alcott, and Lucy Maud Montgomery, Sally decided to write about the elegant, complex world of centuries past.

Sally graduated from Brigham Young University in 2007 with a bachelor's in English, her emphasis on British literature. She met and married her husband not long after and they've been building their happily ever after since that day.

Vincent Van Gogh is attributed with the quote, "What is done in love is done well." Sally has taken that as her motto, for herself and her characters, writing stories where love is a choice.

All of Sally's published works are available on Amazon.com and you can connect with Sally and sign up for her newsletter on her website, AuthorSallyBritton.com.

Made in the USA
Columbia, SC
13 August 2021